ARES

Michael Aye

BOOK 8 OF THE FIGHTING ANTHONYS

Published by Boson Books

An imprint of Bitingduck Press
Formerly an imprint of C&M Online Media, Inc.
ISBN 978-1-938463-78-5
eISBN 978-1-938463-79-2

For information contact
Bitingduck Press, LLC
Altadena, CA
notifications@bitingduckpress.com
http://www.bitingduckpress.com
Cover art by Johannes Ewers
www.zazzle.com/seawolf

Author's note

This book is a work of fiction with a historical backdrop. I have taken liberties with historical figures, ships, and time frames to blend in with my story. Therefore, this book is not a reflection of actual historical events.

ARES

THE FIGHTING ANTHONYS
BOOK EIGHT

MICHAEL AYE

Books by Michael Aye

Fiction

To:

Doctor Lawrence K. Cook, Oral Surgeon and Friend.
You were a very positive influence.

HM2 Paul Dover, Admin Chief, Branch Medical Clinic, MCLB, Albany, GA
You made my job as the Base Medical Officer a lot smoother.
Thank you, shipmate

CHARACTERS IN THE FIGHTING ANTHONY SERIES

Navy and Marines:

Vice Admiral Lord Anthony – Commander in Chief, West Indies. Returns to England for further assignment.

Captain Stephen Earl – Flag Captain, Vice Admiral Lord Anthony

Bart – Vice Admiral's cox'n

Captain Sir Gabriel Anthony – Captain, HMS *Ares*, a forty-four gun frigate.

Dagan – Gabe's uncle and advisor.

Jake Hex – Gabe's cox'n

Con Vallin – First Lieutenant, HMS *Ares*

Ronald Laqua – Second Lieutenant, HMS *Ares*

Bryan Turner – Third Lieutenant, HMS *Ares*

Randall Scott – Master, HMS *Ares*

Robert Cornish – Surgeon, HMS *Ares*

Gerald Myers – Gunner, HMS *Ares*

David Stubbs – Bosun, HMS *Ares*

Brian Heath – Midshipman, HMS *Ares*

Joshua Delsenno – Midshipman, HMS *Ares*

Zachary Massey – Midshipman, HMS *Ares*

Henry Easley – Midshipman, HMS *Ares*

Vaughn Corwin – Midshipman, HMS *Ares*

Philip LoGiudice – Captain, Marines, HMS *Ares*

Robert Hurley – Captain, HMS *Ludlow,* a thirty-two gun frigate

Louis Haven – Captain, HMS *Lark,* a twenty gun frigate

Spies:

Sir Lawrence Cook – Physician, Foreign Agent

Leo Gallagher – Foreign Agent

Lord Randy Skalla – Foreign Agent

The Ladies:

Lady Deborah Anthony – Lord Anthony's wife

Faith Anthony – Sir Gabe's wife

Holly LoGiudice – Marine Captain Phil LoGiudice's wife

Maria Dupree – Gabe's mother and Dagan's sister

Becky English – Gabe and Lord Anthony's sister

Gretchen English – Becky and Hugh's daughter

The Men:

Francis Markham – Royal Navy captain and Gabe's friend

Noble "No" Pride Stanhope – Homeless boy, later a midshipman HMS *Ares*

Lord William Stanhope – Earl of Gladstone, Noble's grandfather

Hugh English – Becky's husband, Gabe and Lord Anthony's brother-in-law

Paul Dover – Noble Pride's tutor

Simon Davis – the hanged man.

The Spy

They whisper in silence
As the man walks by
Careful what you say
That man be a spy.

He goes ashore
Along the enemy's coast
He moves in the shadows
Like some earthly ghost.

He carries nothing
But his pistol and wits
It's death if he's caught
Would you do it?

He's met his contact
Made his rendezvous
He sails home to England
With the enemy's news.

-Michael Aye

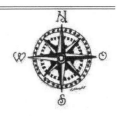

PROLOGUE

IT WAS A HAZY *day, and with the land breeze it made for a chilly morning. It would be considered no more than a brisk morning were it Portsmouth or London. But it wasn't Portsmouth or London, it was English Harbour, Antigua. It was a cold day for English Harbour, and Christmas was only a week away. The year 1780 was almost to a close. First, there was the terrible hurricane that they were calling the worst ever...the Hurricane of 1780; and now this cold weather. The hurricane would no doubt be recorded as one of the most devastating to be recorded, but that was a natural disaster.*

What was about to take place would pale in comparison...at least for one man. He would die today. There had been many deaths during his time spent in the Royal Navy. Men died at sea, even without a war. This was different though. A man was to be executed today...hanged! The day was not only contrary to the normal temperatures but it seemed the whole island of Antigua was in such a state. Gabe had never witnessed an execution, but more importantly, none of the islanders had ever witnessed a sailor hanging from the yard arm. The seaman, to make it worse, was one of SeaHorse's crew; Gabe's brother's flagship.

He'd like to have avoided it, but all of Lord Anthony's captains were required to be turned out with all ceremony as described by the "Principles and Practices of Courts Martial Manual." Gabe took this to mean in dress uniform.

Hex commented, as Gabe was rowed out to the flagship, "The signal of death is already being displayed." By that, he meant an assembly of boats had been manned with armed men and surrounded the flagship, where the execution was to take place. Room was made so that Gabe's gig was allowed to approach the entry port.

Gabe looked down at the battens as he was announced and, not surprisingly, saw Hex was scaling SeaHorse's side behind him. He was escorted to Lord Anthony's cabin with Hex still on his heels. Even in these circumstances, Gabe had to stifle a smile. A seaman, who'd moved aside for him to pass, not only moved but also knuckled to Hex. *He looks more like an officer than I do,* Gabe thought... or *he looks that much more menacing.* In his brother's cabin, a group of officers were standing and adjusting their uniforms. *Damn, I've almost cut it too late,* Gabe thought.

Vice Admiral Lord Gilbert Anthony looked at his brother. "We'll speak after," he said, and then headed topside.

Gabe stood aside as his brother, Rear Admiral Dutch Moffett, and lastly Captain Stephen Earl, his brother's flag captain, marched past.

Bart whispered, as Gabe fell in line, "Iffen yews can't get here's on time, just get here when yews can's."

Damn, Gabe thought again. *When the admiral's cox'n scolds you, what are the others thinking?* Hearing a "he-he", Gabe snarled, "Hush Hex, or you'll be joining that poor bugger at the yard arm."

***

THE DECK HAD CHANGED drastically since Gabe had been piped aboard. In keeping with the rules of the service prescribed for executions, the entire ship's company had turned out. The glitter of gold on the officers' uniforms stood out, even with the misty haze. The master, surgeon, and other warrants were all in their prescribed uniforms, while most of the crew wore slops from the purser. A few men wore checkered shirts, and their hair was combed, tarred, and some even had their hair pulled back in a queue. They all had solemn or firm looks on their faces. Some of the men had their heads tilted back so that they could see the yardarm.

A rope had been run through a single block with a sliding noose at one end. A few feet above the noose, a small toggle was securely fastened. The purpose of the toggle was to check or stop the body as it is hauled up rapidly. When the body is checked, it springs out into the air and falls with a violent jerk that breaks the man's neck. As Gabe watched, he noticed more than one man swallow with a grim look on his face.

The prisoner was brought up from the after hatch as the bell struck once in the forenoon watch. He was guarded by four marines, with a sergeant in charge of the detail. On reaching a spot under the mainmast yardarm, the guard halted. The man was ghost-white pale but seemed resigned to his fate. One of the masters-at-arms took a step forward and put a blindfold on the man. His arms were pinned behind him and secured with a rope, as his feet were also tied. The collar of his shirt was rolled back and tucked in. The noose was then applied and the master-at-arms stepped back.

Captain Earl stepped forward and took out a rolled up document. Reading from the document in a clear voice, Earl said, "Simon Davis, having been found guilty of Article 27, which states all murders committed by any person in the fleet shall be punished by death with the sentence of a court martial." As he stepped back, his First Lieutenant Peckham called to the bosun, "All ready."

A cannon boomed at that time, making more than one of the crew jump. Gabe waited for them to haul the man up as the smoke cleared away.

Captain Earl, instead, stepped forward again. He

slowly and coolly drew out another document. It took Gabe an instant to realize that what Captain Earl now read was a reprieve…a miraculous reprieve. The clemency for the condemned man was based on his actions in saving a life aboard SeaHorse during the hurricane in October, 1780.

***

BACK IN LORD ANTHONY'S *cabin, refreshments were served to Rear Admiral Moffett and Gabe. Captain Earl had not finished his duties on deck. Bart and Hex were sitting off to one side with a cup while the officers were being served a cup of Silas' special coffee. The sun was starting to heat up the day but it was still damp, so a cup with just a dollop of brandy seemed to be called for and no one disagreed.*

"That went damn well," Moffett said.

"I think it drove the point home, yet it also showed that some sins can be forgiven under the right circumstances," Lord Anthony replied.

"It definitely changed the crew's mood," Moffett responded.

"How can you pardon murder though?" Gabe asked.

"I'm not sure that he committed murder," Lord Anthony replied. "Had you been here when expected, you wouldn't be asking that question."

Gabe could think of several excuses but only replied, "Yes, sir."

Seeing his brother's look of repentance, Lord Anthony spoke again, "Davis was found by the purser pulling a knife from the murdered man. It was on the purser's testimony that the court martial came back with the guilty verdict. Davis says he found the man face down at the foot of a ladder. He rolled him over and saw the knife and, thinking that he'd be helping the man, he pulled it out. The surgeon said it had pierced a lung, but of course Davis didn't know this." Lord Anthony then seemed to change the subject. *"How are you coming along with crewing Ares?"*

"I'm still about seventy short," Gabe replied.

"You're sixty-nine short now. Captain Earl is having Davis gather his slops and put in your gig. There's no way we can keep him aboard SeaHorse." Saying this, Lord Anthony raised his cup in salute.

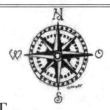

CHAPTER ONE

CHRISTMAS DAY, 1780, AND the year was almost at an end. Several people gathered about in the dining room in the small cottage that Gabe and Faith had rented just up the hill overlooking English Harbour. If there had been more room, at least another six people would have been invited. Dagan, Hex, and Bart lounged about on the small porch, while Deborah and Ariel were chatting away about children inside. Ariel was pregnant and, even though she was not showing yet, it had been two months since her monthly curse was upon her. The women discussed all the aspects of pregnancy, as the men talked of the war.

Vice Admiral Lord Gilbert Anthony, 'Gil' to his friends in private circles, had just stated that England could not continue to fight the Americans, the French, and now the Spaniards. "It won't be long before the Dutch will throw in with the rest," he said.

"Aye," Stephen Earl, flag captain to Lord Anthony, replied. "I remember when the war started and an admiral at Scoffs rebuked a captain who said the war wouldn't last a year. The admiral said to the captain, 'You wouldn't want to stake your flag on that would you, sir?'"

Lieutenant David Davy, captain of *HMS Tomahawk*, then spoke, "I'm not for the war, especially now that Ariel's with child. But I recall the first day that I set foot aboard ship, a snot-nosed midshipman. I was the youngest middy and Gabe was the senior if I remember right. I'm a lieutenant now with a ship to command, and Gabe's a captain and has commanded a squadron. None of us would have advanced so quickly, were it not for the war; nor would we be as financially sound as what the prize money has made us."

"Aye, that's all true," Gabe agreed. "I'm not sure though, that it's been worth all we've done and the men we've had to kill to get it."

Inside the kitchen, Nanny, with the help of Josiah, had prepared what Faith described as a traditional Christmas meal. Gabe was astonished at all the different types of foods. When he'd strolled through the kitchen, he'd seen enough so that it made him think of ship captains dining with the admiral in command.

The dining table was not big enough for everyone, so a couple of small tables had been set up. When Faith called everyone in, a sideboard had been set up for the food. Gabe and Faith's guests had their choice of ham, beef, turkey, and mincemeat pies in one section. The next one had oysters, shrimp, and different vegetables to include buttered carrots, new potatoes, creamed corn, and peas. The last section had the desserts. Tonight, a large chocolate cake had been sliced; a lemon pie had also been cut, and apple tarts were also available. The beverages were wine, rum, and rum punch.

There was an abundance of conversation and merriment around the tables until Bart and Hex both grabbed for the last slice of chocolate cake. Laughing, Bart broke it in half, with Hex swallowing his half in one bite. The men and women then divided up, allowing each group to take care of nature and a quick cigar or bowl of pipe tobacco if desired.

When the men had relieved themselves and gathered on the porch for a smoke, Stephen Earl asked

Gabe, "How's the refit coming along?"

"Slowly, but surely. Con Vallin is worth his weight in gold," Gabe replied, speaking of his first lieutenant. "I am still seventy...er...sixty-nine men short, including a master, gunner, and Marine officer."

"I might have a Marine officer for you," Lord Anthony responded. "My captain of Marines wishes to stay here and I'm sure that with the hurricane destroying Barbados, I will be recalled to England."

"I hope not, Gil."

"Aye, Gabe. Deborah would rather not go back either. She doesn't say that but this is home for her."

"Will Dr. Cornish stay on?" Davy asked.

"Aye, he'll stay." This came from Dagan. "He likes the way we do things. It makes his job easier." This brought forth a chuckle from the group.

"Finish up your cigars," Faith said, standing in the doorway and waving away a cloud of cigar smoke that wanted to enter the cottage.

Coffee was offered to those who wanted it, but the men continued with the wine and rum. Everyone followed Faith into the parlor and stood around as she spoke, "At home in South Carolina, Christmas was a day we used to celebrate the birth of our Lord Jesus Christ. As Christ was a gift to the people by his father in heaven, some have even took to giving gifts. I understand George Washington, our American general, gives gifts to his children as part of the celebration."

Gabe looked about at their guests' faces when Faith had described George Washington as 'our American general.' If anyone resented the comment, they didn't let it show.

Faith spoke again, "We began our Christmas morning by attending church. We would then have dinner, and we often attended parties where there was much singing and dancing. I thought I'd read about the first

Christmas, since we don't have church services here on Antigua. It begins in Saint Matthew, chapter one. I'll start on the eighteenth verse and read through to the second chapter, verse fourteen."

Gabe looked about discreetly as his wife read the verses in a surprisingly strong voice. Everyone appeared to be listening intently. When Faith finished the reading, everyone bowed their heads while she said a short prayer.

She then looked at the group and said, "For your entertainment now, Jake and I have been practicing a song that Lum taught me as a child. Lum," Faith called.

Lum came in with his flute, licked his lips, and then played a measure, after which Faith and Jake joined in. Everyone was amazed at how well they sang together. Jake's mandolin really added to Lum's flute. When they finished the song, everyone applauded.

"What was the name of that song?" Captain Earl asked.

"Joy to the world," Dagan responded. He grinned and then said, "Lum told me back when we had *Sea-Wolf*."

"Yes, Lum sings it every year," Faith added. "It was written by a man named Isaac Watts, from Virginia, in 1760."

The furniture was pushed back, after that. With Lum on his flute and Jake, first on his banjo and then the mandolin, they played and sang, while everyone danced for several hours. When they were thoroughly exhausted, everyone broke up and took their leave.

Captain Earl, walking up to Faith, took her hand and said, "So much was the love you set forth unto our Christ, that I myself felt improved."

Faith gave a small curtsey, "Thank you, Captain. I'm glad you enjoyed it."

Damn, I believe he means it, Gabe thought, and then had to agree with him. *Faith's celebration was divine.*

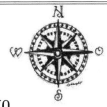

CHAPTER TWO

THE SUN BURNED AWAY the early morning mist that hung over English Harbour, as it rose higher over the horizon. Faith stood looking out the stern windows of *HMS Ares...Ares...*the mythical Greek God of War. The ship was what Gabe called a razee. It had been a larger ship, a sixty-four gun French ship of the line. It appeared that the French, like the British, were coming to the conclusion that the sixty-four was too slow to be used as a frigate and not strong enough to stand alongside the larger ships, like *SeaHorse*, in the line of battle. At least, that was what she understood from her husband's explanation. She had dined aboard *Ares* last evening with the officers and midshipmen. She knew most of the men from Gabe's last command, but there were a few new faces. The conversation was polite, all seemingly pleased that the captain's lady was willing to dine with them.

The one thing Faith had picked up on during the dinner was that every man was in fact proud of their ship. *Like a mistress*, Faith thought. *Ares*, enchanting, mysterious, and alluring, enjoyed a love affair with every man and boy. The promise of adventure, of riches...Faith turned away from the windows. *Siren*, her previous name, better fitted the ship from Faith's point of view.

She heard noises coming from the pantry. Josh Nesbit was with the new man, the one that was almost hanged. They were undoubtedly preparing breakfast for her and Gabe. She needed to get dressed. Closing the stern windows, she looked out once more at the distant sea. The ship...the sea, she could never compete against them. She had come to accept that. She had to become a part of it.

The war...it had been going on so long. She'd married a man who was her own country's enemy, but she loved him. He did his duty sailing against all of England's foes, and had grown very wealthy doing so. He did so with reluctance, though. He was very in tune with his wife's feelings. Dagan and Hex had both said that he'd let smaller vessels go that were known to be Colonials. He did this for her.

Faith thought of Ariel as she dressed. She was an American also, married to a British officer. Did Ariel have the conflict of emotions that she had? Did Davy understand her feelings? How would he handle going to sea knowing his wife was pregnant? How could the sea have such a hold on a man that he could sail off leaving all he loved ashore? Why ask why!

"I sees ya done stirred yo lazy bones, girl." It was Nanny. She'd come aboard to help with James.

"Is James awake?" Faith asked.

"He was, but after bouncing on his daddy's knee and going over the ship, he took a bottle and is now sleeping again."

Faith smiled. James was at that age where he'd found his legs and was into everything. Sam tolerated his laying on him or pulling on his ears. The big dog would just look at Faith as if to say, 'are you coming to get this rascal?' Whenever James happened to see the cat and headed toward her, she'd scat. Faith smiled suddenly, wondering what the ship's men thought seeing their captain playing with his son and talking baby talk. Well, those that didn't know it would realize that their captain was human, with a son he loved.

Faith heard a discreet knock, "Yes?"

"It's Nesbit, Madame. I've sent for the captain. If you'd like to break your fast, we have coffee or I can heat up some cocoa. We have the usual pastries that the captain likes for breakfast. I could fix you some toast, if you prefer."

"Thank you, Joshua," Faith replied, seeing the man smile at the use of his first name.

"We'll get the carpenter's mate to take the measurements for the captain's furniture you spoke of after breakfast," Nesbit said. "Most of what's here is not fit for a bum boat."

***

THE LONG ROOM AT Government House echoed as Governor Burt's shoes clicked on the plank flooring. The new year, 1781, was only a few days old. Vice Admiral Lord Gilbert Anthony and Rear Admiral Dutch Moffett were with the governor. A courier brig with dispatches had dropped anchor earlier that morning at English Harbour. Lieutenant Rice was confused as he looked at the vice admiral's flag that flew over *SeaHorse* and wondered if his orders to report to Rear Admiral Moffett were still valid. A 'captain repair on board' ended the quandary for the young officer. The news that he brought from the Colonies was dismal.

Lord Anthony could not help but recall the words of his friend, Commodore Gardner, so many years back, when the war had just broken out. He'd predicted all of the events that had taken place. "We've bitten off more than we can chew," Commodore Gardner had said. "The Americans will not just roll over. France, and probably Spain, will come to their aid before too long. The Frogs and the Dons hate us anyway. Why in God's name wage a war that we can't win against our cousins?" His words had all come true.

Lord Anthony had reported the loss of Barbados to the hurricane in late October.

The courier brig that had arrived that morning brought orders for his recall. His squadron was to return to England as soon as his ships could be assembled and the necessary repairs to make them seaworthy could be done. Admiral Rodney would be his replacement. Rodney's second in command was Rear Admiral Samuel Hood. They were expected in the West Indies soon. Lieutenant Davy was asked to report to Government House to receive his new orders. He was to sail to Barbados to advise Captain Markham of the recall, instead of his usual patrol.

A servant came in carrying a tray with a decanter and several glasses, as Governor Burt continued to pace. Each man took a glass of the governor's preferred hock. "A toast, gentlemen, for a quick end to the hostilities," Burt said.

"Hear, hear," Anthony and Moffett joined in.

Burt set down his glass and said, "Gentlemen, I'm being replaced as well. Sir Thomas Shirley is to take over as governor. I expect he will be here by the summer."

Neither Lord Anthony nor Moffett were sure how to reply to this. Burt did not seem to be overjoyed or morose. He had done all he could to support the Navy, so he was well liked by both men.

"You've done a lot for us...for the Navy," Lord Anthony said. "I will always be in your debt."

"Nonsense," Burt quickly replied, but with a hint of a smile. "Lord Anthony, before you leave, allow us to have a dinner in your honor."

"As you wish, sir."

Burt continued to pace, his glass in one hand and a sheaf of documents in the other. "It appears we are about to declare war on the Dutch. The Americans, the Frogs, the Dons, and now the Dutch," he snorted. "Do they intend for us to take on the world? Damnation!"

By the use of 'they', Anthony and Moffett knew Governor Burt was speaking of Parliament.

"I believe it was in 1778, that Lord Stormont declared during a session of Parliament that if Sint Eustatius had sunk into the sea three years before, the United Kingdom would have already dealt with George Washington," Moffett said, adding to the dismay of their government's actions.

"Aye," Lord Anthony agreed. He also knew that the Dutch neutrality was something of a farce. It was a known fact that nearly half of all the American's military supplies were obtained through the island of St. Eustatius. Lord Skalla had said as much one night when they had dined together on Barbados. He had also said that most of the communications between the Americans and Europe first passed through the island.

St. Eustatius had a large Jewish population who were notorious in their support of the Americans and the French.

"I would not be surprised to hear that our new commander may have orders to take St. Eustatius," Lord Anthony said.

"I agree with you, my Lord," Burt responded.

"I wonder how much bounty will find its way into the Rodney coffers instead of the treasury," Moffett chided.

Rodney had, more than once, taken the opportunity to capture prizes over the fulfillment of his assigned duties.

"Let's hope we will not suffer long from this," Burt said, setting his glass on the table and turning as his secretary knocked, stuck his head in the door and reminded the governor of his next appointment.

Taking this as their cue to leave, Vice Admiral Lord Anthony stood, followed by Rear Admiral Moffett. They shook hands with Governor Burt and thanked him for such a fine beverage. A liveried footman handed their hats to them and bid the two good day.

Bart had been standing just outside the entrance to Government House, and as Lord Anthony approached, he declared, "I's bet the Dutch is going to regret saluting the *Andrew Doria*."

Lord Anthony and Moffett looked at each other. They'd just heard the news themselves, and here was Bart, obviously well informed. Anthony didn't bother to ask Bart where he'd gotten his information. Crumbs were scattered on his jacket. He'd no doubt been in the kitchen. The servant's line of communication was amazingly fast.

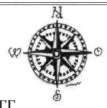

CHAPTER THREE

RODNEY'S FLEET ARRIVED IN Antigua the last day of January, 1781. Merchant ships under Rodney's protection, to be more specific, sailed into English Harbour. His fleet of fifteen warships, troop ships, and supply vessels sailed on to St. Eustatius. Rodney was en route to attack the small Dutch island, according to one of the merchant captains. The captain also said sailing with Rodney was General Vaughan, who had under his command three thousand soldiers.

"That's a sizable force for St. Eustatius," Admiral Moffett said to Lord Anthony.

"Aye," Anthony agreed.

"I doubt the Dutch even know that war has been declared," Moffett continued. He was perplexed that Rodney hadn't even come ashore to at least advise the naval authority on Antigua about what was happening. In fact, it spoke volumes in regards to respect for one's peers, meaning both Vice Admiral Lord Anthony and Rear Admiral Moffitt. It did not sit well with the governor either.

"Damn that man," Burt cursed. "He believes that since he is now the commander in chief that he's above communication to us underlings."

Later that evening, as Lord Anthony and Lady Deborah enjoyed a cool breeze on the porch of her cottage, she asked, "Is something bothering you, Gil?"

"I was just thinking how Rodney felt that he had no reason to stop at English Harbour. He didn't even send a courier to enlighten us on the state of British relations with the Dutch. If war has been declared, and I think it has, it would have been a pertinent piece of information for us to know."

"You don't like him, do you," Deborah said, more a statement than a question.

"He's not my most favorite officer. I think he puts himself before his country. He's done that since he made captain back in 1742."

"He's senior to you?" Deborah inquired.

Gil smiled at his wife, "Much senior. He also has numerous political allies."

"I didn't know his family was so...so influential," Deborah replied.

Gil took Deborah's hand and said, "He married well."

This caused Deborah to smile, "Are you ready to retire, dear husband?"

"I never thought you'd ask," Gil said, as the two of them stood so that they could see the moon over the water.

"Such a peaceful sight," Deborah said, speaking softly. "I will miss this little cottage." It was where they had first made love.

"I will do what I can to see us back as soon as possible."

"I know you will," Deborah replied, and then smiled. "You want to know who else will miss the island?" They looked at each other and smiled together, "Bart!"

***

HMS Storm, a thirty-eight gun frigate, dropped anchor in English Harbour on March 7th at six bells in the afternoon watch. Captain Joseph Galicky noticed the anchorage was very crowded with warships. He spoke to his passenger, Doctor Lawrence Cook, about the assistant, Leonardo Gallagher, who was traveling with the doctor. Cook always called the man 'Leo,' instead of his full name. When Galicky asked about the nickname, Cook responded with, "Leo is a lion."

Galicky had never heard this before, so during a quiet time, he summoned the ship's surgeon and asked about Leo the lion. The surgeon told his captain about the Greek and Chinese astrologers. The Greek zodiac follows a lunar calendar, with each month having the name of an animal.

The surgeon continued, "Leo is the fifth sign in the zodiac. I believe the dates are in July through August, but I don't know the exact days. I have a chart in one of my books below. I can get you the days, if you desire."

"No, that won't be necessary," the captain replied.

"I'm a bull, Captain. The sign, Taurus, is a bull. I was born the first of May. When were you born, if I may ask, Captain?"

"November...November the first."

"You are a Scorpio, Captain."

"A Scorpio?"

"You are highly ranked by the Greeks," the surgeon said.

Galicky thanked the surgeon but wondered if he was being sincere.

Dr. Cook interrupted Galicky's reverie. "Seems to me, that's a lot of ships, Captain."

"Yes, it is, Doctor. Are your things ready?"

"I believe they are bringing them forth now, Captain."

Galicky's first lieutenant walked up at that time. "Lookout reports a 'captain repair on board' signal, sir. How he sighted it is beyond me. What?"

Cook smiled, the first lieutenant was a man that

took some getting used to.

Admiral Moffitt sent word to Lord Anthony and Governor Burt requesting a meeting as soon as convenient, after hearing Galicky's report. It was the night of Lord Anthony's squadron's farewell dinner. All the ships' captains, their first lieutenants, and wives or girlfriends were invited. The meeting Moffitt had requested was scheduled for an hour before the dinner. This gave Captain Galicky, Dr. Cook, and his special assistant, Leo Gallagher, time to pack their bags and get ready to go ashore. They had to meet with the governor, so hearing that he had a function that evening they were rushed.

Gabe and Faith were busy getting ready for the dinner after a quick, impromptu round of making love. Faith had just finished with her bath. An overwhelming urge swept over Gabe as she stood letting the water drip from her body. He was holding the towel for Faith to dry off with, but as the humors boiled, he picked up his wife and carried her to the bed. They were now both flushed and a bit rushed.

When a gentle tap on the door was heard, Gabe had just gotten one boot on. Faith went behind the little dressing screen as Gabe spoke, "Come in."

Nanny opened the door. "Lawd, Captain! You need to open a window. You two have gotten it hot in here."

Faith, seeing it was Nanny, stepped from behind the screen as Nanny opened a window. "You know how uncontrollable these sailors are," Faith said, with a smile.

"I noticed you didn't cry for help," Nanny threw back. "Lawd, child, the sun ain't even down."

Gabe smiled, "She's a wanton wench, Nanny. A poor sailor has no power over her charms."

"Huh, I reckon there's something to be said for that. You need to put that other boot on, as you have an officer here to see you most urgently."

Gabe put his other boot on and stomped it in place. He then walked to the living room where he greeted Lieutenant Mahan, his brother's flag lieutenant.

Lieutenant Mahan spoke, as the two men shook hands, "An urgent meeting has been scheduled with the governor, Sir Gabe. Your presence has been requested. I have a carriage waiting if you are ready, sir."

Damnation, this was short notice, Gabe thought. He thought then, *better now than half an hour ago*. "Let me get my coat and hat," he said. "I need to tell my wife as well."

"I'm to return for Lady Deborah and Faith," the flag lieutenant volunteered.

"Thank you," Gabe said as he entered his bedroom.

"I heard," Faith said before Gabe could speak.

She's smiling at least, Gabe thought. He then had a second thought. *If she heard his conversation with Lieutenant Mahan, did that mean Nanny heard them making love. Hmm!!*

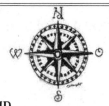

CHAPTER FOUR

GOVERNOR BURT, LORD ANTHONY, Admiral Moffitt, and Gabe, as well as Dr. Cook and his assistant, Leo, were in the room.

"It was a bloodless surrender," Captain Galicky was telling his audience. "Admiral Rodney informed Governor de Graaff that Britain had declared war on the Republic of the Seven United Netherlands on December 20, 1780. He then told the governor that he had over a thousand cannons on fifteen warships plus an army of three thousand on transport ships. De Graaff only had a garrison of sixty or so men and a dozen cannons. He knew that resistance would be futile, so he surrendered. Rodney did allow the governor to fire two cannons, for honor's sake." Galicky paused for a second and took a deep swallow from his glass.

Galicky was a stocky man of medium height. His face and hands looked like leather, with crow's feet at the corner of his eyes. His hair was once black, but now had a salt and pepper look and was shorter than most men of the time. He had a booming voice, even when he was speaking in a normal tone. *He'll not need a speaking trumpet*, Gabe thought.

Doctor Cook was a tall man, with black hair and a quick smile. He had a firm manly handshake. Leo, his assistant, was much shorter, with a darker complexion, and seemed to steadily take in everything with his eyes. Other than a quick introduction, the man's function had not been addressed.

Yet, to Gabe, Leo Gallagher had foreign officer written all over him. He was not sure about Cook. No, his function would come out in due time, but Gabe felt his presence was more to do with the good doctor and his assistance than what occurred at St. Eustatius.

Galicky set his now empty glass down, cleared his throat and continued, "Inside the harbor lay some one-hundred and thirty merchantmen, as well as an old Dutch frigate, and five smaller American armed merchantmen. It's said that Rodney told General Vaughan just the prizes would buy him a new townhouse in the finest section of London." He paused and took a deep breath, and then gave a sigh. "Rodney's next moves were not what one would expect from someone of Rodney's status, who was supposed to be representing our government. Everything was searched. Men and women were stopped and searched in a most disconcerting way. They took everything. They even broke into the tomb of former Governor Jan de Windt. The British soldiers opened the tomb and took all of the silver decorations off of the casket."

Galicky's audience stared in disbelief. It was unspeakable that such a thing would be allowed.

"Rodney will answer for this!" Burt exclaimed.

"Aye," Galicky said.

Cook spoke then, "There'll be a trial but such was the wealth he'll be acquitted."

Galicky agreed. "He's loading up several ships full of plunder to be taken back to England. The ships that were sent to discourage the French here in the Caribbean and the Colonies will now be used to escort the treasure."

"Damn the man," Burt snapped. "I'm sorry," he said, speaking to Galicky.

"It's alright, Governor. Several of Rodney's captains feel the same way." Galicky looked longingly at his empty glass, which prompted the governor to refill it himself, rather than call a servant. After taking a generous swallow, Galicky cleared his throat and resumed his narrative. "Once the island was in Rodney's hands, he sent word for all the adult Jewish males to report to him. When they had done so, he herded them aboard a ship and deported thirty-one heads of families to Saint Kitts. This was done without allowing them to speak to their families or collect any belongings."

The men could not believe what Galicky was saying. His report went against all of Britain's tradition and sense of fairness and honor.

"The Americans were next to receive Rodney's notice. They were expelled on the 23rd of February and the merchants from Amsterdam the next day. The French and other Dutch citizens soon followed. The crews of the Dutch ships were stripped of all their belongings and sent to Saint Kitts as well. Rodney was more generous to the French and Americans. He allowed them to take their belongings."

"He was worried what would happen if British ships were taken," Lord Anthony said. "Turn about is fair play, after all."

Cook now stood and walked to the governor's conference table, setting his glass down. "It seems the Jewish community was the ones to suffer most of Rodney's wrath."

"He even went so far as to have the linings of their clothes cut open searching for money or valuables. That's not the worst though, in addition to looting Jewish homes, warehouses, and personal possessions, he even ordered the Jewish cemetery be dug up looking for treasure."

"The man has gone mad," Moffitt said. His words echoed everyone's thoughts.

Cook spoke then, "The admiral and I had several disagreements about his conduct. I have it from Captain Galicky that the word was passed that no letters or correspondence by me was to be carried back to England. Gentlemen, be that as it may, I have a letter for Edmund Burke that I'd like to see find its way to him." Cook said this looking at Lord Anthony.

"I assure you, sir, the knowledge of how the correspondence arrived in England will never be divulged. I will see to it, Dr. Cook," Lord Anthony replied.

"Thank you, sir."

Governor Burt rose, sensing the meeting was finished. "I believe I have picked up on the arrival of our dinner guest."

As the men followed the governor out the door, Dr. Cook hung back and fell in line with Gabe. "When it's convenient, sir, may I call on you at your house?"

"Certainly," Gabe responded but thought, *now what*.

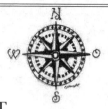

CHAPTER FIVE

FAITH AND ARIEL WERE talking about the pleasures and trials of raising a child. "Nanny has been a God-send," Faith said. "I don't know how I would have gotten by without her and Lum, especially when Gabe was at sea."

"She certainly has impressed me," Ariel said. "You were lucky to find her."

Faith laughed, "Nanny and Lum were slaves on our plantation in South Carolina before I was born. Mama made daddy give them their freedom before she died. Nanny raised me." Ariel was all ears now.

Hex and Gabe sat on the porch discussing the readiness of *Ares*. Lord Anthony had sent over twenty hands and there was talk that some of the free blacks on the island were interested in joining.

Gil and Deborah were coming over for dinner that evening and bringing the marine officer, Captain Philip LoGiudice; and his wife, Holly. This would be Gil and Deborah's last night on the island for the foreseeable future. They would sail with the tide on Saturday morning. Few sailors ever set sail on a Friday if there was an alternative. Sailor superstition!!! Friday was considered an unlucky day. Gabe never subscribed to the superstition, but he didn't go against it, if possible.

A carriage pulled into the yard. Gabe threw away his cigar and Hex knocked the ash from his pipe. Dr. Cook and Leo stepped down from the carriage. Gabe called Lum and asked him to make the driver comfortable. Dr. Cook and Leo had met Faith and Ariel the previous evening at the governor's farewell dinner, so Gabe didn't call out the women for pleasantries. Dr. Cook had scheduled the meeting in the afternoon between the midday meal and dinner, not wanting to intrude on family time.

Gabe introduced Hex and told the visitors to speak freely in front of him. "There are no secrets between my cox'n, my Uncle Dagan and myself. So saying what's on your mind now will just keep me from having to repeat it later. Dagan is expected back at any time, so if he arrives just continue as if he'd been here all along."

Leo smiled, "We were told that you had your inner circle."

"I suspect from Lord Skalla, which means you are both from the Foreign Services office," Gabe replied. The two men acknowledged that they were.

"Dr. Cook is actually Sir Lawrence Cook," Leo Gallagher said, introducing him. "He is a Cambridge physician of some renown. His usage of doctor instead of sir seems to eliminate certain barriers. He is new to our office. His cover is to see why certain sailors succumb to the tropical illnesses while others flourish. We will discuss his real reason for being here later. I... we understand your new ship will be ready to sail in a few days." Gabe acknowledged this with a nod. "We will speak to Admiral Moffett and show him our and your orders."

Gabe started to speak and paused, "I guess for the time being I will be under independent orders."

"That is correct, sir. The first place we'll sail to is Saint Kitts."

"Aye," Gabe responded.

Both men stood then. "We will check back in with

you on Monday, sir. Enjoy your evening with your family."

***

THE DISTANCE FROM ENGLISH Harbour to Saint Kitts was roughly sixty miles, according to the master's charts.

Mr. Randall Scott, *Ares'* new master spoke to Gabe, "Taking into consideration all the variables, I figure the trip will take nine to ten hours if the ship is able to log a constant eight knots, sir."

"I don't intend to sail directly to Saint Kitts, Mr. Scott. I would like to put *Ares* through a few evolutions before arriving."

"Aye, Captain, vary as you may, I'll put us on Saint Kitts." This caused Gabe to smile.

Mr. Scott had come over from *SeaHorse*, volunteered in fact, was Gil's words. Mr. Scott liked the idea of the smaller ship compared to the seventy-four gun *SeaHorse*. He had become a master with the Honest Johns, but after a night of wine and women, he found himself under the guns of a press gang. His exemption papers were never found. However, he soon proved himself and was rated a master's mate. He was now beached, thanks to the October hurricane. He was taken as an extra aboard *SeaHorse*, but with a chance of being disciplined, he spoke to a sailor he was standing by, that it was too bad his master's papers were lost in the recent storm. The sailor looked at Scott as if he was daft, but Lieutenant Mahan, the admiral's flag lieutenant heard the exchange as Scott planned.

"You there," Mahan called. "Come here."

Scott stepped over and knuckled his brow, "Yes sir."

"Did I hear you say that you were a master, a

36

certified master with certificates?"

"Aye, sir, that I be."

"With the Royal Navy?" Mahan asked.

"It was with the East India Company, sir, but other than the document stamps, they be the same."

Mahan paused a second and thought it over. When he decided, he spoke to Scott, "Go get cleaned up and then report to me at the quarterdeck."

Scott was back, looking as polished as he could with little to wear other than the slops from the purser, in fifteen minutes. Mahan was waiting and took Scott to Vice Admiral Lord Anthony's cabin. Seated there were Captain Earl, *SeaHorse's* captain; John Waters, the ship's master, Lord Anthony, and just behind him was his fierce-looking cox'n, Bart. Scott stood, with his hands at his side, as no offer of a chair was given.

Lord Anthony spoke, "My flag lieutenant tells me that you are a master."

"Yes sir."

"Why haven't you spoken of this before?"

"It was my intention, sir, but when I heard the ship was returning home, I just decided to wait until we got home."

"I see," Lord Anthony said. "Captain Earl said that you were listed as a master's mate when you came aboard."

"That's true, my Lord. I was in my cups when taken by a press gang, and being the worse for drink, I didn't realize my whereabouts until we were out to sea."

"You didn't tell the captain?" Earl threw out.

"I did, sir, but he wasn't going to come about for the likes of me." This gained a few chuckles from the group. "It wasn't right away that I was allowed to speak to the captain, as it were. When I finally did get to speak to him, he related that I was not the first mistake made by the press gang. He asked me several questions to be sure I was who I said I was, but he didn't care about my certificate. He said he already had one master and that was all that was needed, so he rated me as the senior master's mate with the promise to set things right when possible."

"I see," Lord Anthony said. He then added, "I have a ship needing a master...my brother's ship. You wouldn't mind answering a few questions from Mr. Waters, would you, before I send you to my brother?"

"No, sir, I welcome them and the chance to serve in my rightful place."

Captain Earl asked, "Mr. Scott, tell me, is it hard to make master with the Honest Johns?"

Scott replied, without blinking, "You almost have to wait until someone dies." The group of men chuckled at this. He then volunteered, "I had fifteen years in service; ten of them as a master's mate. I knew I'd never make lieutenant, without some influence, so I went before a board of the senior captain and three senior masters." Waters had been standing behind Scott when he was speaking. He nodded this to be the way to achieve the rank.

Captain Earl spoke, as Waters and Scott left the cabin, "You might have Gabe a master."

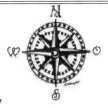

CHAPTER SIX

IT STILL LACKED TWO more days for March to end and April to begin, but the weather had a time frame of its own. It had been miraculously sunny when the carriage with Faith and the new marine captain's wife pulled away as *Ares* got underway. A very smooth evolution, but with Con Vallin at the quarterdeck Gabe would have been surprised had it not been.

It seemed that the sky became moody with a distant rumble of thunder, and dark clouds were dimming the sun's rays as the carriage pulled out of sight. The rain came once *Ares* was free of the harbour. A torrential downpour that lasted all of twenty minutes, which coincided with the new master's prediction. 'Heavy showers off and on until midday, I'm thinking,' were his exact words. He'd been right, so far.

Hex came in, pulling his dripping tarpaulin off, just before entering the cabin. The marine sentry at the door made no announcement.

Captain Philip LoGiudice, captain of the marines, had had an early dinner with Gabe and Faith the night before. Faith and LoGiudice's wife, Holly, had taken a liking to each other instantly. Gabe thought that was a good thing, since most of her friends were leaving with the squadron...it was a godsend actually.

After the meal, and over cigars and brandy, Gabe introduced his uncle, Dagan, and his friend and cox'n, Hex, to LoGiudice. He said, "As far as these two, they have an open door, to come and go as they please. The only time they are to be announced is when Faith may be aboard."

LoGiudice smiled, "Aye, every courtesy for the captain's wife."

"My servant need not be announced as he spends most of his time in the pantry, and will announce himself before he ventures further into my cabin," Gabe continued. With a smile creasing his face, he added, "Josh Nesbit is like no other you will find. He is an outstanding chef but he's also a gentleman's gentleman. He is far more educated than most men. It has been a bit of a transformation for him, learning the language, traditions, and ways of the Royal Navy. But he has done very well. He also stands in for my clerk. Our surgeon, Dr. Robert Cornish, is the best of his kind that I've ever met. He is often found with Dagan or Hex when not attending to his duties. I've known most of our crew for some time. We've one new officer and several new midshipmen. It will take a while but you will get to know them all."

Gabe then explained *Ares* was a new command, that she was a razee, like *Drakkar*, his first ship with his brother in command. LoGiudice had not heard the term razee before, so for the next hour, they talked about *Ares* and what makes a ship a razee.

"Simply put, it is when a larger ship, usually a sixty-four or a seventy-four gun, has the upper deck removed and is converted into a heavy frigate. The razed ship will have the strength of construction to carry heavier guns with more firepower. They are also able to take more punishment than the usual frigate. Another bonus is their increased length tends to make them fast sailors. We've taken *Ares* out and she is indeed fast, and has excellent maneuvering qualities. We took her out with a reduced crew, so I've not been able to test her as I'd like, but we will on the way to Saint Kitts. The only thing I've noticed, so far, which may not be so when fully loaded, is that she tends to roll more than needed to leeward. She is a fast lady in a strong wind. *Ares* was originally a French ship that we captured after the big hurricane. I hope that she serves us better than she did the French," Gabe said.

"I noticed that they were putting a new cannon aboard her a few days ago," LoGiudice said.

"Her armament is all new," Gabe replied. "On the upper deck, we have 12 twelve pounders on the quarterdeck and we have 4 forty-two pound carronades. Plus on the forecastle, we have 4 twelve pounders and 2 forty-two pound carronades. We also have 26 twenty-four pounders on the gun deck."

"That's forty-eight guns!" LoGiudice exclaimed. "I thought that she was a forty-four gun ship." Gabe, Hex, and Dagan all grinned this time.

Hex had slipped off and returned with the brandy bottle. He topped everyone's glass and relit his cigar.

Gabe continued, after Hex took his seat again, "She is classified as a forty-four, but most ships carry more guns than classified. In addition to the gun deck and upper deck, we have 2 twelve pound stern guns and numerous swivels."

LoGiudice had been listening to Gabe and let his cigar go out. He got a light from Hex and realized over the next few minutes this trio of men was like no other group he'd ever met in the Navy. Lord Anthony and Bart might be as close but he'd never spent time with them as he had this evening with Gabe, his uncle, and cox'n. Gabe had not once been addressed as anything other than 'Gabe' by Dagan, and 'Captain' by Hex. Hex, in turn, was called Jake. Sir Gabe was not used one time during the conversation. *I've learned a lot and I feel that I've not scratched the surface*, LoGiudice thought.

***

"IS EVERYTHING FINE ON deck?" Gabe asked Hex. With anyone else other than Dagan the official answer would be 'aye', but Gabe was after the truth... the truth of someone other than an officer.

"There are one or two hard bargains that will have to mend their ways," Hex answered. "I expect Mr. Vallin will have a private word with our new bosun about the use of his starter."

"He has a zeal for it." Gabe and Hex turned. Dagan had entered without their hearing him. "Mr. Scott is assembling the mids together just to see who knows what a sextant is."

"Does anyone?" Gabe couldn't help but ask.

"Aye, two of them, the oldest and the youngest," Dagan said smiling.

"Looks like our new master will have his work cut out for him," Gabe replied.

A knock at the door was heard, "First lieutenant, suh."

"Enter," Gabe replied. "Nesbit, a glass of refreshment for Mr. Vallin."

"Aye, Sir Gabe." Nesbit set a glass of lime juice down for the lieutenant. He asked, "Would a glass for everyone be appropriate?"

"I think so," Gabe replied, seeing the glass sitting on Vallin's knee.

"With your permission," Vallin started, "I think we'll spend the afternoon in sail drill."

"That's good," Gabe said. "I want to see how our new ship handles. The skies are darkening again, so we'll see how her sailing abilities change with the weather."

Without another word, Vallin downed his glass. Overhead, through the skylight, the sound of raindrops was heard again.

"My cloak, Jake," Gabe ordered. "Let's see how the ship handles in a squall." He looked back as he made his way out the door.

"I'll stay here...out of the rain, " quipped a smiling Dagan.

***

DOCTOR LAWRENCE COOK, HIS assistant, Leo Gallagher; Doctor Robert Cornish, First Lieutenant Con Vallin, and the two senior midshipmen, Brian Heath and Joshua Delsenno, joined Gabe as dinner guests that evening. The talk centered on the new ship, *Ares*, how she handled before, during, and after the showers that day.

Doctor Cook spoke of some new studies that he and Doctor Cornish would discuss in detail at another time so as to not burden the non-medical people with such talk. They were midway through the main course of apple and herb roasted pheasant, which was one of Nesbit's specialties, served with buttery new potatoes, carrots and a pleasant white wine. Doctor Cook asked the midshipmen how they liked their new ship.

Brian reported that he'd never been aboard another ship before, so he had nothing to compare *Ares* with. He then smiled and said, "If the food is this good, I'm glad father sent me."

This caused a big smile to appear on Vallin's face. He looked at Gabe who smiled back. "Always enjoy a good meal when it's offered, young sir, as you are bound to find them few and far between."

Heath was about to say something in response but a quick nudge from Joshua Delsenno caused him to close his mouth, leaving his comment unspoken.

"And you, young sir, have you been on another ship?"

"Aye, I was aboard *Tomahawk* with Captain Davy, sir," Joshua replied.

"How long were you with Captain Davy?" Gabe inquired.

"Five months, sir."

"Did you like *Tomahawk*?"

"Aye, sir, she was a fine ship."

"Are you from Antigua?" Gabe asked, wondering why the young gentleman asked to be assigned to *Ares*.

"Yes sir. My father is the tailor that most of the officers use at English Harbour. Captain Davy recommended the transfer, sir. He related that *Ares* and his first ship, *HMS Drakkar*, are similar. He said that I'd learn more here than tied up in Portsmouth."

Gabe thought, *that sounds like Davy.* "Did he tell you we were both midshipmen on *Drakkar*?"

Joshua smiled, "Aye, Captain that he did. He said you were the senior and he was the most junior."

By the twinkle in Joshua's eyes, Gabe guessed that Davy may have said more. "Yes, we did have some fun times back then. We also paid the price. I can't tell you how many times I was sent to the tops or had to kiss the gunner's daughter."

This comment caused Doctor Cook to speak, "Please take pity on a lubber and explain the phrase. I sense that it has nothing to do with a romantic kiss." Everyone at the table smiled at Cook's question.

"When a young gentleman does something where he needs to be punished, he is frequently bent over one of the cannons and the bosun lays on a dozen with his ratten or starter."

"That's a harsh form of discipline," Cook said in awe.

"Aye, one that seldom has to be repeated," Gabe responded.

"I see," Cook replied.

It appeared that young Mr. Heath did as well, as his appetite suddenly seemed to have left him.

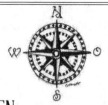

CHAPTER SEVEN

GABE HAD THE LOG cast at times when the sun was out, when a squall was approaching, and again in the midst of the squall. Not a single cast came back at less than eight knots, and for the last hour *Ares* had surged along at ten knots. *She'll do better under full sail and once we get her weight balanced*, Gabe thought to himself. A note had been made prior to sailing that the ship was a bit down aft.

"Land ho, off the bow, dead ahead."

Gabe couldn't recall the man's name so he looked at Hex. "That's Seaman Parker, Captain, with young Mister Corwin with him."

"Vaughn?"

"Aye, Captain, Vaughn Corwin. His father has his hand in several enterprises. Shipping is one of them."

"He's the youngest son?"

"I believe so, Captain. His papers are on your desk."

Gabe had accepted several of the midshipmen as a favor to the governor. He'd not actually looked over their papers or letters. In fact, other than having the two to dinner the previous evening, he'd only spoken to the young gentlemen once very briefly. He was now being reminded by his cox'n that he'd been remiss in his duties.

Gabe was about to speak but Hex spoke again, "I believe Dagan has spent some time with the young sirs and feels that they all have promise. Maybe because he's the youngest, but he seems to be drawn to young Corwin. I've seen them speaking a few times."

Another I've neglected...Dagan, Gabe thought. He'd remedy that now. "Well, Uncle," Gabe spoke to Dagan. "It's not our first approach to the island, is it?"

"No, but things are in the process of changing, I fear," Dagan replied.

Gabe stopped. *What was Dagan's meaning? We'll have to speak of it soon.*

***

THE SHOWER THAT HAD come with the dawn had moved on, but the sun was yet to shine at its usual brightness. It had warmed up and a bit of wind blew the gray clouds to the west, since that early squall. The bow was put into the wind and the anchor let go. The chain made its telltale sound as it followed the anchor running forward and down, creating a splash as the anchor hit the water. Several fishing boats moored to larboard seemed to bob up and down. A man was leaning off the bow on one of the larger boats, untying a line and tossing it back on board the boat.

Dagan volunteered as he walked up, "He's off to make a catch."

Wavelets slapped up against the rocks along the shoreline and a brown pelican flapped its wings and hopped up on a higher rock.

Doctor Cook and his assistant, Leo the lion as Hex had started calling him, but not in hearing distance, came on deck. "I can smell the salt in the air," Doctor Cook said. He then looked up and pointed at the gull riding the wind upward and then gliding off in another direction without even flapping. "There are only a couple of ships in harbor," Cook said as he approached Gabe. "I'd have thought that there would have been more."

"They are probably with Rodney or escorting his

prizes," Gabe responded.

An old twenty-gun frigate and a newer looking thirty-two gun frigate were all there was for the naval presence at Saint Kitts.

"A boat has shoved off from the smaller ship," Hex informed his captain. Within a few minutes, the challenge 'boat ahoy' was given at the entry port and the reply *Lark* came back.

A youngish, almost boyish-looking captain made his way up the battens and through the entry port. He doffed his hat and reached out to shake Gabe's hand. "Louis Haven, sir, *HMS Lark* of twenty guns," the captain said, introducing himself.

"Gabriel Anthony," Gabe replied. "Welcome aboard *HMS Ares*." He wondered as he introduced himself if he had looked so boyish when he made post.

Hex had already gone down to make sure Nesbit would be ready with refreshments. To give Nesbit time to get ready, Gabe introduced Captain Haven to Lieutenant Con Vallin and then to Doctor Lawrence Cook and his assistant.

"Captain Robert Hurley of the *Ludlow* is waiting upon the governor, sir. We were sent here to Saint Kitts with several Jewish families and were told to wait upon the governor or the senior naval representative for further orders. Captain Hurley was the senior naval authority until you arrived, sir."

"How are your ships in regards to a state of readiness?" Gabe asked.

"We were next in line to be sent to Bermuda for overhaul when we were assigned to Admiral Rodney's command, sir."

Hmmm, Gabe thought to himself, and then said "Let's go below and see what my man can provide by way of refreshments."

***

GABE, WITH DOCTOR COOK, Leo and Dagan went ashore to see the governor. Gabe was a bit surprised that the two frigate captains had been given such hazy orders. Rodney must have had his mind on his fleeced treasure more than the welfare of his ships.

The temperature was at least ten to fifteen degrees cooler upon entering the Government Building. The group had paused a moment in Basseterre to watch a street vendor doing tricks with his little monkeys. A woman had colorful parrots in a cage for sale and still another was offering hand rolled cigars. At the end of the square, they obtained a coach for the ride to the Government Building. During that short time, even with a land breeze, Gabe's uniform had become wet with sweat and was sticky, so the cooler building was appreciated. He'd noted that the roof had been made with a white terracotta tile. *They must help reflect the heat*, he thought.

The doorman led the group to a modest sized office. *It must be the governor's private office*, Gabe thought. General Shirley had succeeded his father as the governor of Saint Kitts. Shirley did not keep the group long. When he came in, Gabe introduced himself and the rest of the men with him.

"I was glad to see your ship enter the harbor. I was just talking to Captain Hurley about the needs of his ships and that of *Lark*. Frankly, I had no idea as to the best course to follow. When I saw your ship, Sir Gabe, I was relieved. I will, therefore, turn the decision as to what course of action to take, over to the new naval authority." This he said with a smile. *Shat rolls downhill*, Gabe thought.

The governor ordered refreshments and then took up the subject of the two ships again. He walked over to the far wall, where a large map hung. The map included the West Indies and the Caribbean, and went as far north as Bermuda. It also showed the southeastern part of the Colonies, with those bordering the Gulf of Mexico in detail. Using the stem of his large pipe, he pointed out Saint Eustatius. "Here is the island of Saint Eustatius where Admiral Rodney laid waste and pillaged the place." Gabe didn't miss the disdain in the governor's voice.

Governor Shirley continued, "And here is Saint Kitts. Gentlemen, between the two islands lies Antigua. Please explain to me why Rodney would bypass Antigua, which is far more capable of handling the needs of the Navy's ships and displacement of honorable citizens. Civilians who are noncombatants, who have never taken up arms against anybody and their only crime is being on a Dutch island." Before anyone could comment, Governor Shirley answered the question he put forth. "I will tell you why. He didn't want to face the scrutiny of Admiral Moffett, much less Lord Anthony." He then turned and, walking to his desk, he tossed his pipe on it, scattering ashes everywhere and breaking the stem of the brittle white clay pipe. "Dammit," Shirley swore when he saw the mess that he'd made. He waved his hand as if dismissing the incident. "I've news for our admiral," he said, looking directly at Gabe. "I'm sending the Jews right back home...such as it may be. Hopefully, they'll come to understand that not all of our countrymen are cast from the same die." He paused then for a moment. "I apologize for my rant, gentlemen, but I have to consider that should we get attacked, which I feel is very likely, we will be subjected to the same abuse as our esteemed admiral and his general have meted out."

One of the governor's secretaries knocked discreetly and reminded Shirley of the time. "My cue, gentlemen, please feel free to enjoy the island's comforts. I hope you find the answers to your questions, Doctor Cook, but I must tell you, that it's not just the sailors who succumb to the island's ill vapors. It's often the soldiers and others sent from England in support of the crown."

"Thank you," Doctor Cook responded, his assistant Leo giving a slight bow.

Gabe reached out to shake Shirley's hand. The governor grasped his hand and spoke, "If you can transport any of the Jews home it will be appreciated. Also, if the other ships need to go for their repairs then so be it. However, if it's not an undue hindrance, if they could take as many as possible of the displaced home before they go to the dockyards, so much the better."

"I was thinking about one of the ships going with me and when their overhaul is complete they would come back and relieve the other. That way you'd have at least one warship here if needed."

Shirley nodded, still holding Gabe's hand. "I appreciate your concern. We do live in fear of an invasion, but in truth, one small frigate offers little, Sir Gabe. If we were attacked, it might be better if they were not here. Besides, we have the fortress at Brimstone Hill. I hope that you have time to visit it. I will put a carriage at your disposal. I'm sure that you will be suitably impressed."

Gabe thanked the governor and walked out. Doctor Cook and Leo were in conversation with one of the secretaries.

"Asking directions to an import export company," Dagan volunteered. "It is such an original place to put a spy." This made Gabe smile. His uncle had a way with words.

Before taking the offered carriage to Brimstone Hill, Gabe decided to send the two frigates to dry dock at Antigua. They then would come under Moffitt's orders. Feeling good about his plan, he climbed aboard the carriage.

CHAPTER EIGHT

THE FORTRESS AT BRIMSTONE Hill was, in fact, something to behold. Gabe was in awe, as were Doctor Cook, Leo, Dagan, and Hex. The fort had been designed by British military engineers and constructed using slave labor. The fort was built on a very steep, sloping hill. It was situated so that you could see for miles. Any ships approaching from the western Caribbean would be sighted long before they arrived.

Gabe heard Hex comment to Dagan, "They have about every caliber of gun imaginable." Looking about, Gabe realized he was right. Fort Charles was nothing compared to Brimstone Hill.

A major walked up to Gabe inviting him and his guest to dine with the officers. "Your man," he said, meaning Hex, "has an invitation to dine with the sergeant major, who will be along soon." Looking up, a red-faced man was approaching. The major said, as if reading Gabe's mind about how flushed the man appeared, "Irish," as if that would explain it all. The Irish, in general, were fair complexioned; and being on a tropical island wearing full dress was bound to make the man appear flushed.

The group gathered to depart after a very agreeable lunch of cold meats, bread and cheese, with the artillery major. "It's been a very pleasant visit," Gabe told the major and invited him and a guest to dine aboard *Ares*.

As they left in the carriage, Doctor Cook remarked

that he'd never seen a more formidable fortress.

Hex spoke up, "The sergeant major says that if a force fights its way up the hill, at this time, the lower emplacements will be overrun. However, once inside the actual fort, the likelihood of the enemy broaching its walls is almost none. The problem then becomes supplies, mostly food." Gabe had noted a large number of people working inside the gates and the numerous huts built in the compound.

"The hospital I noted," Doctor Cook interjected, "is on the lower aspect of the fort, almost overlooking the sea, where the sick can take advantage of the sea breeze. Should the fort be attacked, will the sick be deserted?"

"Not likely," Gabe answered. "I've never known the enemy, though, to not act honorably to the sick and wounded." Doctor Cook acknowledged the statement but it seemed his mind was thinking on something more distant.

***

THE SUN WAS STARTING to set and creating such a view that Gabe wished that he had Faith with him. Josh Nesbit had just left to get ready for the evening guests. Gabe had invited First Lieutenant Con Vallin, Doctor Cook, Captain Hurley of *Ludlow*, Captain Haven of *Lark*; the artillery major, Major Rich from the fort, plus Marine Captain LoGiudice and Dagan to be his dinner guests. Josh Nesbit was in a good mood as the island had provided all he needed to show off his culinary talents. Gabe was sure the meal would be one to remember.

Josh had also taken the time to apprise Gabe of the new man, Simon Davis' (referred to by the ship's company as the hanged man) many talents. He was a man who knew his numbers and letters. In fact, he was a merchant's son from the coastal village of Polperro, on Cornwall's southern coast. It was a small fishing village, but was also known for its notorious smugglers. Contraband goods were smuggled across from Guernsey. Many of the fishermen supplemented their income acting as crewmembers for the smugglers. The Davis family had prospered and so young Simon had benefited from better than average tutors. What the young Simon hadn't learned was to stay away from another man's wife; especially when the man was the most noted smuggler in Polperro with dozens of black-hearted henchmen.

John Quiller, the leader of the smugglers, had a friend who was much in debt to the smuggler's banker. Quiller paid off the father's debt, and in turn was able to wed the friend's much younger daughter. She and Simon were of the same age and had been friends for some years. When the new husband was out to sea, Simon would prevail upon himself to keep the lass company. This meant that he often bedded her as he gave comfort. A gale rose up one night, and the sea was too high for the usual run, so Quiller came home much sooner than usual. Hearing the front door, Simon grabbed his clothes and exited the window, and was hurried along by a pistol ball that grazed his naked arse. Simon ran right into the midst of a press gang and, stammering excitedly, told the lieutenant in charge that he wanted to volunteer. The lieutenant responded, 'Aye, it's eager you are, I see, but wouldn't it be more fitting if you were to dress before you sign the papers.' This brought a chuckle from Gabe and Dagan as Nesbit told the story.

***

THE MEAL THAT EVENING was one to remember. Nesbit served the first course, which consisted of turtle soup with bread that was thin and crusted, but otherwise not unlike a ship's biscuit. The main course was served and consisted of a blackened tuna with a slightly seasoned sauce to pour over it, and greens with bacon bits mixed in. Jacket potatoes were halved, buttered, and had a cheese topping that was cooked to a crust to the delight of all of Gabe's guests. Nesbit had brought out a few bottles of a captured French white wine.

"This is a fine wine," Doctor Cook said, congratulating Gabe on his wine selection. Gabe quickly passed the compliment on to Nesbit.

After the meal was completed, hot coffee and apple tarts were served. A warm, thick sweetened cream was spooned over the tarts, making the dessert a crowd pleaser. Brandy and Cuban cigars or pipes followed the dessert.

"Better enjoy the Cuban cigars," Major Rich volunteered. "They will become a precious commodity with Spain in the war now and the supply drying up."

"Not if I know my captain like I think I do," Con Vallin responded.

Philip LoGiudice took a puff and thought, *there's no doubt our first officer has every confidence in our captain.*

Doctor Cook heard the exchange but his eyes fell on Dagan. The captain's uncle seemed to wince at the comment. Did he feel something was up? Cook had talked to the second lieutenant, Lieutenant Laqua, when he had watch during the voyage from Antigua. He too praised the captain, but he didn't stop there. He commented that Dagan was a mystery, a friendly, capable man, but very dark and mysterious at times. One who the captain held above all others outside of his wife and child. 'You want to know how the future is going to play out, then pay attention to Dagan...

he knows,' Laqua had said. Cook was certain that he placed little regard as to one seeing the future. He did not doubt the man had a certain 'sense' about things.

Cook was sure of one thing, though, after his and Leo's meeting with the Foreign Office's agent here on Saint Kitts, it was a certainty the island would be a prime target for the French...and maybe with the help of either Spain or the Dutch. He took the last swallow of his brandy. Trying to discover why some seamen suffered from tropical vapors more than others would probably lessen, compared to trying to save those cut down by a ball or blade. If the first officer was right, his captain was a magnet for drawing enemy ships to battle. *How will I act in battle*, Cook wondered. He was so deep in his thoughts that he was totally surprised when Dagan touched his shoulder and spoke.

"You will be helping Doctor Cornish in the cockpit on the orlop deck should we go into battle."

Damn the man reads minds, Cook thought. "Thank you," he replied.

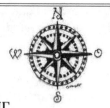

CHAPTER NINE

DOCTOR COOK HAD WATCHED with intrigue at what he would have described as organized chaos as *HMS Ares* got underway. *HMS Ludlow* and *HMS Lark* with their decks full of Jews from Saint Eustatius took station on *Ares*, as Saint Kitts and Nevis slipped astern.

The master, Randall Scott, was in conversation with Vallin, the first lieutenant. "I can smell a blow coming on," Scott said. Without questioning the master, Vallin called for the bosun and ordered that everything be secured and battened down.

Cook found himself looking up at the sky and the horizon. As he turned, he looked into the eyes of Dagan and Captain Anthony. "Your master says he can smell a blow," he said.

"Aye, his kind usually has a feel for the weather," Gabe replied.

Leo, who'd been standing by the rail, volunteered, "It looks clear now, but I've learned never to doubt an old shellback."

"Nor would I," Gabe and Dagan replied in unison.

"It will not be anything of significance, but if we prepare for the worst, we will have done what's prudent," Dagan added.

"Aye, and nobody likes a wet hammock," Gabe responded.

When the gale did arrive, it roared in with a blinding vengeance, low and level from across the open sea. The first warning was the chop of the waves, followed by the wind and rain. A pelting rain that stung the skin as it peppered the faces of the crew. The lookout had called down, 'Here she comes,' and the next instant the riggings started to sing. Cook looked behind him but the *Ludlow* and *Lark* were no longer visible.

Cook, not wanting to be in the way but desirous of seeing the storm firsthand, was given permission to remain on deck. He donned a tarpaulin and secured himself to the fife rail. He watched as the bow plunged down and the sea crashed over it, sending water across the deck and cascading down the channels and out the scuppers. He realized that he was completely soaked, even with the tarpaulin. As quickly as it had come, it was gone and Cook marveled at how he could see it continuing on its path as he watched.

The coolness from the squall didn't last long, and the ship's deck grew hot. Tar bulged in places along the seams between the deck planking. The sails dried quickly, between the breeze and the warmth of the tropical sun.

The third lieutenant, Mr. Bryan Turner, spoke to Second Lieutenant Ronald Laqua,"Are we in for another blow? I think I hear the sound of thunder."

Lieutenant Laqua had his head turned and his features changed. "Lookout," he yelled. "What see you?"

Gabe heard Laqua's shout, as did his first lieutenant. They both knew for Laqua to make such an inquiry something had to arouse his suspicion.

"Nothing but haze to larboard, all else is clear," the lookout replied.

Gabe approached his third lieutenant, "What do you hear?"

Young Turner answered, "Thunder, I believe, Captain."

"It's the thunder of cannons, sir," Laqua threw out.

Hex and Dagan were close by. They both heard the sound and were about to speak when Gabe spoke, "I hear it now." Seeing Midshipman Delsenno, he called to him, "Take a glass and up you go, young sir." Delsenno grabbed a glass from its rack and with a bound he scurried up the ratlines.

Marine Captain LoGiudice was standing next to Doctor Cook. "The urgency of youth," Cook said.

"Aye, that and knowing that his captain had his eyes on him," LoGiudice said.

Cook smiled and replied, "Aye, there is that as well."

Once in the tops, the young gentleman scanned the horizon. "Mist is lifting to larboard," he shouted down. Shortly after his first report, Delsenno said, "Two ships attacking a ship with our colors, Captain. One appears to be a brig and the other one is flying French colors and appears to be a corvette. The British ship is a sloop, Captain."

"Mr. Vallin, wear ship if you please and have the master set a course for yonder ships," Gabe said.

"Mr. Heath," Gabe called. "Signal our two frigates, 'enemy in sight.' *That should require no more explanation or signals,* he thought.

The sound of cannons going off was now plainly audible on deck. Gabe, still not able to see the fighting ships from the deck, took the glass Hex offered and climbed up several feet in the ratlines. "Mr. Delsenno has a good eye, Mr. Vallin, that English vessel is indeed a sloop."

The sloop was being chased by two ships, as reported. It would have been a long chase but one the sloop would have lost. Gabe could now make out the French colors but he couldn't see any from the other enemy vessel. She did appear to be a brig, but seemed to carry a wider beam. It dawned on Gabe then—she's got to be Dutch. They didn't wait too long to show their ingratitude for Admiral Rodney's exploits, if she was indeed Dutch.

"Mr. Vallin, beat to quarters if you will. Once our men are at their stations, have Mr. Myers make our presence known with our bow chasers."

"Aye, Captain." The bosun's pipe whistled out and the drummer was quickly beating out 'Heart of Oaks.'

Cook stood aside as the deck vibrated with the stamp of feet across its deck and the sound of the cannons' carriage wheels being pulled into place. *I thought getting underway was something, but that pales in comparison as going to quarters,* Cook thought. He suddenly realized that his name was being called. "Er...yes, Captain."

"I was saying you may remain on deck for now but should the enemy engage us, please make your way to the cockpit."

"Yes, Captain, by all means."

One by one the stations reported their readiness. The first officer snapped his watch cover shut and reported, "Eight minutes, Captain, not bad."

Gabe looked at his first officer and saw the thin smile. "You are either a liar, Con Vallin, or need a new watch," Gabe whispered. He then said in a louder voice, "Closer to eight and half minutes, I'd say. The men are improving, thanks to your drills, sir."

One of the gun captains heard the conversation and whispered to his mate, "'Ear that did ya? The first lieutenant ain't such a bad bloke, after all. Covering for us with the cap'n, he is."

"Forward guns are ready for a ranging shot, Captain."

"Thank you, Mr. Myers," Gabe responded to the gunner. "You may fire as you will."

The forward guns quickly fired. **BOOM...BOOM!** The gun captains' shouts could be heard as they quickly and professionally barked out orders for reloading. **BOOM...BOOM!** The guns continued to fire and an acrid smoke drifted back. Doctor Cook quickly put a handkerchief to his nose and shielded his eyes. The sloop had changed her course and now made directly for *Ares* and her consorts.

"The enemy has broken it off, Captain," Delsenno called down.

Damn, Gabe swore to himself. He'd forgotten to call the midshipman down. Almost as if reading Gabe's mind, Dagan spoke, "Had a bird's eye view that one did. I've no doubt he'll explain where every shot fell to his mates when he's off duty."

"Aye," Gabe replied, but wondered how many hours he'd spent in the tops because someone forgot to call him down.

CHAPTER TEN

H*MS PICKLE* WAS A fine looking ship. A Bermuda sloop, Dagan advised Doctor Cook as her captain made his way up the battens and through the entry port. Mal Nicholson was a cheerful man. He doffed his hat and shook Gabe's hand and introduced himself.

"My thanks to you, Captain," Nicholson said. "You showed up at the most opportune time. I was fell upon by the French corvette but felt we could out sail her when the Dutch brig came in off the bow and fired upon us. We never expected the Dutch to fire on us."

"You haven't heard then," Gabe responded. "We are at war with the Dutch, Captain Nicholson."

"We've just come from Bermuda," Nicholson explained. "The news hasn't reached there yet."

"I see," Gabe replied, and then asked, "Where are you headed, Captain?"

"Antigua, sir."

"We will sail as a group," Gabe ordered and then added, "Once we are at English Harbour, Captain, I would like very much to visit your ship. She is a fine-looking vessel."

"By all means, Captain," Nicholson exclaimed. "Let's make it at such a time that you can have dinner after your tour."

"Done," Gabe answered with a smile, liking this ruddy captain.

Nicholson made his way back aboard his ship and *HMS Pickle* fell in with *HMS Ludlow* and *Lark*.

***

THERE WERE ONLY THREE ships at anchor in English Harbour. Doctor Cook was on deck and Gabe pointed out the elevated plateau that was Shirley Heights.

"Shirley Heights is a welcome sight for any ship that's been at sea for a month or so. The landlocked harbor offers a sheltered refuge not only from the elements but enemy cannons as well," Gabe said, pointing out Fort Berkeley.

"The island has many forts, does it not, Captain?"

"Aye it does, but Fort Berkeley is the one that protects the harbor's entrance," Gabe replied.

"Is English Harbour the only suitable harbor the island has?" Cook asked.

"No, there is Falmouth Harbour as well, but English Harbour is the largest," Gabe answered.

"I see it's still a work in progress," Cook mused.

"What's that?" Gabe asked.

"I'm sorry, Captain, I was just thinking that there seems to be a bit of construction still going on."

Gabe smiled, thinking of his first trip to English Harbour. "It's been constant construction since my first trip to the island," Gabe replied. "I was a midshipman then. Commodore Gardner was in charge of the dockyard at the time. I recall him saying that English Harbour was the biggest dockyard outside of England. I don't know if that's really true or just his pride speaking. I do remember him saying they had over one-hundred and fifty workers. Sadly, most of them were slaves. They did have many shipwrights, some sawyers, and blacksmiths, sail makers, caulkers, and such."

Cook noticed that as Gabe spoke, he also kept a keen eye as Vallin, the first lieutenant, expertly brought the ship in.

"Ready to fire the salute," Vallin said to his captain.
"Very well. Proceed, Mr. Vallin."

Cook thought the business of firing salutes a bit of waste and would broach the subject at some point. Seeing the captain was now employed with bringing the ship in, Cook walked over to join Leo. The sound of the first cannon booming out its salute startled him, making Leo laugh. He asked Leo, "What now?"

They had been given a fair amount of information by the agent on Saint Kitts, along with a dire warning of the likelihood of a French invasion. Rodney should have been headed to the Colonies with his fleet, if the report of a French fleet coming to the aid of the Americans was true, instead of plundering a helpless island and then sending a good many of his ships back to England as escorts for his plunder. "If the fleet arrives as expected and we're not there to defeat it, the war is lost. Admiral Comte de Grasse is a most able man." This warning struck home to the experienced Leo Gallagher.

CHAPTER ELEVEN

THE SLAP OF A halyard and the flap of the pennant overhead caused Gabe to look up as *Ares* sailed along under a fresh breeze. Dagan had walked up just as the sun set over the horizon. He brought a tinderbox and two cigars. The groan of spars grew in frequency and looking over the stern the foaming wake grew wider. *Ares* had proven a good sailor. Gabe was more than just satisfied, he was happy with the ship. There was time enough to load extra provisions, water and articles to be used by the soldiers being carried to the island of Roatan. More than one seaman and even a few officers questioned the why of it. What was the island worth? Most didn't know or care. To Gabe it was a welcomed voyage. It gave him time to train his men. Since leaving Antigua, he had drilled the crew in every imaginable drill...sail drill, gun drill, and fire drill. He marked key men as dead during each drill so the next crew member in line would have to step up. He met with all the hands after each drill.

"What's the biggest sin a seaman can commit?" he asked the crew. After several hands had volunteered their answers, he told his version, the version Lord James Anthony had passed down to each of his sons. "Not being prepared for any situation that might arise was to my father's mind the one sin, the mortal sin of a sailor. Were I to fall, it would be a mortal sin for Mr. Vallin to not be prepared to take over. Were a gun captain to fall, the next man must be prepared and ready to take his job. That goes for every man and every task."

They had called all hands for sail drill in a blow. The wind had all but died at one time and Gabe had all sails furled, long boats taken out and tow lines rigged. Now according to Randall Scott, the master, they should sight the island of Roatan by the first dog watch.

HMS Pickle had brought dispatches from Commander Edward Marcus Despard on Roatan requesting men and guns to protect and defend the islands and English settlers from raids by the Spanish. Commander Despard used Roatan as a base for hit and run or, as termed by the Americans at the battle known as the Battle of Lexington and Concord, guerilla style operations. He did this to extend and maintain England's influence along the Mosquito Coast and wreak havoc against Spanish shipping. His success made it likely that Roatan would be attacked.

Men and weapons, including four six-pound field pieces, were aboard *Ares* and the smaller frigate, *Lark*, and were being taken to New Port Royal. They would be used to fortify Fort Dalling and Fort Despard. Port Royal, located at the western end of the island, had at one time been a pirate stronghold in the old days.

Gabe puffed on the cigar Dagan had brought him and watched as the white smoke drifted up and aft. "That's a good cigar," he said. "Where did you get these?"

"Lieutenant Kenneth Collier gave me these," Dagan replied.

Lieutenant Collier was Captain Nicholson's first lieutenant. They had met while in Antigua. Baxter, Nicholson's cox'n, had delivered the invitation to tour the ship and dine the evening before *HMS Pickle* sailed for Barbados. The sloop was indeed a Bermuda sloop. Her hull was constructed of Bermuda cedar. She mounted ten guns, and was a fast sailor and definitely a beautiful ship. Two of her seamen, a man named Karl and the other one, Mason, pointed out certain features of the ship as only a seaman could appreciate, as Gabe and Dagan toured the ship. The master, Harry Harrison, joined Captain Nicholson and First Lieutenant Collier in welcoming Gabe and Dagan that evening at dinner.

Gabe learned that Captain Nicholson was from Burringham, North Lincolnshire, which is where Captain Stephen Earl was from and, not surprisingly, the families knew each other.

The cigars were known as Fonsecas, and Collier had picked them up in Bermuda. No doubt, from a merchant with ties to illegal trading with Cuba, but for these fine smokes one would be willing to forgive the activities.

Gabe saw his new clerk, Simon Davis, as he was enjoying his cigar. "Davis," he called to the man. "Would you be so good as to have my coxswain attend me and bring his guitar?"

"Aye," Dagan volunteered. "He's been working on some lyrics since he got that guitar on Saint Kitts."

Hex showed up with the guitar he'd bought from one of the deported Jews. It came with several replacement strings and a case of sorts. As with the cigars, trading was prohibited, but if Governor Shirley was disposed to treat the Jews well, Gabe allowed his men to follow suit.

"Let's hear that new song you've been practicing," Dagan said.

"Aye, and if it's good, Dagan will reward you with one of these fine cigars," Gabe said.

Dagan elbowed Gabe in the ribs gently and then said to Hex, "Aye, Jake, I'll gladly give you the cigar I'd saved for your captain." They all laughed, including a voice from the side. Con Vallin had walked up. "Join us, sir," Dagan offered before Gabe could speak. "Our captain is of a mind to give away cigars." Vallin had his pipe lit, "Maybe later, but thank you."

"This song is based on a man, whose wife has died and he's raising his daughter by himself," Hex said.

Gabe knew where the song came from...a planter on Antigua that Lady Deborah knew from years back. His wife had caught the fever and died suddenly. Hex strummed the guitar once, and fine tuned the lower string and started singing.

> *We lay on a blanket – down by the lake*
> *The moon on the water had taken us away*
> *Spent from our passion we cuddled so tight*
> *The smell of the blossoms filled up our night.*

> *I wish that somehow I could go back there*
> *The stars had shown down and danced in your hair*
> *I feel your closeness as if we could touch*
> *Now the world is so lonely, I miss you so much.*

Chorus
I miss you so much the tears I have cried
Lord, what I'd give to be by your side
The memories I hold fill up my dreams
While I try to tend to the little one's needs.

> *I've planted some flowers for the blossoms that bloom*
> *You said it filled the air like a sweet perfume*
> *And I call her Blossom for the blooms that you loved*
> *Me and little Blossom miss you so much.*

Chorus
I miss you so much the tears I have cried
Lord, what I'd give to be by your side

The memories I hold fill up my dreams
While I try to tend to the little one's needs.

As I hold her close
I tell her of you
But there are so many things
A man just can't do.

Hex noticed that as his voice faded away with the words of the last verse, a crowd had gathered. When Gabe looked up, many of the tough seamen were wiping their eyes. He was not surprised as he felt a lump in his throat.

CHAPTER TWELVE

"Sail ho! Three sets of sails to midship larboard side." The lookout's report had been clear and precise. Gabe had felt something that morning when Nesbit had awakened him. They were not far from the coast of Roatan, the master had said, so Gabe had expected sails. Hopefully British sails, but Spanish or French would not surprise him. Scott, the master, had related that there were several bays where they could anchor but the Mesoamerican Reef nearly surrounded the island. The biggest portion of which was on the leeward side of Roatan.

"They be Dons, Cap'n," the lookout called down, having identified the ships.

"Mr. Vallin, beat to quarters, if you please."

Turning to his signals midshipman, he ordered, "Signal to *Lark*, 'enemy in sight'. Follow that with 'three sails.'"

"Aye, Captain," Heath answered as he bounded off.

Gabe could see as the ships grew closer that one was an old fifty gun double-decker, the next in line was about the size of *Lark*, and the third was much smaller, closer to the size of Captain Nicholson's *Pickle*.

Vallin asked, standing next to his captain, "Do you think the little sister will join in?"

"I would think not but it wouldn't hurt to keep an eye on her."

"Do you think they've been to Roatan, Captain?"

The question came from the Third Lieutenant, Mr. Turner.

"I'm not sure," Gabe responded. "We may be too late with the reinforcements and artillery, if so."

"I don't think they have been," Scott, the master offered. "They were too far to the north when we spotted them."

Seamen were busy sanding the decks, so the officers moved out of the way rather than make the men wait.

Scott continued, once they were out of the way of the seamen, "Had they been sailing from Roatan, I would have expected them much further to the south and coming from the west."

"They're tacking," the lookout called down.

"Do we split up, Captain, or go in line."

"I think separately. The *Lark* would never stand a broadside from the big girl," Gabe replied.

"Look, they're not tacking, they're turning away," Turner said.

"Aye," Gabe said. "Let us give chase."

Vallin replied smartly, "Aye Captain."

"Bosun, pipe up sail handlers," Vallin shouted.

"Do you think they are running from us or to help, Captain?"

Gabe looked at his young third officer. His look showed no fear. *Too young*, Gabe thought, but replied, "Time will tell, Mr. Turner."

Ares surged forward with the added canvas. They were soon almost up with the smallest ship. She was the *Zabra Julia*.

"Mr. Heath," Gabe called. "Signal *Lark* to put a prize crew on that ship," he said, pointing with his glass.

The next ship in line appeared to be a frigate. "A thirty-two gun, would you say?" Vallin asked. Gabe nodded but didn't speak.

"She's faster than the two decker," Dagan said.

Gabe put his glass to his eye. Dagan was right. The frigate appeared much newer without the gaudy stern the Spaniards were noted for.

"She will pass the two decker to larboard," Dagan guessed. She was definitely heeled over in that direction.

"Mr. Vallin, I expect fire from that big girl now that the frigate is out of line. Have the forward guns ready."

"Aye, Captain."

The lookout called down from above, "*Lark* has taken the prize, Captain."

BOOM...BOOM!!! The Spanish two decker fired her guns.

"Mark in the log, fired on by a Spanish vessel," Gabe ordered.

The Spaniard's shots were both wide and short.

"A point to larboard, Mr. Scott."

"Aye, Cap'n."

Gabe called out, taking up the speaking trumpet, "You are at liberty to fire, Mr. Myers."

The gunner waved his arm in recognition. He then sighted down his starboard chase gun. He fired with the lookout shouting, "Just short."

"We are gaining," Hex volunteered, and then smiled at having spoken out. Gabe smiled back, taking no offense at his cox'n.

BOOM...BOOM...BOOM!!! The enemy's ball was wide and fell where *Ares* had been before Gabe ordered the change.

The lookout shouted from the tops, "You hit her, I saw railing flying."

"You have her now," Gabe called. "Keep it up."

The gun crew's forwards were working like devils,

firing, reloading, and firing again. Each shot was hitting now. Suddenly the ship swung to starboard. Gabe thought, at first, that it was a maneuver by the Spanish captain, but then a mast went over.

"We've parted her rudder cable, I believe," Gabe said. "See how she slewed around."

"Aye," Vallin answered.

"She's listing as well," Dagan added.

"No white flag," Vallin noted.

"Bring her around for a broadside, Mr. Scott."

"Aye, Cap'n."

"Mr. Laqua, be ready to give her a broadside."

Lieutenant Laqua saluted and turned to his larboard gunners. Ports were opened and carriage wheels rumbled across the deck.

"Fire when ready, Mr. Laqua."

Laqua threw up his sword and then brought it down. *Ares'* full larboard battery cut loose a fiery hell, almost at once, with flames belching three feet out of the cannons' snouts.

"A white flag," the lookout yelled.

"Take a boat, Mr. Vallin, and assess the situation."

"Aye," Vallin replied.

"Mind if I go over?" Marine Captain LoGiudice asked. He said smiling, "You've left no work for my marines so I thought I might gaze upon your handiwork."

"You've my permission, Captain, just be careful. I don't want Faith and Holly both mad at me." LoGiudice smiled, came to attention and then was off.

"I think Hex and I will take a look," Dagan said. *No asking from that one*, Gabe thought. With Hex as his partner, there was no limit what the two might pilfer...*Dagan's retirement fund had to be bulging and Hex's nearly full*, Gabe thought. *The larcenous louts.*

***

THE *SAN LORENZO* WOULD not sail again. She had already been leaking so the pumps had to be manned one hour in four. She was to have traveled to Havana to join forces with Matias de Galvez. They had sailed from Belize City, so Scott had been right in his assumption as of where the ships had come from.

Gabe was now stuck with what to do with the prisoners. He was certain Despard and the people on Roatan had no means to keep them. Simon Davis spoke a bit of Spanish, as he put it. He was now looking through some of *San Lorenzo's* papers. The ship's captain had been an old man and died at sea days before the encounter. The next officer was in place by family connections only. It had been the second lieutenant who had sailed the ship and ordered the frigate to flee. This lieutenant, Hugo de Medina, was now in bad shape. He had been hit with a foot long piece of railing that impaled his abdomen. To pull it out would cause immediate death. Gabe spoke to the officer and asked if there was someone he could write or notify.

"Do not send Lieutenant Gomez back please," de Medina pleaded. "He will lie about my Capitan and do much to disgrace him. For me, there is no one."

Gabe nodded. How many times had influence put people in positions of authority in the Royal Navy? It seemed to be in all walks of life. Gabe decided that he'd do as de Medina asked. He'd make Gomez a prisoner of war and somehow he'd send the rest back to Belize.

Vallin had said the ship carried munitions and food, but felt it too risky to bring out of the ship. Dagan had said the captain's cabin offered little. Gabe thought, *it must not have, as they brought back no chest or bags and they didn't clink or jingle when they returned aboard Ares.*

"Hardly worth the trip over," Dagan said.

Hardly worth, did that imply that they had found something? Well, it must be small, Gabe decided.

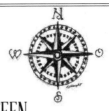

CHAPTER THIRTEEN

A SHIP'S CAPTAIN ALWAYS HAS reservations when he's given a new master who is not a known quality and when he knows that he's possibly putting his ship in danger. It was true that the charts showed a channel through the reef to the anchorage at Port Royal. They were coming in slowly under reduced sail with a man in the chains with his lead line taking soundings. Gabe's apprehension eased as the soundings were called out. He gave a sigh once they were across the reef. The waves could easily be seen breaking over the reef, not a hundred yards to larboard.

"I was a bit anxious myself," Vallin said.

Gabe smiled, only a fool would not be. Looking toward Mr. Scott, he realized that his trust in the master had risen considerably.

Two ships lay at anchor in the harbor. They both flew the British flag but Gabe was taking nothing for granted.

"Take a boat and go ashore, Mr. Vallin, and take Captain LoGiudice and some of his marines with you. In the meantime, we will have the cannons loaded. Any sign of the Spanish, and we'll open up on the shore."

A few people seemed to be wandering about, and on the nearest ship a seaman noticed *Ares*. He pulled on the shoulder of another seaman and pointed toward the new arrival.

"Damn lax watch, if you ask me," Lieutenant Laqua

volunteered. "Surely they have a lookout somewhere."

"At the fort," Dagan said as he pointed out a watch tower ashore.

Vallin was back within the hour. His boat had been followed by another that held Commander Despard and his second in command, James Lawrie.

Edward Marcus Despard was an Irishman. He held the rank of colonel. After brief introductions were made, Despard revealed the two ships at anchor were private vessels. They were both smugglers but they also did a bit of privateering, which kept the Spanish ships busy protecting their harbors and merchant ships. Plans were made to offload the reinforcements and supplies.

"Our island is small," Captain Despard said with his Irish accent. "It would, therefore, be a good place to allow your men a bit of liberty."

Captain Haven of *HMS Lark* had been aboard during the meeting. When Colonel Despard was shown over the side, Haven turned to Gabe. "I see trouble on the horizon, Sir Gabe."

Puzzled, Gabe asked, "How so?"

"Major Conway, the officer in charge of the reinforcements, has shown his dislike for the Irish. You rarely hear of a major speaking to a common soldier, but the good major has gone out of his way to make life hell for two privates. My first lieutenant is named O'Brien. He said something to him about his Irish heritage. I couldn't let one of my officers be subjected to that sort of thing, especially in front of the crew."

Gabe listened intently. It was not good business to have ill feelings between the services. "What did you say?" Gabe asked.

"I told him he was, in fact, a guest aboard our ship so I would not allow Mr. O'Brien to seek satisfaction. I told the major that the lives of him and all of his men might well lie in the hands of the first lieutenant. I then told the major in a whisper that it was not uncommon for hands to vanish over the side, never to be heard from again. I told him that were I him I'd do nothing further to antagonize our Irish brethren."

"Did he change his ways?"

"Aye, Sir Gabe, but being ashore might bring back to his old ways."

***

ARES AND *LARK* LAY at anchor for five days. The crews were allowed ashore, fifty men at a time, during that time. Nesbit and Simon went ashore almost daily, bringing back coconuts, mangoes, bananas, some bags of coffee, and bread that was made by a woman who put corn in her batter when she baked the bread. Nesbit also got a recipe to make conch fritters to go with coconut conch chowder. He had gotten the ingredients so that he could prepare it that evening.

Dagan and Hex accompanied Gabe as they took a boat out to the reef. The water was so clear that it was easy to see all the vibrant colors. The reef was alive with fish of various colors; gold, green, blue, and silver. They each had been given large glass jars, and by pushing them down part way they were able to see the shallow bottom. Lobsters, starfish, two small octopus, and a moray eel. Sitting up straight, Hex called to his companions as a huge sting ray swam by the boat.

Captain Haven, Con Vallin, Scott, the master, and the two youngest gentlemen, Vaughn Corwin and Henry Easley, joined Gabe for the evening meal, which consisted of conch chowder and fritters, and also a delicious lime pie for dessert. After the meal, Hex serenaded them with a few songs. When at last Gabe went to bed, he thought of how it would have been a perfect visit had Faith been along. Would she have enjoyed the reef and all its inhabitants? He was sure that she would.

They would sail back to Antigua tomorrow. Gabe had traded some of the gunpowder and ball to Isaac Zeilistra, in return for taking the Spanish prisoners to Belize. Unfortunately, Lieutenant Hugo de Medina had not lived an hour after Gabe had spoken to him. Gabe kept his word and took Lieutenant Gomez back as a prisoner of war. He'd receive no thanks from Admiral Moffitt, but hopefully he'd understand. What he knew about the Spanish lieutenant was enough to want to be rid of him right away. Gabe had even thought of putting him off on Captain Haven, but his conscience wouldn't allow that. The prize money from the little sloop would make it worthwhile, hopefully. *If not...who's to say he couldn't go over the side. Hmm... that's not a bad thought.*

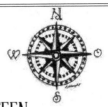

CHAPTER FOURTEEN

THE SHADOWS LENGTHENED AND a bit of welcome coolness greeted the evening. Gabe was only too happy for the respite. He had been aboard the flagship in a meeting with Admiral Dutch Moffitt and the two foreign agents, Leo Gallagher and Doctor Lawrence Cook. Gabe was surprised, at first, to see both of the agents, expecting one to have sailed back to England in *HMS Pickle*. Plans had changed though. News arrived that Sir Rodney was still at Saint Eustatius and showed no sign of an early departure. Therefore, with recommendations from Governor Burt, Admiral Moffitt had sailed to the Caymans, back to Jamaica, and then to Bermuda. The only ship not assigned to other duties was *Ares*, so within the week *Ares* would sail to England and deliver the foreign agents. She was expected, unless they were overruled by the Admiralty, to return within a short period of time. Gabe had learned long ago not to trust politicians.

Once ashore, Dagan was waiting with a carriage and a driver. "We going to England?" he asked.

"Yes."

"I would think it advisable to take Faith."

"I was thinking of that," Gabe replied.

Dagan nodded, something made him feel their stay would be a short one, but it would be good for her to spend time with Gabe and to visit family in England. They would stay in Portsmouth at Gabe's mother's house.

"Jake," Gabe called to his cox'n. "When we get home, take the carriage to Philip LoGiudice's house and ask if it would be convenient for him to call upon me this evening. Holly is welcome to join us."

Hex nodded, "Aye, sir."

***

ANTIGUA'S WHITE GLISTENING BEACHES got smaller and smaller as *Ares* put distance between herself and the shore. A clump of seaweed had torn away from the ocean bed and floated to the surface drifting silently away. They were still close enough to land that a few seagulls crying out to one another flew overhead. A group of gray clouds moved quickly overhead and for a brief moment they blotted out the sun's intense rays.

Lieutenant Laqua was talking to Doctors Cook and Cornish. Faith had listened to the lieutenant bragging about what a fine ship *Ares* was. Gabe's shadow announced his arrival.

Faith looked up as he peered down on her. His boyish smile was much like when they had met. "Is she, dear?" Faith asked.

"Is she what?"

"The eagle of the sea, that's how Lieutenant Laqua described this ship."

Gabe grinned, "I hadn't thought about it but I would not disagree with our good lieutenant. A man's last ship is usually, if not always, the best. Darling, like you, *Ares* is a lady. I've loved all my ships but I must say I've never had a finer ship."

Faith looked at her husband as he said this. He was sincere. Gabe turned his head as something, a sound or noise caught his attention. Is the white streak, where a pistol ball had once creased his scalp, wider now? Or was it gray starting to find its way into his coal black hair? His face was more weathered as were his hands. *My boy captain is starting to show the signs of stress and always being at sea.*

It was April, and in another week, April 18th, little James would be two. It was hard to believe it was already 1781. The war had gone on forever, at least it seemed that way. Gabe had confessed his doubts about England winning the war. There had been too many military setbacks, and men placing greed before duty. He had been livid when he heard that Admiral Rodney had not sailed to the Colonies as he was supposed to.

The news that the Colonies could well win the war was not unwelcome to Faith. *Should I feel differently*, she wondered. It was her country. Gabe had told her right after they had married that he knew where her sympathies lay, but to keep her thoughts private. It would create problems for the Anthony's, the whole Anthony family, otherwise. Gil and Deborah had always been so kind. How could she do or say anything that would hurt them? She could not.

"The wind is freshening a bit," Gabe said. "I better rescue uncle from little James if I want any time with him before it gets any rougher."

Faith had looked about to see who had her son. It was Dagan. She should have known, but it could have been Hex...Uncle Jake. How many captains had a cox'n who was called Uncle Jake. She didn't know any, other than Gil and Bart. But how many captains owed their life to their cox'n? Gabe did. She'd be a widow had it not been for Hex, so naval protocol be damned. She would always be appreciative to Hex. And...anybody who got their nose out of joint over him being Uncle Jake, could just damn well get over it.

PART II

Noble "NO" Pride

Fate had dealt him...A dirty rotten blow
His mum had died...He had no place to go.

He slept up under...The baker's stoop
What little he earned...Barely bought food.

The incident happened...On a bright sunny day
"No" ran their errand...But they refused to pay.

Two Navy captains...They saw it all
They collared the rogues...And made 'em stand tall.

Pay the lad they warned...Or you'll taste my blade
One rogue he cowered...But from his purse he paid.

Vengeance the rogue vowed...On these King's men
They'll never interfere...In our doings again.

It was very dark...And the shadows loomed
It was time for the blackhearts...To make their move.

But "No" took action...Their plan was ruined
Yet he suffered...Such a terrible wound.

Seeing his bravery...Fate changed once again
"No's" future was bright...He was taken in.

He was no longer...That little gutter snipe
He stood like a man...Young Noble Pride.

...Michael Aye

CHAPTER FIFTEEN

GABE JUMPED QUICKLY DOWN from the carriage and held the umbrella furnished by the carriage driver. When the driver had first handed the umbrella to Gabe, he had to show Gabe how to open it. Gabe saw several men along the waterfront carrying similar contraptions as he looked about.

"It's called a Hanway or Hanway umbrella after the writer Jonas Hanway, who made them so famous. They're the latest thing for men," the driver said, somewhat surprised a decorated Navy captain was so backwards.

"We've been away from England for a few years," Gabe said, by way of explanation. This seemed to satisfy the driver.

"They are available at Foxx's here in Portsmouth," the driver said, thinking the information might add to his tip.

Dodging a horse and carriage, Gabe and Faith jumped over streams of water that ran down the street. Holding the umbrella so it kept most of the rain off of Faith and little Jake caused the water to cascade down the side and straight down the collar of Gabe's uniform. Gabe, gritting his teeth, held back the curses on his lips. Faith had already warned him to watch his language around little ears. Stepping under the porch of his mother's house, he told Faith to knock while he carried the umbrella to Holly. She could hold it herself as she had no baby to tote.

Handing the blasted umbrella to Holly, Gabe helped her down from the carriage. While she walked to the porch very ladylike, Gabe was across in three bounds. Thinking that he was through, Faith said, "Take it to the second coach now for Nanny."

"Damnation," he swore aloud this time, only to receive 'that look' from Faith. Gabe handed the umbrella to Nanny and helped her from the coach. About the time that Nanny was down, another carriage plodded down the street hitting a puddle and splashing water over Gabe's legs. "You blind whoreson," he shouted.

The maid had opened the door just as Gabe was splashed. The ladies, hearing his outburst, all turned and started laughing at his outrage. "I'll have you all flogged," he growled. Lum was getting Samson out of the carriage, and hearing Gabe's tone, the big dog growled. "I'll shoot you...you mangy cur. Have you forgotten it was I who saved you?"

Dagan stepped out of the house onto the porch with Maria. He had come ahead to greet his sister and to let her know of the family's arrival.

Gabe was still complaining, "I should have let the beast drown."

Faith knew that while Gabe said this, he didn't mean it. She'd be dead, and most likely Lum as well, were it not for Samson. "Come to mama," she said, handing James to Grandmother Maria's outstretched hands. The dog's demeanor changed at once. His hackles went down and his nub of a tail started wagging, which made his whole rear end wobble. He strained at the leash to get to Faith, and licked her face when he did get close.

Gabe thought to himself, *I'm supposed to kiss you after that*. He'd once said it out loud to which Faith had retorted, "Sam doesn't complain about your kisses."

Everyone was greeted with hugs and kisses. Maria even hugged Holly. The maid helped Lum and Nanny with the luggage and showed them where they'd stay.

"Mother," Gabe said, "I simply must get changed out of this uniform before I soak the floor."

"You and Faith go ahead. I'll show Holly her room... and I'll watch James while you are getting changed," Maria replied. The look in her eyes let Gabe and Faith know that Maria had some grandmotherly catching up to do.

***

GABE HAD REPORTED TO the port admiral immediately upon arriving in Portsmouth. He'd arranged transportation to London for Gabe via post-chaise, which was only marginally better than horseback. The trip would take fourteen hours if the road was good, but it had been raining. They'd spend at least one night at a coaching inn, hopefully one with little or no vermin. The port admiral also promised to send a message to the Admiralty via semaphore.

"This will be done tomorrow with our routine messages," the admiral said with a wink, "now go visit your mother." It was only later that his mother mentioned that Admiral Webster and his wife attended the same church.

***

GABE AND FAITH WERE enjoying the sun as the two of them lay close in the hammock on the observation deck at his mother's house. It was the house his father had bought and left to Gabe's mother. Leaving his wife and taking Maria as his common law wife had cost the admiral his career. He had maintained the respect of all his peers but he'd been doomed to never set foot on a man o' war again as admiral. He had built the observation deck atop the Portsmouth house so that he could see all that was taking place with the Navy at Spithead, the dockyard, and also the harbor. The warmth of the sun felt good.

Marine Captain LoGiudice had taken Holly to visit some old friends. Hex and Dagan had run off to see their agent with a chest that they'd brought off the ship. There was no telling what the two had in the chest. Gabe didn't want to know, in truth. Plunder, no doubt, but he could honestly say he had no knowledge of it. The large ruby that Dagan had given to Gabe years ago was now a pendant that was always around Faith's neck...a symbol of their love.

Maria was with little James. The two of them were inseparable. "We've a lot of catching up to do," Gabe's mother declared.

A messenger had arrived inviting all of them to Deerfield Manor for a holiday. Hugh and Becky would be there with Macayla, who when Gabe saw her last was turning into a beautiful young lady. Gabe sent a message to the port admiral stating that he'd been invited to Deerfield Manor. The messenger unexpectedly brought back a quick reply written in the admiral's own hand, "Enjoy your holiday. Give Lord Anthony my best."

***

THEY TRAVELED BY COACH to Deerfield, since Gabe's mother's carriage was too small. Hiring two coaches was not as easy as it once had been, but placing a guinea in the right hand caused things to move along much faster. That and the promise of two men serving as guards with no pay due sealed the deal. The highwaymen were not as bad on the Kings Highway as they were on the old routes. With the coaches loaded up and everyone in as comfortable a place as they could be, they started off. The recent rains hadn't done the roads any good. Potholes seemed to jar the coaches every quarter of a mile or so.

Gabe snarled, "Damn that man. Do you think he's missed a single hole?"

Maria smiled at her son, "I'm sure that he's doing his best."

They stopped at noon at a coaching inn called the Red Lion. "Looks more like a red herring," Gabe muttered, only to get an elbow in the ribs from Faith.

The inn's yard was a quagmire from the rain and constant use of horses and coaches. A couple of planks were put down as the coaches pulled up. Gabe helped Faith and his mother down.

"We've another coach that needs planks," Gabe said to the man.

"They be for the gentry, yer Lordship. Not 'is servants."

"You'll see the planks are laid down if you want a tip."

Marking Gabe as one not to truck with, the man replied, "As ye say, Guvner, but the keeper don't let jus' anyone in the common room."

"We aren't just anyone," Gabe quipped.

Faith saw the barn and paddock as she made for the door. "There must be three to four hundred horses out there," she said.

"They are for changing the horses when the coaches need them."

She nodded and then put her handkerchief to her nose as the wind changed direction and she got a whiff of the wet horses and horse manure. "Glad I wasn't hungry," she volunteered.

Hex was down and he opened the door to the inn. A man, the owner Gabe assumed, looked up when they entered. He turned his attention back to what he was doing when something caught his attention and he looked up again, seeing Nanny and Lum. Whatever he started to say was left unsaid when he saw the look on Gabe's face and realized that he was backed up by Dagan and Hex.

"Let's move over to the area by the far wall," Dagan recommended. "There's more room and a large table."

Small beer, ale, and sherry for the ladies was offered by a tavern wench who recommended the cold meats, warm bread, and cheese. *She wants us gone*, Gabe thought and then changed his mind. The Red Lion put on a good spread.

The door opened and the two drivers came in. They were recognized by the owner and pints were brought to their table with meat and cheese without asking what their pleasure was. The door opened again, and with a glance outside, Gabe could see the hostlers were changing the horses. Gabe gave Hex the money to pay the bill. He smiled to himself as the cox'n dropped a shilling down the wench's more than ample bosom. Neither Faith nor Maria missed how the wench leaned extra low for Hex to see her wares.

"Catheads," Hex whispered to Dagan as they left. Neither of the women let on that they had heard.

CHAPTER SIXTEEN

THE TRIP TOOK LONGER than expected. The rain came down in sheets, making it difficult to see the drive. After passing one coach on its side, they decided to stop at the next inn, even though they'd only traveled a few hours since the lunch stop. The rain was so bad that the driver of the first coach blew his horn to announce their arrival. Flagstones marked the entrance which was an improvement on the previous inn.

Hex held up his tarpaulin as first Faith and then Maria got out. Lum helped Nanny inside. *Where's those umbrellas*, Gabe thought. He looked up at their luggage atop the coach.

"Don't 'ee worry, zur, I'll send your chest in for the innkeeper to store." Gabe thanked the man, placing a coin in his hand.

Gabe stepped inside the door and threw his boat cloak off his shoulders, with little puddles of water cascading to the floor.

"Never you mind, sir, and welcome to the White Horse Inn. The weather 'as been bad but will get worse, I fear. There's room for the ladies, but you men will have to find a spot by the fire."

The weather did get worse as Grogan, the innkeeper, predicted. The wind, at times, was so violent that it rattled the shutters, but the fire was warm and the inn was cozy. The man had good food and passable wine. Twenty-four hours later, they started their trip again, leaving the man's coffers replenished.

Gabe glanced at his mother as the coach turned down the narrow lane with the gray stone fence on either side. She had refused to visit the place that her man had turned his back on. It was different now. She knew everyone now and Lord James Anthony's wife had been dead for years.

Cobblestones lined the circular drive, causing the horses' hooves to clatter. Several servants rushed from the house followed closely by Gil and Deborah.

"Welcome to Deerfield," Gil greeted Maria. "We are so glad that you came."

As they entered the large two-story gray stone house, several maid servants passed by to collect the chests . Maria stopped after walking down the flagstone hall and into the main room. Her hand went to her heart as she gazed at the large painting of her man, Admiral Lord James Anthony, with his stained meerschaum pipe. Deborah placed her arm around Maria's shoulders.

Gil looked at Maria, whose eyes had moistened, "He sure loved you, Maria. Father told me that he'd never felt such love as you offered." Maria managed to smile.

It was then that Gabe decided to hire an artist to make a painting of his mother and father together... and damn the cost.

***

THE NEXT FEW DAYS went by fast. Becky, Hugh, and Gretchen were there for three days. Gretchen, acting all grown up, attached herself to Faith and talked girl talk. She was starting to attract boys, which Hugh felt was the worst thing possible. Gretchen made Faith promise to visit them in London if time allowed. Hugh was now a major factor in Parliament. He had long since gained the ear of the Prince Regent.

Hugh had arranged for Gabe and Gil to meet with different financial advisors. Both men were doing well and saw no need to change agents or solicitors, thanks in part to Hugh's ever watchful eye. An agreement was made where the three would pool some of their resources to purchase properties. The war had ruined several men who had made their living in shipping. Insurance had not covered everything, so their properties could be bought cheaply.

They had an unexpected but welcome visitor on the fourth day...Captain Francis Markham. He was one of Gabe's best friends, since their midshipman days. He was on loan to the revenue service as commander of a squadron of revenue cutters...temporarily. After a pleasant visit, Markham invited Gabe to Deal to see his command.

"Bring Faith," Markham added.

"No," Faith replied. "I've been to the coast. We visited both Walmer Castle and Deal Castle. I will rest here for a few days. We have to go back to Portsmouth soon."

Gabe agreed to visit and would bring Dagan if he cared to come along. Hex was off and not expected back until Sunday.

***

DAGAN AND GABE RODE over to Deal in one of the manor's carriages. When they arrived at the pier, they could see the gentle rise and fall of the revenue cutters as the waves came in and washed ashore. Gabe remembered the times when as a youth he went out in a similar vessel with his father, Dagan, and his father's cox'n.

"Brings back memories, does it not?" Dagan said, seeing his nephew's face, a hint of a smile appearing.

"Aye, Uncle, fond memories. The cutter may look like an ugly duckling to some...no figurehead, no stern galley, nothing to entice a soul except her sailing qualities."

The cutter closest to Gabe and Dagan was seventy feet long and had a blunt bow that reminded Gabe of Faith's dog, Sam's, nose. Her beam was twenty feet if it was a foot.

"She be a massive brute, yer 'onor," a seaman said, seeing the men looking at the cutter.

"Aye, she is that," Gabe agreed, as he mentally counted the guns. Ten per side, six pounders he guessed.

This cutter was single-masted. Her foot sail and top sail were furled and the hands were working on a jib sail. She looked as clumsy as anything that sailed, but from his days with his father, he knew her capabilities.

"'Ere comes her cap'n now," the seaman said.

Gabe's reverie broke and he looked up as Markham and another officer, a lieutenant, walked up.

Markham greeted Gabe and introduced the lieutenant. "Gabe, this is Collin Mitchell. He's the commander of the cutter, *Swift*. Lieutenant Mitchell, meet Captain Sir Gabriel Anthony."

The men shook hands and then Dagan was introduced. "Dagan, the master of *Eagle* is an old friend of yours, John Copeland," Markham said. Dagan smiled now. It had been years since they'd seen each other. "Lieutenant Mitchell and I were headed to the Customs House to give them the latest reports," Markham said, addressing Gabe. "You care to come along? And then we'll have something to eat."

"I'll carry the reports, sir," Mitchell volunteered. "You go visit with Sir Gabe."

Taking Mitchell up on his offer, Markham and

Gabe had reached the end of the pier when they heard an outburst of cursing. "Pay up! You promised me a groat if I got you the bucket."

"Off wid ye, ye gutter snipe."

"Not until ye pay me what you owes."

Wham! One of the four men slapped the boy, knocking him down and bloodying his nose. Gabe reached down and helped the boy to his feet. He picked up the boy's hat and dusted it off and handed it to the boy. The four men sat as they had been, but they now appeared nervous as they looked at the two naval officers.

"Did you promise the boy a groat to bring you a drink?" Markham asked.

"Admiral, not strictly speaking. I may 'ave said it to be worth a groat to me but no promise were made to 'im."

"You lie," the boy threw back, struggling to get lose from Gabe's grip.

"Pay the boy," Markham said firmly.

"It's like this, yer Lordship, we already gave the little bastard…" the rest of the sentence was left unsaid as Gabe's temper flew out of control. He backhanded the man, grabbed him by the shirt and slapped him again and shoved him against the building. Gabe reached in the man's pocket, while he was dazed, and took out his bulging purse.

"Broke, you say," Gabe snarled. He opened the purse and took out a guinea and handed it to the boy.

"Oh no sir," the boy stammered through busted lips. He put the guinea back and took a shilling, holding it for Gabe to see.

"Fair enough," Gabe said. "Be off with you now, and stay away from such trash."

One of the men, a man with a faded red shirt laughed, "'Is mum's a whore, trash is all 'e be."

"Not so," the boy said. "My father was a gentle-man, but he died." Gabe calmed the boy and sent him on his way.

Markham looked at the men, "Stay away from that boy. If I hear he's come to any harm, I'll come looking for you four personally."

The man Gabe slapped swore, as Markham and Gabe walked off, "I'll see 'is bloody 'eart cut out for this."

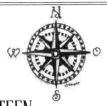

CHAPTER SEVENTEEN

GABE AND MARKHAM WALKED down to a tavern called The Fisherman. "They serve a good tankard, oysters, fresh bread, and cheese," Markham quipped. Once they were seated and a tankard put before them, the tavern owner came back to their table saying he still had some smoked herring left from breakfast. This appealed to the two men, so they ordered it as well.

***

NOBLE PRIDE, KNOWN TO the locals as No, sat under the porch in back of the bakery eating a loaf of fresh, not moldy bread, with some marmalade left in the bottom of the crock. The marmalade was given to him with the promise that the crock would be returned. Meeting the naval officers had proven to be rewarding. This was the first that the boy had eaten in two days and he still had money. Across the alley from where he sat was the back entrance to the tavern that the officers were in.

"They're still there," a voice said.

Lying flat, No could see the legs of the men who were talking. He couldn't see their faces but he didn't have to. He recognized their voices.

"It's getting late," one of the men said.

"Aye, tis better for our purpose. I promised myself that I'd 'ave 'is 'eart and I will," one man growled. "Nobody slaps the likes of Peter Bently and lives to tell the tale. What would me mates think?"

"Aye," they all agreed.

"You keeps a sharp lookout," Bently said to one of the men. "Let us know when they comes out. We'll go down close to the pier where there's not many about and jump 'em." Bently waved his knife so that the sun glinted on the blade. "Once 'e's down, it's 'is 'eart I'm after, but if somebody comes shoot 'is bloody arse and lets be off."

No listened as the men plotted. He slid out from under the porch when they walked off and ran around to the window to look inside the tavern. "Damn," the boy swore. What a fiddler's luck, he looked and saw the men walking at a distance. He called out but they didn't hear him. He ran back around to his hiding place under the baker's porch and got a belaying pin that he'd pinched off a drunken sailor who was rough with his mum. Running, he saw a broken rum bottle in a pile of garbage. Hardly slowing down, he scooped it up as he ran. Looking ahead, he saw the rogues. Two of the men went between two buildings while the other two went past the building and turned. No thought, *so this is it*. He was running as fast as he could but he dug deep for one last burst of speed.

He came around the corner of the building shouting, "Lookout, lookout."

Two of the rogues, by this time, had stepped out to confront Gabe and Markham from the front. The other two approached from behind. One of the men behind the two captains raised his pistol as they stopped. Out of breath and unable to speak, No brought the belaying pin down hard on the man's outstretched arm. The wrist bones made a loud cracking sound as they were snapped by the force of the belaying pin.

The man screamed in pain as his wrist was broken.

A spasm still caused him to pull the trigger but the ball went into the dirt. The other man in back of Gabe and Markham whirled, slashing as he did so. No felt a burning, stinging sensation across his chest. The knife wielder had lost his balance as he slashed and fell forward. No thrust his broken rum bottle upward without thinking and the shards of the glass cut the side of the man's face and neck, slicing the jugular vein and carotid artery as it penetrated the sheath that held the vessels. Blood spewed out of the rogue's neck. He clamped his hand against his neck but nothing would staunch the blood flow.

Gabe and Markham's opponents were not so brave. They had both been knocked down by the captains but got up and ran. The man with the broken wrist tried to get up but Markham knocked him down again. People were milling about now, and as they gathered around, the man with his neck cut slumped to his knees and then fell forward, dead.

A watchman walked up and seeing the dead man, he said, "That's one wrecker you won't have to deal with, Captain Markham."

No, for some reason, was feeling weak and nauseated. He started to weave and Gabe caught the boy as he passed out, and then felt the wetness on No's shirt. Looking at his hand in the lantern light, Gabe swore, "Damnation, the boy is hurt." Speaking to the watchman, he said, "Hold that lantern closer." The watchman did so as Gabe ripped open the boy's shirt. He was cut from his right shoulder diagonally across to the lower ribs of the other side.

"He'll likely die," the watchman said. "His mother's dead, and he hasn't got anybody to care for him."

"Damn you, man," Gabe snarled. "Somebody go get a doctor."

Someone whispered in the crowd, "'E's a good boy,

but 'e's dead anyway. If 'e lives, the freebooters will get 'im."

Gabe, taking the lantern, looked at the watchman, "Go get the doctor!"

"It's better to take him home. He'll make it." Gabe looked up and saw it was Dagan. "We'll dress it and take him home." Dagan looked at a girl standing near, "Go get me something to dress this with...a sheet."

"Poor No," the girl said as she ran off, but quickly returned with a not too clean looking sheet.

Dagan said, seeing a seaman, "Get me some straps." He folded the sheet several times and then strapped it across the boy's cuts. Picking up the boy, they made their way to the carriage.

"Home and don't spare the horses," Gabe growled.

CHAPTER EIGHTEEN

THE HOLIDAY WAS OVER and it was time to return to Portsmouth but Gabe was a bit apprehensive. The boy, Noble Pride, had pulled through as Dagan had said. The doctor came and cleaned the wound, and then spent nearly an hour suturing the boy up. No kept ranting during all that time about his bag. He wanted his bag, but the surgeon had said that he was not to be moved.

Dagan had surprised Gabe when it was time to return to Portsmouth, "I'll stay here until the boy can move. Bart and I will then take him to get his bag. He seems to value it dearly."

***

THE HORSE CLATTERED ON the stone drive at the Admiralty. A doorman opened the coach door and held it open while Gabe stepped out. At the entrance of the Admiralty, another doorman opened the door for Gabe to enter. The day after arriving back in Portsmouth, a messenger had arrived with a short note requiring Gabe to report to Phillip Stephens, the first secretary, as soon as convenient...so Captain Sir Gabriel Anthony KB reported.

Gabe checked his hat and cloak and then made himself known to one of the clerks. He was shown down a hall to a small private waiting room. Gabe asked, knowing these clerks were growled at often enough, "How are you today?"

The clerk shocked to be spoken to so pleasantly replied, "Main-well, Captain, just topping."

"Good," Gabe responded. He then asked the clerk, "Your name?"

"Pervis, sir."

"Thank you for escorting me, Mr. Pervis."

"My pleasure," the clerk said and then hurried out the door to his desk. It was less than twenty minutes when the clerk was back. "If you will, Sir Gabe, follow me please."

Just before they made it to the common room where numerous out of work captains and lieutenants sat impatiently, the clerk turned down a side hall. They made a couple more turns and then came to the first secretary's office. *He's skirted around the common room to avoid officers who'd probably been waiting hours,* Gabe thought to himself.

When Pervis knocked on the door, Gabe whispered, "Thank you again, Mr. Pervis." He then slipped a shilling into the man's hand. "Enjoy a wet on me." Pervis didn't say anything as he slipped the coin into a vest pocket.

Entering the office, Gabe was invited to take a seat after shaking the first secretary's hand. Secretary Stephens had aged since Gabe had last seen him. Years of stress dealing with the war with the Colonies had taken their toll. The stress would be worse now, with all their old enemies coming to aid the Americans.

"Lord Sandwich sends his wishes and will stop by if time allows," Secretary Stephens said. Gabe wondered if he was working, gambling, or topping one of his mistresses. "I understand you've had a short holiday at Deerfield."

Damn, Gabe thought, *does the man know everything, do they keep close tabs on everyone*? He then recalled his conversation with the port admiral who likely passed on the information.

"I hope Lord Anthony is well, and his family also," Stephens added. Gabe acknowledged all was well with the family.

"Are you ready to put to sea?" Stephens asked the pleasantries over.

"Aye, sir, there's always a few things a ship could use, but if needed we could weigh anchor as soon as I step aboard," Gabe replied. Thankfully, Con Vallin had come by last evening and brought him up on the readiness of the ship.

Stephens smiled, and Gabe knew that was the answer he wanted. Taking a pipe down from the fireplace mantle, Stephens packed it with tobacco. He sat down next to Gabe as he lit his pipe.

"It seems, Sir Gabe, that you've garnered much affection from the Foreign Services office. Lord Skalla not only wrote letters to the King on your behalf, in regards to the unpleasantness with Admiral Kirkstatter, but Sir Lawrence Cook and his mentor, Leo Gallagher, have praised your leadership to the heavens and back." Stephens paused, "Did you know Gallagher was captured in France a few years ago? He killed seven men in his escape."

"A capable man, I'd say," Gabe responded.

"Aye and I tell you, Philip Stephens will never take the man lightly. In truth, I feel better knowing he's on our side."

"I, as well," Gabe agreed, remembering that Dagan said he saw a dangerous man when he looked upon Gallagher.

Stephens, pausing to relight his pipe and getting a little cloud of smoke going, spoke again, "You are to transport Sir Lawrence and Gallagher to the Rock of Gibraltar."

"When do I leave, sir?"

Stephens said with a smile, "Not as soon as the gentlemen would like. We can't just send a crack frigate off every time the Foreign Office has a whim. You'll be one of Admiral Sir Raymond Knight's escort ships." Gabe's eyes lit up as he recalled serving with Knight in the Caribbean some years ago.

Stephens asked, seeing Gabe's expression, "Do you know the admiral?"

"Yes sir," Gabe answered and told him of their time together in the Caribbean.

Voices could be heard just outside the door, and Stephens stood, the cue that the meeting was over. "I'm sure that the admiral will welcome you to his squadron. You never have enough frigates. I know escort duty can't be to your liking, but it will fill a vacancy and help out the Foreign Office, as well. Are you staying in London for a few days?"

"Aye, at Hugh and Becky's house," Gabe replied.

Stephens nodded and said, "Give the address to Pervis. A messenger will bring you your orders." Grasping Gabe's hand, Stephens shook it. "This should not be a long trip and then you'll return home. I know that you've rarely set foot on English soil since the war began."

Gabe mused over Stephens' parting words, as he took his leave. Damme, if the man doesn't think it's been a sacrifice being in the Caribbean. Well, he'd let him think that ...for now.

CHAPTER NINETEEN

THE ANCHORAGE AT SPITHEAD was full of ships. Waves were choppy as the wind blew a driving rain across the Solent. Admiral Sir Raymond Knight, KB, aboard the flagship, *Triumph*, met with his officers. They would sail on the morrow if the weather moderated. Sailing to Gibraltar and beyond was now far more dangerous since Spain had joined the war, aiding the Americans. They'd angered the Dutch, as well.

Knight's flag lieutenant passed around a copy of Knight's private signals. As the meeting broke up, the flag lieutenant asked Gabe to wait on the admiral. When the last of the captains had taken their leave, Knight came over and pumped Gabe's hand vigorously.

"It's been a long time, Gabe. Let's go to my cabin."

A list of beverages was offered once they were in the admiral's private cabin. Gabe chose coffee.

"It's not Silas' coffee," Knight apologized with a smile.

Gil's servant, Silas, was noted for his coffee flavored with brandy. It would be welcome on a night like this. The two men sat back and talked of old times and mutual friends until finally the flag captain was announced. Seeing the admiral's time was called for, Gabe made his departure. He couldn't help but notice the glare he got from the flag captain, as he left.

The flag lieutenant, on deck, spoke softly, "Our flag captain is envious of anyone who holds any weight with the admiral. You have, this evening, spent more time privately with the admiral than our flag captain has in the year he's been in his position."

Gabe thanked the lieutenant for filling him in. Climbing down the battens, he realized that the rain had stopped and the wind died down. As he lay in his cot later that night, he thought about his last few days with Faith. They had attended the theatre with his sister, Becky, and her husband, Hugh. They'd taken horseback rides through the park. Gretchen had become quite the equestrian. The last day in London they toured a couple of galleries, making Gabe think of his promise to have a painting made with his father and mother together.

Hugh had told Gabe that the man who painted his father's portrait was still alive. He was a young man when he'd painted that first portrait. Gabe visited the man, who took him by the arm and led him to the back of the studio. He looked about and pulled out a sketch that he'd done of Gabe's father. He continued to look about and came up with a painting of Maria that was unfinished. "Your father commissioned it just before he died."

Gabe looked at the painting. It was his mother, but her face looked younger. *Of course it did*, Gabe thought. It was six or eight years ago.

"Can you do a painting of them together?" Gabe asked.

"Certainly."

"Do it then," Gabe instructed. "How long will it take?"

"Three or four months with the commissions that I have now."

Gabe looked at the man, "I will give you your regular commission plus a bonus of twenty-five pounds to have it completed in one month. If I am at sea, see

Hugh English. He will pay you."

"It will be done as you say, sir," the old painter promised. The old artist could well use the bonus from the look of his back rooms.

***

IT WAS DAWN AND they had been at sea several days. *Ares* was assigned the larboard flank of the convoy. Gabe was miserable this morning and this caused him to be in a foul mood. He had growled at Hex and Nesbit. Dagan would have called him on his behavior had he been there. Was that it? Was he moody because Dagan wasn't there? Gabe took time to brush his teeth before going on deck. Some of the bristles came loose in his mouth, as he brushed, causing him to spit and curse. Damn the brush anyway.

"Nesbit," he called.

"Sir!"

"Unpack my spare toothbrush and put that on my list of things to buy when we get back to Portsmouth."

"Aye."

The third lieutenant smiled as Gabe came on deck. Before he could speak, though, Gabe growled, "If you say that it's a good morning, Mr. Turner, I'll have you shot."

Con Vallin was in conversation with the master, Mr. Scott. "Our captain needs another cup of coffee," he whispered.

"Aye, or a stiff shot of rum," Scott replied.

It was hazy with a fine mist that the sun would burn away once it rose. Doctor Cook came on deck in a very cheerful mood. He'd won a guinea from Doctor Cornish last evening playing cards. He cheerfully spoke to Laqua, the second lieutenant, who frowned and darted his eyes toward the captain. Cook picked up on the look quickly and didn't say any more.

It was getting lighter and they could see all the way forward now, and to starboard it was possible to make out one of the ships in the convoy.

"Deck thar, ship to larboard, amidship." Everyone thought an escort ship out of place or a raider.

Vallin sidled up to his captain, "I don't get the feeling that it's an escort ship, Captain."

"Nor I," Gabe replied.

The ship did not have stern lanterns lit. Gabe didn't call to the lookout for further information. The man was an experienced seaman. He knew his duties. He'd report when he had something. Minutes felt like hours.

"Deck thar, she be a frigate, Cap'n. No flag be visible but she 'as the cut of a Frenchie."

Gabe was not surprised. The flagship would never see a signal. "Send up a flare, Mr. Vallin. Hopefully, someone is awake aboard the flagship."

This brought smiles to those on the quarterdeck. There was nothing like the promise of action to change the captain's mood. Hex went below for the captain's pistols and sword while Vallin sent the officers to their battle stations.

"Change course to intercept yonder ship, Captain?"

"Not yet, Mr. Scott, let's see what she's about first and if she has any company."

"Aye, Captain."

"Deck thar, another ship...a brig, Cap'n."

Gabe nodded to himself. "Signal to flagship when it gets light enough to see, Mr. Heath. 'Enemy in sight', then add 'two ships'. Mr. Massey!"

"Aye, Captain."

"Go aloft and see if you can spot any more ships."

"Aye Captain," the fifteen year old replied excitedly.

"Mr. Massey."

"Sir."

"Enemy ships."

The boy smiled, "Aye, Captain, enemy ships."

Gabe had every confidence in the lookout but felt the midshipman could learn from the seaman. He also provided a set of fresh eyes.

The sun was up and bright, and the haze was gone. The second ship was a corvette. Two ships, a frigate and a corvette. Go after one and the other one could make a run after the convoy. The two ships sailed along keeping pace with the convoy, but making no movements to attack.

"You think there are others on the starboard side of the convoy?"

"I wouldn't doubt it," Gabe replied to his first lieutenant. "That or they're expecting company ahead."

Gabe finally called to his signal midshipman. "Message to the flag, Mr. Heath, request permission to investigate."

"Aye, Captain."

BOOM...BOOM...the French frigate had fired its forward guns, water splashing inboard as the ball landed close to the ship.

"Mr. Heath, forget my previous signal. Send fired on by the enemy. Mr. Scott, make an entry in the log. Mr. Laqua, you may fire the larboard side as they bear. Mr. Myers, I'd admire it were you to knock off the frigate's bowsprit."

"Aye, Captain," the gunner grinned.

If the French ships thought they could force *Ares* to give up protecting her escorts, they were wrong. *Ares'* cannons thundered forth their deadly loads while maintaining her station. The hours at gun drill were paying off. The French frigate was hit several times with *Ares'* broadside. The forward guns smashed away at the enemy's bow. When the corvette closed to within range, the quarterdeck's carronades and long guns threw forth their own lethal loads. The twelve pounders scored at least two hits. The two French ships quickly grew tired of the onslaught and hauled their wind.

"From the flag, sir," Mr. Heath volunteered.

"Go on," Gabe prompted.

"Bloody good show, with our number."

"Send a response, Mr. Heath. Make it short and polite."

Dagan would have followed the midshipman to make sure it was done right, had he been here...but he wasn't. Gabe turned to Hex and made a motion with his head to follow the young man. Hex tilted his head in reply to his captain and followed the midshipman.

"Mr. Vallin, let's check the damages."

"Aye, Captain, but I don't believe that we have received any, beyond scratched paint."

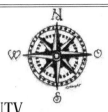

CHAPTER TWENTY

GIBRALTAR, WHAT *ARES* COULD have sailed in nine days alone, took thirteen with the convoy. Entering the Bay of Gibraltar, Gabe recalled Scott's words, 'It was once known as Algeciras Bay'. Gibraltar was also known as 'the Rock'. This was only the second time that Gabe had been to the Rock. The first time he'd been a young middy.

Gibraltar was a peninsula on the southern tip of Spain. It was notable for its strategic rocky promontory that rose up fourteen hundred feet. It was only two and a quarter square miles, and it was situated so that it proved the ideal location for controlling the Straits of Gibraltar separating the Atlantic Ocean and Mediterranean Sea.

Gabe received his instructions for anchoring, and they turned into the soft breeze and let go with the best bower while the salute from Knight's flagship still echoed across the bay. Gabe had felt somewhat excited about entering this new anchorage. His second time, to be sure, but his first as a captain. Part of this was probably due to the huge ship of the line flying a vice admiral's flag. He had little doubt, knowing the habits of his brother and his flag captain, that there were several telescopes trained on *Ares*. He meant to give them no cause to criticize his ship. Being the brother of a vice admiral, the scrutiny would be much more than for others.

Con Vallin walked over to Gabe, "Shall I send for

boats for our...er, guest, Captain, or send them ashore in one of ours?"

"I think my gig will do nicely, Con. I don't think I will be summoned anytime soon.

Vallin smiled, "No sir. I think our admiral will be taking care of the convoy's business for a while."

Hex had been standing close by. "I'll have the cox'n call your gig, Captain."

Mr. Heath came running forward, as the bosun's whistle filled the air with its shrill call. "Our number, sir. 'captain to repair on board.'"

Vallin looked at Gabe and then at Heath, "Which ship, young sir? I think there must be forty at the anchorage."

"Sorry sir, the *Triumph*, Admiral Knight."

"Very well," Gabe responded to Heath. "Never assume, Mr. Vallin, is that not what they say?"

"I guess you are right," Vallin responded.

Hex came down to buckle on the captain's sword, as Gabe switched into a better uniform coat. Nesbit and Simon had made a fair copy of his reports the previous evening. These were now put into a leather bag. Simon Davis, the hanged man, as many referred to him, was indeed a good man at the clerical duties. He was also well spoken.

Gabe found Doctor Cook and Leo Gallagher waiting on deck. "Gentlemen, you may have to wait until the admiral is finished with me before I can put you ashore."

"That's alright," Cook replied. "We'd appreciate your coming ashore with us once your duties are completed."

"I see," Gabe responded, unable to think of any other comments. "You may wish to wait here until I return."

"Gladly," this came from Gallagher. "Your officers

have been the perfect hosts. We simply must get some provisions while we are ashore to repay their generosity."

"I'm sure they will appreciate that greatly." In fact, he knew they would. While Doctor Cook spent a lot of time with Doctor Cornish, two extra mouths with few shipboard duties bit into the ship's wardroom supplies quickly.

With his thoughts on this, Gabe called Vallin over just before he went down to his gig. "Send Nesbit ashore to replenish my larder. He knows where my money is to pay for the supplies."

"Extra mouths means extra outlays," Vallin replied..."and I hear the costs here on Gibraltar are much higher than in England."

Gabe grimaced. "Better tell that to Nesbit," he said as he went through the entry port and down the battens into his gig.

Hex shouted, "Cast off," as Gabe settled in his seat. "Let fall, give way lads, pull. The admiral is watching, together now." Gabe smiled; Hex knew how to get the most out of the gig's crew.

"It gave me a bit of unease entering the Straits of Gibraltar now that we are at war with Spain," Admiral Knight admitted to Gabe, as they were taken to see the vice admiral. "A British convoy would have attracted more attention, I would have thought," Knight added.

Gabe had gone to the vice admiral with Knight, in case there were any specific questions in regards to the attack on the convoy. Gabe had not been spoken to, other than the greeting and the admiral asking about how his brother, Lord Anthony, was getting along until after the meeting was over.

"I understand that you carry two men of the Secret Service," the admiral said.

"Aye, sir."

"It's best..." the admiral said, and then paused as if choosing his words. "It's best that you don't find yourself overly attached to that group. It often keeps you busy, but does little for promotion or prize money."

"Yes sir," Gabe replied, wanting to say he didn't ask for them or knew he had a choice.

Knight whispered, once on deck, "You handled that well."

"It seems that our admiral is not fond of the Foreign Service office."

"You are right, Gabe," Knight responded. "It seems that he missed the Battle of Quiberon Bay. His orders were superseded by the Foreign Office and his junior, Samuel Graves made the battle. Had he been with Hawk as they broke the French Navy, he'd be in the House of Lords now."

"He made vice admiral," Gabe said.

"Aye, while others were instantly recognized."

Humph, something to think about, Gabe mused.

The next day Gabe watched as water hoys, powder barges, and various supply boats made their way across the anchorage. A boat passed below and the sentry called, "boat ahoy." "Passing," came the reply. Gabe had gone ashore with his 'guest' as promised. He had dined that evening at a little place specializing in Mediterranean cuisine. It was delightfully delicious. He hired a boat to take him back to *Ares* after the meal, having sent his gig back to the ship.

The next morning, Nesbit came from his venture ashore in a hired boat. He spoke to Lieutenant Turner, the duty officer, as he came aboard, "I have supplies for the captain. Our guests have also sent cases of beverages and various food items for the wardroom."

Turner brightened at this news. He called to a nearby bosun mate, "Get a group of men together to bring the supplies aboard."

"Yes, sir. Stir your selfies," the petty officer called to a group of men.

"'E thinks 'is nibs is going to share a wet, 'e does."

"Shh!" the seaman's mate said seeing Lieutenant Turner turn toward them.

"Ye be slower than a whore headed to confession."

A shadow suddenly fell over the group of men. It was Stubbs, the bosun, holding his starter in one hand and tapping the side of his leg impatiently with the business end. "Top o' the morn to ye, bosun," the laggard said as he stirred himself.

CHAPTER TWENTY ONE

Went to the Government House
Had to pay my respect
Flowing in the wind
I saw our nation's flag.

Suddenly I felt a change
A ghost within my soul
I was taken away
To a place I didn't know.

I heard the cannon's roar
I saw the Redcoats stand
Battle smoke filled the air
Then I felt his hand.

Chorus
Take these colors, hold 'em high
Don't let them hit the ground
I've gave my life protecting them
Don't you let them down
They've been shot and battle scarred
I think they've even bled
Carry them with pride, son
It's your heritage.

I watched the soldier fade away
I returned to here and now
I thought about the war he fought
How he died so proud.
Repeat chorus.

HEX AND ONE OF the seamen, who could play the banjo, sat below the mainmast singing and playing for the crew.

"You have a talented man there," Doctor Cook said to Gabe.

"Thank you, Sir Lawrence," Gabe responded, using Cook's title. "I've no doubt that Jacob Hex couldn't be successful at any number of professions. He'd even be a good sea captain."

"I don't believe I've heard that song before," Gallagher threw in.

"It's probably one that he wrote," Gabe replied. "He writes a lot."

It was a clear night with the clouds rolling along overhead, darkening the moon at times but never blocking it. The waves rolled along, occasionally the lapping sound of the ship passing through the waves was carried inboard and up to the quarterdeck. The wind blew fair for sailing. The men with no hats could feel the breeze lifting their hair or tugging at their shirts.

Lieutenant Laqua had the watch. He judged the captain's mood and conversation tones. When he was certain all was good, he walked over. "Evening, Captain."

"Mr. Laqua," Gabe greeted his lieutenant.

"I wanted to say thank you to Doctor Cook and Mr. Gallagher for their generosity to the wardroom. I've never tasted such fine wine...except at the captain's table," he quickly added.

"I do believe that we have encountered a merchant who was a tad unscrupulous, Mr. Laqua. I think that we've been drinking wine that has been placed off limits by our government."

"I suggest then that we drink up the evidence before we reach Portsmouth, sir." Lieutenant Laqua said this so firmly that Gabe and the two guests looked at each other totally amazed, and then burst out laughing.

Gabe said, with tears coming from his eyes from laughing so hard, "I believe you've spent too much time around Dagan and Hex, Lieutenant. You sound just like them."

Laqua wasn't exactly sure what caused the captain to laugh, but it made him smile to see the captain in a good humor.

"I see that I've missed something," Lieutenant Vallin said as he walked up. He had cigars in his hand offering them to the group. Gallagher and Gabe each took one, but Doctor Cook turned one down.

"I know of no science to back my theory," Cook said, "but something that creates such a fog of smoke and smells so foul, surely has to affect the body in some harmful manner."

"If you find out, good doctor, don't tell me until it's too late," Vallin quipped. "I can think of very few vices a man can enjoy at sea."

Cook smiled, "I will go challenge Doctor Cornish to a game of chess while you men smoke those vile sticks."

Gabe realized just how alone they were as he smoked his cigar and talked to Vallin. One ship full of men with no one else in sight in the Atlantic. It was an eerie feeling to be so isolated.

Vallin was talking about how fast the voyage back to Portsmouth was compared to the slow trip to Gibraltar. "What was our speed with the last cast of the log?" Vallin asked Laqua.

"Nine and a half knots, sir. We are like a thoroughbred racing across a watery track."

Gabe smiled. Laqua's reply was a bit embellished. Nine knots was more like it, but the man was proud of *Ares* and was trying to impress their civilian guests. A thought came to Gabe, *just like I'd tried to impress Faith showing how much I missed her.*

***

THE PORTSMOUTH REUNION WAS all Gabe could have asked for. He was welcomed back by the port admiral. His mother was so glad that he was back, she cooked his favorite meal. They usually had a cook do this but Maria wanted to do it herself.

There was Faith's welcome then. It started on the observation deck while they were lying together in the hammock. She could make out all the smells, being so close to Gabe. The hint of tar, the smell of salt, and the sea on her man still lingered even after a bath and change of clothes. Their kissing grew more passionate, and Faith found herself beneath Gabe as he kissed her lips, her face, neck, and her chest. He tugged at her gown then, until her heaving breasts were exposed and he took her nipples in his mouth, sending shivers through her.

"Me thinks that we'd better go below," Faith said trying to steady her breathing. "We don't want to create a scandal for your mother."

"No one is out," Gabe mumbled as he hungrily devoured his wife.

"Are you sure?"

Gabe rose up and when he did so Faith pulled her gown up over her breasts. Gabe slung Faith over his shoulder and headed for the door.

"Gabe, put me down."

"I will, you wanton wench, where there's naught to stop me from pleasuring your body until we are too drained to continue."

Faith laughed and slapped his arse. "Treat me like some little tavern trollop, will you?"

He slung her over and onto the bed in their room. He then grabbed her gown front and ripped it off exposing her ripe breasts and beautiful nakedness. He lowered himself to her then.

"You are certainly randy tonight."

"It's the spell that you cast on me," Gabe muttered.

Faith whispered later, much later, when they were both spent, "You ruined my gown."

"It was in the way."

"It was new."

"They have others, buy a new one."

Faith smiled, "Did you miss me…or just me wares."

It tickled Gabe how Faith sometimes tried to sound like a seaman. "There was wares a plenty on the Rock, but it was you who my cannon was primed for."

"Hmm, was my wares that much more enticing?"

"There was this one particular wench who dared a second look…but compared to you, my love, they were nothing but two pence wenches."

"What am I?" Faith asked.

"Oh…a shilling at least."

A pillow was used to slap Gabe in the face. "Nay, my darling, you are the air that I breathe; the blood that fills my heart. You, dear Faith, are what I live for and all that I have is for you and little James."

"Would you do anything I asked?" Faith said.

Gabe rose up on outstretched hands. He smiled, not sure where this was leading. "Anything that would make you happy," he replied.

"Make love to me again," Faith whispered as she pulled his head to her breasts.

***

DAGAN WAS AT THE table the next morning for breakfast and with him was the boy, Nobel Pride. Maria talked with the boy and after breakfast they played with little James. Dagan had Gabe follow him up to the observation deck, while Maria had Noble engaged. Once there, Dagan pulled out a paper bearing a coat of arms.

"Do you recognize this?" Dagan said.

Gabe looked at it for a moment and then replied, "That's the coat of arms for the Earl of Gladstone."

"Aye," Dagan said. "William Stanhope, Earl of Gladstone. When Noble was well enough, we went back to Deal, and under the baker's stoop where Noble had buried a small chest, there were two goblets inside with the coat of arms on them. There was also a certificate of marriage signed by Abraham Rowels, Master of the American ship, *Mary Anne*. Noble told me his mum and his father fell in love while in the Colonies. Noble's father had written his own father about falling in love. Lord Stanhope refused to acknowledge a commoner as a wife suitable for his son. Thinking Glenda would charm his father into blessing the union, they took passage to England. The girl was by that time with child, so the ship's captain married the young lovers. Charles, who was already ill, died during the crossing, unfortunately. Glenda took what little bit of money Charles left her and made it to the estate. She was never allowed in the house. She was broke, by then, and out of food. She took a job as a scullery maid for a tavern keeper. He soon bought a place in Deal, taking her with him. When the baby was born she was allowed two days off and then it was back to work. She soon learned that the gentry who stayed would slip her a shilling or two if she came up to their room at night. In doing so, Glenda eventually saved up enough to get the two of them a private room. She took ill, however, and her savings went for doctor's bills. She died and the tavern owner kicked Noble out saying that he couldn't afford to keep the boy."

"Did Noble tell you all of this?" Gabe asked.

"Some. He didn't know what the goblets meant, only that they were his father's. Other parts were told to me by others. One girl, in particular, who was Glenda's friend, told me most of it so we were able to put the story together. To prove the wedding certificate is not a forgery is not so easily done."

"Why?" Gabe asked.

"We are at war or have you forgotten?" Dagan chided.

Gabe smiled, "How could I?"

"Hugh is going to show the goblets and marriage certificate to Lord Stanhope soon. We've not been able to pin down his whereabouts yet. We thought that we should get the boy cleaned up with some presentable clothes, in the meantime. It would also help if we could get him into school."

"I think a tutor first." Gabe and Dagan turned. Maria stood on the top step of the observation deck. "He will only be ridiculed and teased if we try to put him into school at this point."

"Josh Nesbit, or possibly Simon," Gabe said.

"No, not just anyone," Maria said. "I will ask around at church tomorrow. I expect you all to attend, by the way." She looked at Gabe, "Faith's been every Sunday."

CHAPTER TWENTY TWO

DAYS TURNED INTO WEEKS and weeks into months. *Ares* was assigned convoy duty twice, but no permanent orders were given, nor had he heard from the Foreign Office. The men aboard ship grew restless from inactivity and Gabe grew worried that he might lose his command. What was it his father had said, 'Men are made for ships and ships are made for the sea.'

Gabe had dined with each of his officers, at one point or another, at his mother's house, and once the wardroom had invited him and Faith to dinner.

He spoke with the port admiral after the last convoy about his concern of losing his command.

"Nonsense," the admiral had replied. "In God's time, son, in God's time."

Paul Dover, Esquire had become Noble's tutor. He was a man of middle height and the whitest hair Gabe had ever seen. It was so white, in fact, that Gabe was shocked to find out that they were nearly the same age.

Noble began to make friends, a freckle-faced little girl at church, first, and soon her brother. But strangely, his closest friend was Gretchen, Becky and Hugh's daughter. Putting things together as best as they could, they figured to within a couple of months as to when the boy was born. It put him about eighteen months to two years younger than Gretchen.

One evening, at the dinner table, when discussing the boy's age, Maria said, "Why don't you ask the rector? The church records most births in a village. Even those of...well, like No's." Gabe had noticed that his family had taken to calling the boy, No, instead of Noble.

Hugh had finally gone to see William Stanhope. The man, at first, refused to acknowledge that his son would have a liaison with a commoner, other than for a night's pleasure. Hugh grew tired of fencing with the man.

"You old fraud," he finally said. "Had you not had a good army and capable men, you'd still be a common soldier. You raided, plundered, and killed the king's enemies, keeping all that you could steal. Your only son is dead. He fathered a child, before he died, with a girl that he loved. You are getting up in age, now. Would you not care to spend time with a grandchild rather than being so lonely?"

"Damn you, man," Stanhope said irritably. "Noble has people who love him and will care for the boy as if he were theirs."

"What...what did you call the boy?"

"Call him?"

"Yes, his name."

"Noble...Noble Pride."

"That was my father's name," Lord Stanhope muttered, suddenly looking sad, his eyes became moist and he seemed to stare into the distance. "Noble Pride Stanhope. No one, to my knowledge, knew that."

"Somebody did," Hugh said.

"Yes, Charles. He loved my father and promised that if he were to ever have a son, he'd name him after him, his grandfather." The old man sat there sipping his mulled wine. "Can you arrange a visit with Sir Gabe? I have to be in Portsmouth very soon."

"I'm sure it will be no problem," Hugh responded.

"Thank you," Stanhope said.

Hugh hastily made his departure, seeing that the old man was shaken up by the news. He wrote a note to Gabe and had one of his men take it to Portsmouth.

***

LORD WILLIAM STANHOPE'S CARRIAGE drew up in front of Gabe's mother's house. The emblazoned crest, the same as that on the silver goblets, was on the coach's door. He climbed down and looked about the modest but well cared for dwellings. Gabe's mother was a widow, he recalled Hugh saying. Modest as it was, this was much more than most widows could afford. Lord James would have left Deerfield to his oldest son, Vice Admiral Lord Anthony. Gabe was a sea captain of some renown and had even been knighted. Both men were obviously of considerable means. Further proof was the brother-in-law who was in Parliament. This was not a family who would try to use a boy for further gain.

A gardener was pruning in the yard and a maid stood at the door, looking through the curtains. The house had a staff of servants. All of this seemed to drive home the probability that the boy must indeed be his grandson. Before he could knock on the door, a large burly man opened it.

"I'm Lord Stanhope."

"Nice to meet you, sir. I'm Jacob Hex, Sir Gabe's cox'n. I will let him know you are here and then I must be off."

Cox'n the man said, thought Stanhope. *I would have thought him to be an officer. Maybe even Sir Gabe.* Stanhope didn't have to wait but moments before a woman came in. *She must have been a beautiful woman when she was younger*, Stanhope thought. *No wonder Lord Anthony gave up his career. I would have as well.*

The charming lady held out her hand, "I'm Maria

Dupree, Gabe's mother."

Stanhope took the hand and kissed the back of it. He was still staring at this beautiful creature when Gabe walked in. Slightly embarrassed, Stanhope cleared his throat. "You must be Sir Gabe," he said before anyone could speak.

"Yes, and you are Lord Stanhope."

"William, sir, just call me William."

Gabe shook the man's hand and introduced Faith. Stanhope continued to steal glances at Maria, all this time. Faith nudged Gabe, seeing this. As they walked into the sitting room, Faith watched as Stanhope kept close to Maria.

"I've taken the liberty of ordering some refreshments," Faith said and added, "why don't we all take our seats."

The group seated themselves with Stanhope taking the side chair nearest the end of the sofa where Maria sat. *This is interesting*, Gabe thought to himself, not sure if he liked the idea, but not sure he disapproved of it either.

Tea and cakes were served with much ado about the lemon flavor of the cookies. It was a recipe passed on to the cook by Gabe's man, Josh Nesbit.

Gabe waited until Stanhope had stopped talking and brought up Noble. How they had met and how the boy risked his life for Captain Markham and himself, and the terrible wound that he had received.

He then talked about how they had obtained a tutor for the boy so that he could catch up to others his age. "He is wise in the ways of the world beyond his years," Gabe said. Gabe left off the fact that his mother had become something of a prostitute to provide for the boy.

The group had been talking nearly an hour when Gretchen and No returned from their ride in the park.

Hearing the two, everyone turned to the doorway. Gretchen came in bragging about what a horseman No had become. Stanhope stood up, and a tear came to his eyes. The boy was his father made over, same blonde hair, hazel eyes, and broad shoulders. He was young Charles incarnate.

Stanhope took a step forward, and as he did so, he looked at the boy. Both No and Gretchen looked at the man. "Come here, son. I'm your grandfather."

***

THE FOLLOWING WEEKS WERE like a whirlwind for young Noble Pride Stanhope. He moved to his grandfather's estate, which was just a few miles from Deerfield. Gretchen talked her mother into letting her spend the rest of the summer with Gil and Deborah so that she and No could be close.

A small village separated the two estates. People in the village got used to seeing the two together. Gretchen talked to No about his studies.

"You have the best tutor in the world," she declared. "I wish that I would have had Mr. Dover. My tutor was a nasty old bird, who'd never had a husband."

This was incredible to No. "I've never seen a woman who couldn't find at least one man to like her." He then thought of his mother. All the men liked her. Dagan had talked with No and had told him that his mum had done the only thing she could to support the two of them and that he should never think ill of her or be ashamed of her. No understood, but having said that, it was a topic that he'd avoid for a while when talking to his grandfather.

Dagan had visited the church at Deal. He found Noble Pride had been listed in the parish records as being baptized on January 24, 1769. "This is usually within days or a month of the child's birth," the vicar explained. "I remember well in this case. You see, I was present at the tavern when they sent for the midwife. I heard the lad's first cry. And if for no other reason, how many children are born with such a lofty name as Noble Pride." The vicar paused and looked at Dagan. "Has his grandfather finally recognized the boy?"

"You know who his grandfather is?" Dagan asked.

"Of course, I saw the goblets before the child was born."

"He will be recognized," Dagan said.

The vicar looked closely at Dagan, "It's said that you have a gift. I've long wondered was such a thing possible and if so...who gave it."

Dagan said nothing for a moment. He then said, "While I've witnessed things that would make even you question your beliefs, I believe. I'm no doubter."

"Go with God then," the vicar said. "Go with God."

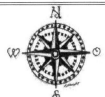

CHAPTER TWENTY THREE

"IF RODNEY HAS NOT taken his fleet and sailed to the aid of Cornwallis, all is lost."

Gabe sat in the secret section of the Foreign Office. He sat in a chair outside an office where the agents for the secret service were in a meeting. From the volume of their voices, there was nothing secret from anyone close by. It was now almost July. *Ares* had just returned from another cruise as escort to a convoy of merchantmen. He received a message, when he anchored, from the port admiral to make his presence known to the Foreign Services Office at once.

Dagan, who had not sailed with Gabe to escort the convoy, now rode with him to London. "We will be leaving soon, I think."

Gabe made no comment. He was used to his uncle's predictions, though this was not much of one. Had they not gotten orders to sail when *Ares* had, Gabe wondered if the anchor would ever be pulled from the mud.

Lord Stanhope had brought No by to see everyone during Gabe's absence. He had also spent considerable time with Maria.

"Do you see this going anywhere?" Gabe asked Dagan.

"I'm not sure. He's at least a dozen years older than Maria. It would hurt nothing for them to enjoy each other's company."

"If you say so, Uncle," Gabe responded, and then

drifted off to a troubled sleep after that.

They had taken a room rather than disturb Hugh and Becky. They were not even sure if Hugh and Becky were in London.

***

"WE ARE GOING BACK to Antigua," Gabe told Faith. "We sail by the end of the week."

Gil and Deborah came by to see them off, and with them was No.

"How old do you have to be to become a midshipman?" No surprised everyone by asking.

"It varies," Gabe replied, not wanting to lie but also not wanting to encourage the boy either. "How are your studies?"

"Mr. Dover said that he was satisfied with my progress."

"I see," Gabe said, glad that he was interrupted.

"There are our passengers now," Hex said, speaking of Doctor Cook and Leo.

Gabe gave the boy a hug. "Take care of Gretchen for me and hopefully we'll see you soon."

"Thank you for everything," the boy said.

Gabe looked back as he approached his passengers. Faith was hugging the boy. She, like every other member of the family, had grown very close to him. He had certainly changed in the months since they had met him, from a streetwise little waif to the heir of Gladstone as grandson of Lord Stanhope.

Gabe thought of his mother's words, 'But for the love of James and the grace of God, you may well have had to live a life much like No has.' Maybe that was what had infuriated Gabe so, that day in Deal. He'd had the most loving father. His father and all who knew him recognized that Gabe was Lord Anthony's son. But still, how many times had he heard

132

the remark 'bastard son.' He understood things better now, but the memory was not pleasant. Nor were the times that he'd heard people speak of his mother as Lord Anthony's mistress. He knew how the barbs could hurt. He also knew how Noble Pride had felt for all those years.

"Sir Gabe, the boat is here."

"Thanks Jake. Have Faith and little James loaded, and then our passengers."

"Aye."

Gabe had said his good-bye to his mother before they left home. He now walked to her. "You've enough money in your account to last you a year or more. But should anything major come up, our agent has been instructed to honor your request. Anything that you have questions about, send a message to Hugh. He will make sure the matter is handled."

Gabe's mother smiled, "You've already told me that and so has Dagan. I believe you worry too much, both you and Dagan."

"I wish that you would go with us, Mother."

"Maybe next time, once you are settled down," Maria replied.

Gabe smiled, "That may be a long time."

"It won't be that long," his mother said, with all conviction in her voice.

***

THE SUN WAS SWELTERING. The skylight was open, as were the stern windows. Nanny was fanning little James, who had beads of sweat on his tiny nose, as he slept on the cushions beneath the open windows. Nesbit had brought both Faith and Nanny some tea. Cold tea as it was preferred in the Colonies. He'd put in sugar while the tea was hot so that it would dissolve. It was refreshing once it did.

The voices on deck were easily heard through the open skylight. One of the bosun's mates cursed a straggler, only to be scolded by Scott. "Watch yer words, you ruffian. The cap'n's lady be below."

Lady, Faith thought and wondered how often a captain might have a lady aboard who was not his wife. Gabe had mentioned that sort of thing happened. The man who cared for the poultry and other animals had his wife aboard *Ares*. She was not only on board ship, but very pregnant. Her name was Nancy Wilkinson, but her husband was called Jimmy Ducks. This was very confusing until Gabe explained that every man who had that job was called Jimmy Ducks. His given name was Christian Wilkinson. Gabe went on to explain that several nicknames were given to specific jobs. Faith understood but felt that it was foolish. There were, of course, a lot of things in dealing with the Royal Navy that she considered very foolish.

Hearing someone enter the cabin, Faith walked over and looked beyond the screen. It was Midshipman Easley...Henry Easley.

The young boy announced, seeing Faith, "The captain's compliments, Madame, and we have been given the signal to get underway."

Faith thought, another foolish procedure, but kept it to herself. "Thank you, Mr. Easley." The boy gave a slight bow and made his way back on deck.

Con Vallin approached his captain on deck, "Anchors hove short, sir."

"Very well," Gabe said absently as he strained to see if his mother's carriage had left yet. He threw up his hand and waved, knowing it was unlikely that his mother would see him. Turning his attention back to his first lieutenant, Gabe ordered, "Get the ship underway if you please."

The bosun's pipe shrilled forth, at a nod from Vallin, and the boatswain's mates took up the cry. "Hands aloft, loose topsails."

Sir Lawrence Cook stood over to the side next to Dagan. He looked on, in awe, as the rigging and shrouds suddenly, with the bosun's mate's cries, came alive with swarming seamen. The top men ran aloft with the grace of big cats. The laggards felt the hard bite of the bosun's starter, encouraging them to move more quickly.

"Break out the anchor," Vallin called to Mr. Stubbs.

The bosun swung his starter against the side of his leg as he yelled, "Heave, put yer backs into it. You move like a used up whimpering old whore." The starter came down across the back of one who showed no effort.

"Ughh!" The man cried out, but put his back into it.

The capstan moved a touch and then cranked steadily as the dripping, foul-smelling cable came inboard.

"Loose headsails, loose headsails." The cry was repeated. Cook looked high above as the loosened canvas fell and then flapped about while men strung out across the swaying yards, fighting with the flapping canvas.

Dagan leaned over and said, "That's a job where you work with your feet and one hand while you hold on with the other. The topmen call it one hand for yourself and one hand for the ship. I've seen more than one man fall to his death who failed to heed that advice." Cook felt a shiver run through him as he thought of falling from such dizzying heights.

Laqua, the second lieutenant, called from the bow, "Anchors aweigh, sir."

Gabe could feel the surge as *Ares* paid off into the

135

wind, the deck heeling sharply as a gust of wind filled the sails.

Vallin's voice could be heard above the wind as he shouted, "Man the braces there! Look alive. I believe your men have gotten fat and lazy, Mr. Stubbs."

WHAP!!! UGHH!!! "Move ye bloody buggers, the cap'n be watching ye. Jones, I'll 'ave yer rum ration for a week, you worthless ape." With the bosun's starter a threat, the men at the braces put their backs into it, heaving and groaning until the yards came around with a grinding like noise at first, and then it went away as the yard moved around.

The wind filled the sails as the yards came around, the billowing canvas flapping hard until it thundered out. Hard and full, *Ares* went about and gathered way. The anchor was soon catted home and made fast.

Faith, in the captain's cabin, looked out the stern windows and saw that the land was fading. "Goodbye Mother Maria, goodbye No."

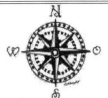

CHAPTER TWENTY FOUR

A CURTAIN OF SPRAY AND drizzle made things miserable. *Ares* had run free, as Gabe called it. Without the hindrance of convoy ships to deal with, the ship proved the theory of a razed ship to be true in regard to speed and sailing qualities.

The master, Scott, was talking to the quartermaster. The two had become friends and spent a lot of time together. The drizzle would be around for most of the day, Scott predicted at dawn. The man's prediction, as usual, had come true. Gabe's confidence in the man had grown to where he now trusted him completely.

It had been three weeks since weighing anchor in Portsmouth. The last week there had been a really good time, not only for Gabe but Vallin as well, if what Hex had heard was true. Vallin had spent several evenings with a young actress. *He deserved it*, Gabe thought, but he wouldn't mention it to Faith. Con Vallin aptly ran the ship, while Gabe spent time with his son. The little mate really liked it forward when the bows would dip into a trough and spray would come over and sprinkle them. The youngster would cackle each time they were hit with the spray. Hearing his son's laughter warmed Gabe's heart. The seamen took to the boy, enjoying his laughter as well.

"'E'll be an admiral one day," one seaman said.

A toothless old seaman with tobacco stains at the creases of his mouth carved a horse from a scrap of wood. Little James took the offered horse, his face breaking into a smile, showing his front teeth. He hugged the horse to him.

"'E'll not be fer the sea, Cap'n. 'E'll take to the fields, I feels it. Nay, the sea is not fer that 'um."

Shocked, Gabe just looked at the man. Would the boy take after Faith's family? A cry from above broke Gabe's thoughts.

***

"Sail ho! Off the starboard bow." The lookout, after a moment, called down again, "She be hull down but she be a ship, I'm certain."

Gabe wiping the drizzle from his face looked at the first lieutenant. "You have a good man aloft today, Mr. Vallin."

The drizzle hung like a curtain across the sky. For the lookout to be able to pick up the ship in this weather meant that he not only had a good eye, but was alert.

"I think that I'll send Mr. Massey up," Vallin said. "It will be good exercise with an experienced hand." Gabe nodded his agreement.

Lieutenant Turner had the watch, so Vallin spoke to him, "I think that I'll borrow your midshipman, Mr. Turner."

"Aye, sir." *What else could he say*, Turner thought. He had been about to send the boy on an errand, but not now.

"Mr. Massey," Vallin called. "Take a glass and up you go. Mind you, if you interfere with the lookout you'll kiss the gunner's daughter."

Dagan had walked up, and hearing Vallin's comment he looked at Gabe, both of them trying not to smile. Thomas, the lookout, was a prime seaman. He was a man who kept to himself, a bit apart from most.

He exercised a lot, drank little, and did not gamble as most others did. He could read, write, and unlike most sailors, he could swim.

Hex had pointed him out once as he went halfway up a stay, hand over hand to the mainmast lookout's platform. "Should I fall, Captain, he'd be the one to take my place."

"He might be my next cox'n," Gabe replied, "but he'll never take your place."

"Thank you, sir," Hex said and then found something to busy himself.

It was several minutes before Massey called down, "Deck thar! She is a frigate, sir, a Frog from the cut of her. She seems to be running parallel to us."

Vallin looked at Gabe. "Nice report," Gabe said.

"Aye," Vallin replied, "right out of Thomas' mouth."

There was little doubt that the experienced hand had told the middy what to say. The report was too precise to come from one so inexperienced.

"Very well," Vallin called up, while Gabe spoke to the officer of the watch.

"Log the sighting, Mr. Turner."

"Aye, Captain. Will we engage her?"

"My orders are to proceed with utmost haste, Mr. Turner. To me that means we defend ourselves but we do not seek out trouble."

"Aye, Captain."

Gabe told the officer that he'd be in his cabin should he be needed. He stepped over the coaming and went down the companion ladder. He took off his hat and slung the water from it,

The marine smiled and said, "Wet day, Captain."

"Aye, it's better down here, at least you're dry."

"Sometimes luck comes your way," the marine said and knuckled his brow in a salute.

Captain LoGiudice had asked Gabe about his

preference as to being greeted or politely spoken to by the sentries. Some captains preferred that they didn't speak at all outside of their duties. Gabe felt different though. You never knew when you needed a man to watch your back. He, therefore, preferred a polite exchange to a hard approach. He'd had no reason to regret his decision, thus far.

Faith put her finger to her lips when Gabe entered the cabin. That meant little James was asleep. "He has called for his father," Faith said softly. "He wanted to go play on deck."

Gabe grinned, his son was starting to speak and put one or two words together. "The weather is not fit for me to take him on deck. We also sighted a ship, probably a Frenchie."

Faith stopped what she was doing and turned to her husband, "Does that mean a fight...a battle?"

"No, not unless he provokes it. I have orders to proceed with haste. Even if I didn't, I carry too precious a cargo to risk it in battle."

Faith smiled, "You know how much I love you?"

Gabe pulled his wife close, "You've shown me a few times but it never hurts to be reminded."

"Remind you I shall. Your prize will be much greater than some stinky old French ship."

Gabe smiled, "I do love you so."

***

DINNER THAT EVENING WAS another of Josh Nesbit's delightful productions. Jimmy Ducks had dispatched two of his fattest ducks. They had been roasted using some of Josh's herbs. Served with the duck were cabbage, mashed potatoes covered with caramelized onions, peas, and carrots cooked in a buttery sauce. A new loaf of still warm bread was devoured before the meal was finished. A bottle of Chianti wine was served with the meal. It was a fine wine that was first produced in 1716 in the Chianti region of Italy. The white wine was a perfect match for the roasted duck. The bottle was part of a case given to Gabe by Doctor Cook. Tonight, in addition to Doctor Cook and Gallagher, who were the usual dinner guests, Doctor Cornish had accepted the captain's lady's invitation. Lieutenant Laqua, and Midshipmen Corwin and Easley were also guests. Easley, sitting by Doctor Cornish, watched his every move; by doing this as recommended by Midshipman Heath, he would not make any mistakes that would embarrass himself.

"Small beer or wine for our young sir?" Nesbit asked.

"Let the boy taste the wine," Faith spoke up. She knew a child's taste buds differed from an adult. She remembered back to her father bragging about how smooth his whiskey went down and its caramel flavor. Faith, wanting to taste this brew her father favored so much, had snuck into his library and taken down the decanter. She poured herself half a glass and smelled the amber liquid, which didn't smell that awful, but not great either. She'd just touched the glass to her lips when she heard footsteps. Rather than taking a sip as she intended, she gulped the half glass of Kentucky sour mash down, not wanting to get caught... but she was. It took her breath at first, and then as the fiery liquid went down it burned her from her tonsils to the pit of her stomach. It burned her vocal cords and made her cough. She repeated one of her father's frequent words then once she stopped coughing. "Shit!" she croaked, and then "Shit, shit, shit".

Nanny came running in, "Child, hush yo mouth, girl. Such words outta a little girl."

Faith could now speak, "Nanny, it burned my guts out."

"Serves you right, child." Nanny could now smell the liquor on her breath. "Yo daddy will make something else burn, he hear you cursing like a field hand. He not gonna be happy wid you messing wid his corn squeezing either," Nanny snapped. "Now go on, get outta heah fo I wash out that mouth you got wid lye soap." Faith smiled, thinking back. It was just before her mother died.

A knock at the door interrupted Cook, who was describing how Cornish had fleeced him at draughts. "Midshipman of the watch, sir," the marine sentry announced.

The skylight had been closed to keep out the rain, so they'd heard nothing on deck over their conversation.

"Very well," Gabe replied.

The senior midshipman, Brian Heath, entered. "Mr. Turner's respects, Captain. He thinks that you should come on deck, sir. He has sent for the first lieutenant as well." Heath had said all this without taking time to breathe. The boy looked apprehensive.

"Excuse me, please," Gabe said to his guests. "Mr. Laqua, would you come topside as well." Gabe thought that if Turner felt strong enough to call both the first lieutenant and his captain as well, it must be urgent.

When Gabe came on deck, Turner had a night glass in hand. One of the helmsmen gave a slight cough to warn his lieutenant that the captain was on deck. *A very good sign*, Gabe thought. Turner had the respect of his men.

Turner turned to his captain, "She is back, Captain. Mr. Heath was talking to Mr. Scott and when the moon cleared the clouds, he spotted her."

"Did you see her, Mr. Turner?"

"Aye, Captain, I did just before you walked up." Turner handed the night glass to Gabe's outstretched hand.

Gabe, taking the glass, said, "When the clouds cover the moon again, I want the ship darkened at once."

"Beat to quarter, Captain?" This was the first lieutenant.

"Quietly, Mr. Vallin, with no drums or pipes." Looking through the night glass, Gabe spoke to Heath, the midshipman. "Mr. Heath, go to my cabin and escort Mrs. Anthony and my son to the cockpit. Have Nesbit and Davis carry down anything she may desire for the baby."

"Aye, Captain."

"Hex!"

"Here, Captain."

"My pistols and sword."

"On the way, Captain."

"She'll not attack tonight." Gabe heard the voice and recognized it as Dagan.

"I hope not, Uncle."

Cook was exiting the companionway as Hex was entering. "French ship," Hex whispered, and then put his fingers to his lips for quiet.

The men went to their battle stations with no fanfare and as silently as possible. When the next dark cloud covered the moon, all of the ship's lanterns were put out.

A gun captain scolded a man down on the gun deck, "Cover yer pipe, you idiot. Yer ember sticks out like a beacon to a bloody knocking 'ouse." The chastised seaman spit in the bowl of his pipe, producing a slight hissing sound.

The ship remained on the same parallel course as *Ares* over the next ten minutes. Gabe walked over to where the master stood and ordered a change in course, but to be done a point or two to larboard at a time. When it was time to change the watch, at midnight, the men remained where they were.

Thankfully, the rain had stopped, but that only made things worse. The men were all wet and now the wind was picking up to chill them. The French ship had not been seen for an hour now.

"Mr. Vallin."

"Here, Captain."

"Have the men at every other gun go below and change into dry clothes. They can return and relieve their mates. Have the officers and midshipmen swap out also. The other men can go below in sections."

"Yes sir," Vallin replied.

The horizon was free of any ships at dawn. Gabe gave a sigh of relief. He had believed Dagan's words. He'd spent too many years with him to doubt him. But Gabe had done the proper thing. He'd done the only thing a captain could do. He suddenly had a thought. *Had things been different and they had attacked would a court martial board find me not guilty based on telling them that Dagan said they wouldn't attack? No, I'll believe him without hesitation but still do what is best for my ship.*

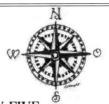

CHAPTER TWENTY FIVE

GABE HAD MIDSHIPMAN EASLEY go find Doctor Cook and Leo, as the men aboard *Ares* knew Sir Lawrence and Mr. Gallagher. Gabe wanted to speak with the gentlemen at their earliest convenience. Mr. Easley wondered if the men knew that when the captain said earliest convenience that meant 'move yer arses', but he didn't feel like it was his place to tell them.

The young gentleman found the two men having coffee in the wardroom. He delivered the message and then found the courage to enlighten the passengers. "Not to be forward, sir, but you being civilians, as it were, you might not know that when the captain sends a message worded in such a manner, it means it's er...urgent. It means right now."

"Why didn't he say that then?" Gallagher snorted.

"He did," Cook said, in as polite a way as he could. "Thank you, Mr. Easley, for enlightening us."

The boy smiled, "My pleasure, sir."

When Cook and Gallagher showed up, Hex nudged the captain, "Your guests, sir."

Gabe turned and greeted the men. "Let's step aft where we might speak privately, Gabe said as he walked toward the stern. "Doctor Cook, Mr. Gallagher, this French ship puzzles me. It's not like an enemy to shadow you unless they are waiting on support or to report your whereabouts. They attack usually, so I'm most curious as to their motive. Do they know something I don't? If so, I need to know what it is. It's not just us men, as you know. There's Captain Lo-Giudice's wife, Faith, my son, and a few others whose lives are at risk."

Cook and Gallagher stood without speaking for a moment. Cook then cleared his throat and said, "We have come upon some information that we must take action against. The French have sent an entire fleet to aid the Colonies. We have orders directing Rodney to sail to the Colonies with all dispatch."

"When is this fleet expected to arrive?" Gabe asked.

"Any day to be truthful, but our best guess is August."

"Damme sir, but that's cutting it close, is it not? This is already July."

"We know, sir, that's why your orders were written as they were. If the French get to the Colonies first, the war is lost."

"Lost," Gabe smirked. "Gentlemen, the war was lost the day it was started." Gallagher looked stunned at Gabe's comments.

Cook hung his head down. "I agree with you, Captain. Unfortunately, we are a minority. So I, like you, will do my duty." Gabe just stood there, looking blank. A thousand thoughts were running through his head.

"Sail ho! It be the same Frog ship, directly astern."

Gabe whirled around, "I'll not be played any longer. Mr. Vallin, beat to quarters. I'll show this bugger." He then turned to the agents, "He is likely spying on us or expecting help. Either way, that puts this ship and our people at a greater danger."

Gabe turned away to attend to his duties when another thought struck him. "The way this ship has shadowed us even when we've changed courses tells me that he knows where we are headed. That, gentlemen, also tells me that you have a spy in your office."

Dagan laughed at Gabe's comments and said, "A spy working in the spy's office, spying for our enemy. It's strange bedfellows you gentlemen keep."

Doctor Cook and Leo were taken aback by those words, staring at one another but not speaking.

***

"MR. VALLIN, HAVE THE guns loaded but not run out. I want to put an end to this. If the fellow follows the same pattern, I will engage as he comes parallel. Have people walking about so that he will not suspect anything. Captain LoGiudice, if you will have your men posted to where they can be ready but not seen. Mr. Laqua!"

"Aye, Captain."

"I think a measure of grape on top of ball on the quarterdeck and forecastle guns would not be amiss."

"Aye, sir."

Faith stood at the hatch against the urging of the young midshipman. Nanny was with James and Lum had already gone down to the sickbay, but she'd stayed at the top of the ladder. So this was her husband, a warrior...her warrior...a man who could only be pushed so far. A man who would charge hell if he felt his family was being threatened.

"Mr. Vallin, I've a feeling today. Put your man, Thomas, in the tops. I want his eyes on the horizon and not that ship."

"Aye, Captain. Pass the word for Seaman Thomas." When Thomas reported, Vallin gave the man his instructions.

Gabe looked about the ship making sure all was ready, and spied Faith. *Damnation*, he thought. He was about to blast her stubborn ways when she blew him a kiss and hurried off with the midshipman, who feared that the captain would blame him.

"Strong-willed woman, Faith is. She wanted to see her husband in action," Dagan said.

"Foolish, she is."

Dagan smiled, "Most women seem that way when their heart rules their emotion."

Hex cleared his throat, "Our foe is almost upon us."

Cook had gone below to help the surgeon if needed, but Gallagher had stayed topside and watched everything: from the gun captain's yell, 'cast loose and provide' to the net being strung up to help prevent any damage aloft from falling debris and striking those on deck.

The captain and his men seemed well-versed in the ways of war. He heard two seamen betting on whether the captain would take the ship as a prize or just sink her. Neither of them seemed to consider just the opposite might just come true. Trust...trust and faith in their captain to see them through and maybe even add to their purse.

Leo Gallagher, a man accustomed to taking chances...a man who had to fight, to kill to survive, had never seen anything to compare with this ship...a war ship preparing for battle.

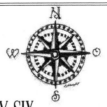

CHAPTER TWENTY SIX

GABE WATCHED CLOSELY AS the French frigate slowly came abreast. "How far away would you say they are, Dagan?"

Dagan, thinking and using his years of experience, finally answered, "I would judge the ship to be between four hundred to four hundred and fifty yards."

Gabe smiled, "You taught me well, Uncle. My guess was less than five hundred."

While the Naval Ordnance Board bragged that a twelve-pound ball at the proper elevation could fire two thousand yards. Most naval officers laughed at this number. One thousand yards was closer to the truth.

Gabe had seen his brother fire at greater than one thousand, but he admitted when he'd done so that it was merely to attract attention. If a hit was scored, unless it was to the sails, riggings, or rails it would do little damage to the ship. It would kill men.

Gabe wanted to do more than just attract attention, with the range of the ship less than five hundred yards. "Mr. Corwin," he ordered, "pass the word to Mr. Laqua, our target is four hundred fifty yards away. I intend to fire the larboard guns." The last should have been obvious, but Gabe didn't take anything for granted. "Mr. Vallin! Mr. Scott!"

"Aye," the two replied in unison.

"I intend to fire and then luff and fire again as we cross her stern."

Both men smiled and replied, "Aye."

Gabe watched closely. Had the distance between the two ships become closer...it had. He was sure of it. Had the frigate's previous tactics been to lull Gabe into "inaction"? Had it been done to set up this moment?

"Open gun ports and fire! Fire as you bear," Gabe yelled. He heard the gun ports slam open, and heard the truck wheels being pulled across the deck. He heard all of this, but at the same time he saw the enemy's gun ports open as well. Had he hesitated a second later it might have been a lost cause.

"I outguessed you, you snail eating Frog," Gabe shouted, shaking his fist. He watched as *Ares'* balls slammed into the enemy's hull, with some of them going through open gun ports. He swore that he could hear the screams on the French ship above the roar of *Ares'* guns, as the quarterdeck's twelve pounders thundered forth.

"Luff," he yelled as the last gun was fired. "Now, Mr. Scott, cross her stern."

"Captain, Captain," Vallin was shouting. "Their flag, sir, they've surrendered. Cease firing, cease firing."

The ship had been hit hard and unexpectedly. They had lowered their sails and now sat a target should they make the wrong move. But, Gabe thought, she could still fight. I would fight her still.

"My gig, Mr. Vallin. Captain LoGiudice, a squad of your marines in a long boat, if you please. Mr. Vallin, should they have treachery in mind, blow them to hell."

"Aye, Captain, usual signal?"

"Yes." A private signal that the men had come up with to alert the other of danger was 'alls well'. Secured meant the ship was theirs.

As Gabe's gig made its way to the enemy, he could see her name across the stern, *Aigle*. Gabe's French was not the best, but he thought the word *Aigle* meant Eagle.

The marines went up the entry port and spread out. Captain LoGiudice stood next to the entry port. "The grape did more damage than I thought possible, Captain."

Gabe looked about and then it hit him: none of the French were in uniform. This was obviously a new ship. A beautiful ship, he had to admit, but it was not the usual French naval ship.

Hex spoke, "I believe this was a private ship, Captain."

"Captain LoGiudice, see if one of those fellows by the quarterdeck will enlighten us. Hex, you know the routine, search the captain's cabin."

"Aye sir, I'll take Mr. Delsenno with me."

Gabe looked over to a seaman, who'd served with him for years, "Twist, take two seamen with you and search the ship." Twist knuckled and grabbed a couple of his mates and made his way down.

LoGiudice returned with a young man. "The captain and first lieutenant were both killed in our attack. The second lieutenant is with the surgeon. He is similar to our midshipman. His ship, this ship, is under contract as a privateer. They are on a mission but he knows nothing else. I believe, sir, if I remember correctly, his official title is that of Aspirant."

Gabe knew the term. "Send your sergeant down to the sick berth with the boy to see what condition this other officer is in." With that, Gabe called out "Secured" for Vallin. As he did so, Hex came on deck.

"There's a box, sir. We pried it open and there are a lot of official documents in it."

"What, no treasure, Jake?"

The cox'n smiled, "Thought you should see this first, sir." It was a large leather folder with the words "des documents top secrete" burned into it.

Gabe thought, *damme, that's either a damn give away, or a hoax or ruse. Ares* had a similar pouch on board, but it was in a bag with a lead weight attached.

LoGiudice was back with the young aspirant. "The second lieutenant is dead."

Damn, Gabe thought. He walked over to the rail. "Mr. Vallin!"

"Aye, Captain."

"Send our guests over."

"Aye, aye."

***

THE DEAD BODIES WERE cast over the side, and while Cook and Gallagher pored over the documents in the captain's cabin, Hex and the marines put the ship's crew to repairing the wreckage. Laqua had been left aboard *Ares* while Vallin came across to assist in making the ship ready to sail. Some of the ship's crew was in the process of being put aboard *Ares* so that the guards wouldn't have to worry about so many on one ship.

"It appears, Mr. Vallin, that you have a ship to command, at least, until we reach Antigua," Gabe said. A forty gun French frigate in good condition would receive a hearty welcome.

"Sail ho!"

Thomas, Gabe thought, *he's still in the tops*. The two ships were now no more than fifty yards apart so Thomas's cry was easily heard.

"Hex, get our guests back aboard *Ares*...quickly."

"Aye, Captain."

"Con," Gabe spoke to his first lieutenant, calling him by his first name. "I've felt all along that we were being shadowed and pushed along knowing that support was soon to appear. I'll send over half the gun crews and enough seamen with some marines. Make the prisoners help and if one balks, shoot him. That will encourage the others to work. I will hoist a French flag over ours and should that be more French ships, we will take or destroy them."

"Aye, I like it," Vallin said.

Thomas called down again, as Gabe made it back aboard *Ares*, "There are three sets of sails, Captain."

Damn, Gabe thought. He'd not thought that there would be more than one, maybe two ships. "Mr. Heath, go over to assist Mr. Vallin. Mr. Myers, make sure your best mates go over."

"Aye, Captain," the gunner replied.

"Deck there, the ships be Frogs...a large frigate, a small frigate, and a brig."

It could have been worse. Gabe walked to the rail. "Did you hear the lookout's report, Mr. Vallin?"

"Aye, Captain."

"I will take the frigate," Gabe said. "The smaller may be a frigate or a corvette. You take it. Keep a lookout for what the brig does. If she invites herself to the music, we'll teach her to dance." This brought shouts and laughter until Laqua shouted silence. "Hex, get the French aspirant up here."

"Aye, Captain."

Gabe looked at the oncoming ships. He had a few minutes. He'd speak to Faith. "Captain LoGiudice?"

"Aye, Captain."

"I believe that you have five minutes, should you care to speak to Holly."

CHAPTER TWENTY SEVEN

THE FRENCH ASPIRANT, LEROUX, was waiting when Gabe returned on deck; not in five minutes but closer to twelve. Faith was trying to be strong but the fear was in her eyes, the tremor in her voice, and the passion in which she hugged and kissed. *If I hesitate a moment longer*, Gabe thought, *the ships will be on us* but was reluctant to push Faith away.

She finally pushed back, "Go fight your ship, my husband. James and I will await you."

Gabe rushed out of the cabin with those words, emotions, welling up inside him.

"M'sieur LeRoux, I want the French recognition signal."

The youth's smiling face suddenly frowned. "You are asking me to betray my country, Capitaine."

Gabe knew the turmoil that the youth was going through. "You have a choice, young sir. Your ship is, was involved in spying. That means that you and every crew member can be shot or hanged. Spies don't get exchanged...they are executed. I will start shooting the crew, in one minute. No one is to know that the information was not found in the captain's cabin. If you cooperate, and the brig does not engage in the fight, I will put you and most of your crew in boats to be picked up by the brig." This last part had just come to Gabe. Seeing the boy was trying to decide, Gabe hurried it along, "Mr. Laqua, have five of the prisoners brought up for execution. Captain LoGiudice, assemble your men for a firing squad."

Laqua had been around his captain enough to know that this was a ruse. He looked at the marine captain and gave a wink.

"Sergeant Daniels, gather a firing squad," LoGiudice spoke firmly.

Cook and Gallagher looked on. Cook, with an expression between awe and fear; Gallagher found it amusing.

"F.C.," the boy stammered. "French Capitaine."

Gabe looked at LeRoux, "You have just saved a lot of lives, M'sieur. If I find that you've tricked me, though, you will die before I do."

"It's no trick, Capitaine."

Gabe nodded, "Remember, the signal was left out by your captain. Mr. Massey, signal the French recognition signal to Mr. Vallin. Mr. Corwin, have a French flag hoisted above ours, please."

"Yes sir."

***

AIGLE WAS NOW IN the lead with *Ares* following behind as a prize would normally do. The French ship was well-armed with twenty-eight eighteen-pounders and fourteen eight-pounders. She carried no carronades. She did carry the usual array of swivel guns. All of which Gabe had seen being loaded. The frigate was built as a heavy frigate, not a razee like *Ares*. What puzzled Gabe was why such a fine frigate was used as a privateer. He had spoken of this with Cook and Gallagher.

Gallagher, being more accustomed to the ways of the secret service volunteered, "As a private ship, she can be used in ways that might bring discredit to France. Also, the French can disavow any knowledge of her. Of course, no one would believe it, but neither could they prove otherwise."

"The lead frigate has signaled *Aigle*, Captain," Lieutenant Turner interrupted.

Vallin quickly sent the reply and so far everything moved normally. More signals were hoisted by the large frigate. *We gained a few minutes*, Gabe thought.

A gun was fired and the signal repeated. *Ares* moved starboard as Gabe had instructed. *Aigle* was now out of *Ares* line of fire. People were hurrying about on board the large French frigate.

"They smell a rat," the master volunteered.

"Take down that French rag," Gabe ordered.

"Now, Mr. Myers," Gabe shouted.

The forward guns roared out their deadly mixture of ball and canister, followed by the deafening thunder of the forty-two pound carronades. Gabe moved to the larboard side of the quarterdeck to see, as the smoke drifted back. They were nearly abreast.

"Fire as you bear, Mr. Laqua. Fire as you bear," Gabe yelled, the smoke and sweat making his eyes water and sting. The French frigate, so far, had yet to fire on *Ares*.

"They manned the guns on Mr. Vallin's side," Scott volunteered.

The frigate suddenly swung around almost like the bow was chasing *Ares* stern.

"'Er wheel 'as been shot away," Gabe heard one of the quarterdeck gunners yell. Mr. Vallin, not one to miss an opportunity when presented, had *Aigle's* eight pounders fire into the stern of the enemy ship. *Ares* was now past the frigate and approaching the next ship. He had been right; it was a twenty gun corvette.

"Fire the forward guns on yonder ship, Mr. Meyers. Mr. Scott, as soon as the forward guns fire, bring her about. I don't relish getting hit by Mr. Vallin's guns."

Ares swung as soon as the guns fired, her deck canting so that Gabe had to grab a rail. The corvette's captain seemed better prepared than the frigate's commander. The corvette's guns were quick to reply. The stern rail burst, sending wood and splinters skyward, the ball continued on, hitting a twelve pounder and knocking the gun off its carriage and crushing a gunner. The stern guns answered the corvette's fire, blasting a huge section of the ship's bow off. They kept firing until their guns were no long able to bear.

Ronald Laqua had fired *Ares* broadside and the guns had been quickly reloaded, knowing that they'd likely be fired on as they passed. The frigate's wheel had been shot away so they might not have the length of the ship as a target. Looking out a gun port, the enemy ship continued in a circle, although someone had gotten the canvas off her.

"'as she surrendered, zur?" a gun captain asked.

Laqua stuck his head further out the gun port. "No, she's still flying her flag."

He heard a thud in the hull nearby. A marksman had barely missed a head shot. The order to fire went out and the great guns boomed forth, their deadly balls pushing back against the ropes that bound them. One of the first shots hit the forward mast, causing the ship to lean over. The next few guns, without trying, fired into the hull, holing her. *She'll never swim again*, Laqua thought, bemoaning the fact that there went the chance of any added prize money.

As *Ares* sailed past the French frigate, Laqua hurried on deck. Gabe, seeing his lieutenant come up, knew that he had something significant to report; otherwise he'd never have left his station.

"She's holed good, Captain. At least, four balls hit as her mast went over. She'll not swim long, sir."

The French flag still flew. Why hadn't they surrendered?

"Bring her about, Mr. Scott. Hold your fire, Mr. Laqua, until we see what happens. Mr. Corwin," Gabe called.

It was the master who spoke up. "The young sir has been taken below, Captain. He's in a bad way."

"Thank you, Mr. Scott." Seeing a petty officer, Gabe told him to go forward and tell Mr. Meyers to hold his fire.

Thomas called down, from aloft, "The corvette has hauled down her colors."

"Where is the brig, Thomas?"

"Off to starboard, amidship."

"Hex!"

"Aye, Captain."

"Take my gig over to the brig under a white flag. Tell the captain that he can come collect the survivors but hurry as I hear the frigate is sinking. Mr. Turner, let's get the boats out and pick up survivors. Use the French as boat crews."

"Aye, Captain."

When several of the French were on deck, Gabe spoke louder than usual, "It was fortuitous that we found the recognition signal in *Aigle's* captain's cabin, wouldn't you say, Mr. Scott? Otherwise, things may have turned out differently."

The master had no idea what the captain was talking about but responded, "Aye, Captain, it was."

Aspirant LeRoux, as well as others, heard the exchange. LeRoux gave a slight nod, as he went down in the boat.

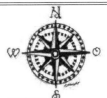

CHAPTER TWENTY EIGHT

THE REST OF THE voyage was uneventful. Gabe met with Admiral Dutch Moffett once they returned to English Harbour. He was being recalled but his relief had not yet arrived. The captured *Aigle* would need repairs but Moffett felt it would be bought in.

"I wish that I could put your Lieutenant Vallin on her," Moffett said. "But..." They both understood and so would Vallin. There was always a 'but.'

Gabe made sure that Faith was settled into Lady Deborah's little cottage atop the hill overlooking English Harbour while the repairs were being carried out on *Ares*.

Cook and Gallagher were in a hurry to get to Saint Kitts to give Admiral Rodney the latest information about the French headed to the Colonies.

"If he doesn't move, I'll kick his butt so hard that he'll wear his arse for a hat," Gallagher had sworn.

The large bundle of French documents was turned over to a local contact that was proficient in French. The morning that they were to sail, the local contact hurried to the waterfront to speak to Cook and Gallagher. The concern over attacks had taken on a new urgency.

"The Dons are going to attack Roatan, and the French are going to attack British held islands in the Caribbean. No specifics were noted, only that it would happen. Each of our possessions is in danger and must be warned."

Gabe cleared his throat, "We've neither the time nor the resources to do that. We need to inform those islands that are strategically important. As far as the other islands, they all know the possibility of an invasion exists. They live with that every day, so what is gained by telling them what they already know. We'll inform Roatan of the impending attack and those islands that are of strategic importance."

"Like Barbados," Gallagher said.

"No, it was destroyed this past October by a hurricane. I doubt the French would want the island at this point," Gabe informed the men.

"It has to be Saint Kitts or Antigua," Cook volunteered.

"I don't think so. There is so much activity going on here at all times, that the French could never be certain what type of resistance they'd meet," Gabe advised.

"It's Saint Kitts then," Cook and Leo said in unison.

***

HMS PICKLE DROPPED ANCHOR at English Harbour that afternoon. Captain Nicholson made his required visit to the flagship and then visited Gabe on *Ares*. The afternoon sun was blazing down on English Harbour's sheltered anchorage. Gabe sat peering out the open stern window at the hill where Faith awaited him in Deborah's cottage. The hillside was a vibrant green, as the island had thankfully received more than the usual rainfall. Lum had been busy cutting back some of the vegetation that was creeping up on the cottage grounds.

Gabe heard the watch give its challenge, and then the reply, *"Pickle." Mal Nicholson*, Gabe thought, *what a pleasant surprise*. Before leaving the cabin, he instructed Nesbit to prepare some refreshments. He then made his way on deck to meet his friend.

With the heat bearing down on them, Nesbit decided to make lemonade and put out the scones that were left over from breakfast. Nesbit's scones were different than the usual English scone, as he made them sweeter and usually added a fruit or berry if available. The scones today were blueberry.

Nicholson looked at Gabe once he was seated with his refreshment, "I have just delivered some dreadful news to the admiral. The French have taken Tobago."

Damn, Gabe thought, thinking of the times he'd pulled into Tobago as Admiral Buck's flag captain. "I hope Lieutenant Governor Peter Campbell and Mrs. Campbell are safe."

"I've no news that they are not," Nicholson said. "I do know that it was Comte de Grasse's fleet. Troops landed and are under the command of General Marquis de Bovillé."

"This war has certainly gone badly for England," Gabe said.

"Aye, if we are to survive, we will need every ship and captain to do their best."

Gabe gave Nicholson a knowing look, as he tossed down the last of his lemonade. He had not missed the term survive. Not win...but survive.

***

A SUDDEN SHOWER HAD come upon the island, increasing the humidity drastically. Some of the seamen swore that they could see steam rising from the rocks along the water's edge and vapors rising from some of the island's rooftops. The afternoon sun struggled to find a clear path to the island through the gray, churning clouds. Dagan and Scott were talking as Gabe and Hex walked toward the entry port.

Scott was saying, "As fast as the clouds are moving, they will be past to the west by dark." Gabe and Hex looked up upon hearing this, but neither of them made a comment.

Gabe made his way to the waterfront. He dismissed his boat crew and took a carriage for hire to the cottage where he and Faith were staying at the top of the hill. The one where Deborah and Gil first made love and where Gabe lay wounded for several days. His hand, without thinking, went to the gray furrow along his head where a ball had nearly ended his life. The cottage had a lot of memories. Smiling to himself, he thought, *Faith and I made a few memories there as well.*

The evening meal had been a simple one. Nanny was now bathing little James while Gabe stepped out on the porch, putting his arm around Faith's waist. He was contemplating telling Faith about the war news but held back. The night was soft, the clouds had cleared, and the sky was filled with stars. A cool breeze could be felt as Gabe sat in a swing next to Faith. It was peaceful.

"I wish every night was like this," Faith said, speaking softly as she moved over until her legs and hips touched Gabe's. "Will you be leaving soon?" she asked.

"In truth, I don't know," Gabe answered. "A dispatch ship came in today so maybe I'll know more tomorrow."

"I'm not sure that I like this assignment you have, ferrying those spies all over the place," Faith said.

"We have been able to spend more time together," Gabe responded, not sure what caused Faith's words. He wondered if the port admiral might have let the navy's negative thoughts on the situation be known to his mother, who said something to Faith.

Gabe asked, when Faith didn't say anything, "Don't you like the gentlemen?"

"Yes...Doctor Cook is the most pleasant and adorable man. Mr. Gallagher...well, it's easy to see him as a spy. He is a very dark, deep man whom I believe would cut your throat without batting an eye."

Gabe thought, *damn she has Leo pegged...if she only knew.*

Any further discussion was prevented when Nanny came to the door holding James, with Sam trailing a foot behind.

"I believe that devil of a dog likes little James," Gabe said.

"Don't you call him that," Faith snapped as she took James. She then knelt and rubbed the scoundrel behind the ears, whispering to him. Sam, to show his appreciation, gave Faith and James several licks. Kisses, Faith called them. When she stood, Sam looked at Gabe but didn't growl.

I should have drowned you, Gabe thought. It was as if the dog could read his mind as he gave a low growl, and then turned and followed Faith in while Gabe brought up the rear.

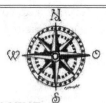

CHAPTER TWENTY NINE

"YOU CHEATED," THE MAN snarled, revealing the brown tobacco stained stumps of his teeth. A muttering ran through the crowd. The man had been an overseer at one of the plantations until his ways were more than the planter could handle.

Simon Davis and Josh Nesbit had been playing cards when the big man asked if he could join in. Midshipmen Brian Heath and Zachary Massey had been playing earlier, until they called it a night and the foul-smelling man sat down and joined in.

The Bucket o' Ale catered mostly to the sailors from the navy ships and the occasional merchant vessel that pulled in. The draw to the tavern that evening was four new lasses straight from London, fresh young lasses and not poxed old crones. Now, hearing the outburst, the spectators and other tavern customers backed up, giving room to what promised to be a fight.

"You cheated," the man said again. "I saw you passing signals."

Simon Davis scraped his chair back on the pine planking. "I cheat no man," he said.

Nesbit stood and backed up, not sure what to do.

"Let's be splitting the pot then," Simon offered.

"You been cheating all evening. One little pot don't make it equal," the man said.

"It seems that you have a problem then," Simon said.

"Me! I'll skin you alive, you bum buster."

"If it's a fight that you want, I'll be happy to accommodate you," Simon returned. "I'm not armed, though." The rotten tooth man laughed, his breath reaching several who stood close by.

"'Is bloody breath smells like a dung 'eap it does," a seaman volunteered.

"You're next," foul breath retorted.

"Not in here," the tavern owner said, walking over.

Foul breath turned and, without a word, sent a huge right into his chin, knocking the owner out in one blow.

Simon stood up slowly, without taking his eyes off of his foe, "Never let it be said that I, Simon Davis, backed down from any man. Nor will I tolerate a man calling me a cheat."

Nesbit, seeing one of *Ares'* petty officers, put a coin in his hand. "You know where the captain lives, go get him. Use the coin if you need but be quick. Otherwise, there may be a killing."

Ashcraft, the petty officer, wanted to stay and see the fight, but if the knowledge came to the captain that he'd refused to go get him...well, he wouldn't be a petty officer long. He took the coin and flew out the entrance. Who knows, if he hurried, he might get back to see the finish.

Simon and the man faced each other, less than six feet separated them. Suddenly, foul-breath charged. His size had intimidated a lot of men. One charge usually was enough. He'd charge, slam into his opponent, and when they went down he'd stomp on them a couple of times. The fight always ended quickly. Not this time though.

When he charged, Simon didn't stand still or back up. He took a step forward, turned a bit to avoid the big man's rush, and stuck his leg out, tripping foul breath. The big man hit the floor hard. He had large scrapes on both arms from the rough plank flooring, and cut flesh hung from his left elbow. His nose was peeled and bleeding as were his battered, bruised lips. He got up, unsteadily at first. Simon waited. Nesbit could not believe the move. Simon was showing himself in a completely different light.

The big man turned and slung a chair out of his way. "Trip me, will ye? I'm going to rip your ears off yer head and make you choke on them."

"Are you no better at fighting than you are at playing cards?" Simon asked. His insult was meant to rile the man into further mistakes.

"Damn you," the man charged again.

Simon turned the opposite way this time, striking out with a quick right to his opponent's ear, splitting it open. Blood was now all over foul breath's face. He touched his ear, and howled as he pulled a bloody hand back. The big man, like a fool, rushed again, but then he stopped short and swung. Had the blow landed the fight would have been over, but Simon ducked and the huge fist grazed the top of his head, dazing him, but not before he put a one-two into his foe's kidney.

***

"Captain, Captain!" Ashcraft shouted as he banged on the cottage's door. Sam gave a loud bark and rushed growling to the door.

Gabe had unbuttoned his shirt but had not taken it off. "What in God's name?" he growled.

Sam was growling as well...growling and scratching at the door trying to get at whoever banged on his door.

"Get Sam," Gabe said to Faith, as he buttoned his shirt.

Ashcraft had backed up to the steps, hearing the dog. Faith retrieved Sam as Gabe opened the door.

Petty Officer Ashcraft was relieved to see his captain. "Mr. Nesbit sent me to get you, Captain. You have to hurry or he's likely to be killed."

"Nesbit?" Gabe asked.

"Er...no sir. Davis...Simon Davis." *Damnation*, Gabe thought.

Lum was at the door with Gabe's pistol and his sword. Nanny held his hat. Gabe took the items from them. Lum had learned for the captain to be called at this hour that it had to be important...trouble, so he'd need his weapons.

Ashcraft had hired the first carriage that he saw. Gabe kissed Faith and promised that he'd be back soon. Hex and Dagan were going to dine with Doctor Cornish, Doctor Cook, and Leo. Hopefully, he wouldn't need them.

***

SIMON WAS SWEATING PROFUSELY. It ran into his eyes, causing them to blur and burn but he couldn't wipe them. Foul breath had hit him several times. They were all glancing blows, but even those carried power and he could feel his energy draining. They had fought, busted out the tavern's flimsy door and were now in the street.

The crowd had now grown and circled, cutting down on the room Simon had to maneuver and dodge. He had just slipped on some loose gravel, and as he fell foul breath grabbed him in a bear hug trying to bend him backwards and break his back. Simon's arms were so wet and slick from sweat that he was able to pull them out from the bear hug. He tried to butt his head against foul breath but it didn't work. His blows to the face had no effect.

Thinking that he was about to lose consciousness, he stretched his arms out as far as they could go and with all his might he slapped his foe over the ears with cupped hands. Foul breath screamed out and released Simon, who dropped to the ground. Gabe saw this as both men, the giant and the smaller man, were trying to catch a breath.

Gabe tried to push through the crowd, but the screaming onlookers couldn't be bulged. He shouted, "Give way there, in the King's name." The King was in England so nobody gave way.

Simon rose up inside the circle. He looked over at foul breath, who was on his knees, his hands still over his ears as blood leaked between his fingers. Glancing up, foul breath could see Simon walking away. The little man had won. He had been beat. A rage went through foul breath. He snatched a knife from an onlooker's belt and charged.

Gabe saw it all, like in slow motion. He yelled at Simon...everyone yelled at Simon. Hearing the yelling, Simon turned, but it was too late. He was dead. For the second time. But this time there'd be no reprieve.

BANG...a shot rang out. Nobody saw who shot. Everyone's eyes were glued on the spectacle in front of their eyes. One second foul breath charged, a large knife raised over his head. He would kill the man who'd beat him...but no. Just a touch to the left of dead center, a hole appeared between his eyebrows.

Everyone, including Gabe, stood in awe. Simon stood in awe. *Twice now...twice he'd cheated death. He won yet again.*

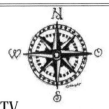

CHAPTER THIRTY

HEX WAS ON THE deck singing for the crew, a fast paced little shanty that had some of the men up dancing. Gabe stood in his cabin staring out the stern window. A bright, full moon was rising and casting its image on the gentle but dark sea. Dagan was smoking his pipe as Gabe puffed on a Cuban cigar. It was a smooth spicy-sweet yet mellow cigar with a Cameroon wrapper. It was not as strong as the dark full-bodied Maduro he'd recently tried. He'd been told the Maduro was a dessert smoke, for after meals, but that particular one had a substantial kick to it. This stogie had been given to him by Leo. The quiet man who you could depend on to come through in a pinch. Simon Davis was proof of that. Just when it looked as if death was imminent, Leo pulled his pistol and shot the man about to stab Simon from behind. After shooting the rogue, Leo simply placed the pistol back in his waist coat and never said a word. The smoke from the pistol barrel was the only clue, had anyone noticed it, as to the direction from which the shot had come. By the time that was decided, Leo had faded into the crowd a few steps to the left.

Dagan had been at Leo's side and even he didn't realize what was about to happen. He couldn't say that he'd actually seen the shooting, if called upon to give testimony. Leo was there one second, and then there was a shot. Smoke floated in the general area but Leo was not there.

Gabe had spoken to Leo the next day. When he said thank you for last evening, Leo gave a hint of a smile and asked 'for what?' Nothing else had been said on the matter.

Doctor Cook was on the opposite side of Dagan and didn't see anything. He said to Gabe, "I was astounded. I thought your man was done for."

Simon still didn't know who his guardian angel was. If he found out it wouldn't be from Gabe, Hex, or Dagan.

Gabe puffed on his cigar as he looked at his near empty glass of brandy and decided he'd not call Nesbit for a refill. Dagan's glass was already empty. "Tell me, Uncle, what do you think of us being a ferry service for spies?" Gabe asked.

Dagan puffed on his pipe but did not speak for a long moment. "It certainly beats convoy and blockade duty. It's not totally without danger, as we saw not long ago, but we do not have to answer to some admiral for our every move."

Gabe nodded, "I said as much to Faith. Do you think it will help the war effort?"

Dagan was quick to respond, "The war is lost, and it has been. This bit with the spies may prolong the inevitable, but the war was lost from the start...certainly by the time the French became allies to the Americans."

Gabe didn't miss his uncle's use of Americans as opposed to Colonials. His love...his woman was the daughter of an American general. Dagan was certainly one who'd like to see the war over.

Dagan suddenly grinned, "You'll not raise your flag in this war but you will in the next."

"Next! Next...," Gabe spoke again. "You think we'll have another war soon?"

"Do you think Parliament is going to overlook the

fact that France sided with our enemies...not likely," Dagan responded.

"Hadn't thought about that?" Gabe said.

Laughter and men clapping could be heard top-side. Hex was good for morale. Tomorrow would see them back in Roatan. Mr. Scott had promised a be-fore-noon dropping of the anchor. Gabe had come to fully trust the master. If he said that they would drop anchor before noon, Gabe considered it gospel.

Ares carried a company of soldiers under a captain who'd not shown his face once the ship had met more than a gentle swell. His lieutenant had taken care of all the matters relating to the company. Gabe won-dered if this was just from his malady or if it was the usual. In addition to the men, four six-pound can-nons and other munitions were aboard.

Doctor Cook had watched the loading of supplies and was a bit pessimistic. "If the Dons want the is-land, they will have it. I just hope our contact and his wife find a way to evacuate," he said.

"He'll not," Leo had said. "Alan and Sandra moved to Roatan long before the war. They are sympathet-ic, being Canadians, to our cause, but they've lived on Roatan too long to give up their homes and way of life. They are very well liked by the islanders, so I doubt anything will be said regarding food, water, and fruits to provision the ship. Our Captain Dunlap and Lieutenant Lewis have no knowledge of their role so they can't tell."

Aye, the more who knew a secret, the less likely it stayed a secret, Gabe thought.

"Other than Edward Despard, no one else knows about the Segarichs," Cook said.

Leo agreed, "I doubt that Irishman would tell the devil, if his arse was on fire." They all laughed at that.

***

A NICE BREEZE WAS blowing through the palms on shore and it was a clear day. True to Scott's word, *Ares* dropped her anchor at seven bells in the forenoon watch. Con Vallin was talking to Gabe when one of the newer hands fell as he went about his duties to anchor.

"Collins, you clumsy oaf, I swear you wouldn't make a pimple on an old whore's arse. Look lively now, here comes the bosun."

Smiling at Midshipman Delsenno's comment, Vallin said, "That one's been around the bosun a bit too much, I'd say."

Gabe had to agree, smiling. He then nudged his first lieutenant and motioned with his head. The Army captain had walked on deck, his first appearance during the voyage.

"That's one I wouldn't waste the wadding to blow his arse away," Vallin offered. Gabe nodded his agreement but didn't speak.

"He has money for his commission," Hex said from behind. "He keeps Lewis around to run the company. He's promised Lewis that every time he increases in rank he'll pay for Lewis's next commission as long as he stays with him."

"Do you believe that?" Gabe asked.

"The sergeant does, Captain. Lewis started out as a sergeant and now he's a lieutenant, obviously Dunlap's father is rich and realized the second son will only make it if he has someone who knows what he's doing to watch over him."

"Like a good master with a young lieutenant on his first ship."

"Similar I guess, sir, but the sergeant said that without Lewis, Dunlap couldn't pour piss out of a boot with directions on the heel." This caused Gabe and Vallin to bust out in laughter.

The helmsman whispered to the master, "Hex be telling a good one, you guess."

"I guess that you need to keep your eyes on the compass. You've drifted off a point." Scott then softened. "Whatever it was I wish we'd heard. It had to be good."

"Aye," the helmsman agreed. "Let a jack be telling a good one and the officer would be screaming bloody silence."

"True," Scott said. "All you have to do now is learn how to sail, get to be a master's mate, pass the lieutenant exam, and you can join in."

"Not bloody likely, Mr. Scott."

"Don't be whining then. The ways open to yew. Think our captain started off as a captain?"

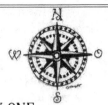

CHAPTER THIRTY ONE

ALAN AND SANDRA SEGARICH lived right on the bay, not more than one hundred fifty yards from the reef. Their house was built on stilts with palm trees surrounding it. Along the drive going from the road down to their house were a few cashew trees.

Gabe listened intently as Sandra explained to Doctor Cook the process of harvesting the nuts. A long wooden dock jutted out from the beach that encompassed their yard, just down from their house. A couple of small fishing boats were tied up to the dock. A youth dove off the dock and his big black dog jumped in after him.

Alan came up to Gabe and offered him a cigar made from tobacco grown on the mainland. "Do you enjoy a fine beer, Captain?"

"I don't know that I've ever tasted a fine beer," Gabe replied with a smile.

"Come with me then, sir," Alan said with a wink. They walked across the yard to a little hut. "This is a spring house. It's one of the few natural springs around."

Gabe had noticed the runoff just to the side. Opening the door, Alan lit a candle and walked in. Gabe could appreciate a big change in temperature.

"It's not like the icehouses that we had in Canada, but it's certainly cooler," Alan said. He reached for a line and pulled it up. A large jar with a lid was attached to the line. Handing Gabe two steins, Alan filled each from the jar. Walking back outside after the jar was closed and put back in the spring, the two took sips from the steins.

The beer had a nice foam head, and was more of an amber color than the usual dark English beer and tasted great.

"I call it Premier Beer, Alan's Premier Beer," he said with a smile.

Gabe had to agree, it was the best beer he'd ever tasted. Alan agreed to send a jar with him when he departed.

"The secret to a great taste is keeping the beer as cold as possible. Warm beer tastes worse than horse piss."

Gabe laughed at this. "I'm happy to say that I've not tasted horse piss so I'll take your word for the comparison."

Over the evening meal, Alan said, "Roatan, at one time, had been the home of over five thousand pirates. One of the most noted is John Coxen. Other famous pirates like Henry Morgan used the island as a lair."

Sandra, who'd been in conversation with Doctor Cook and Leo while the other two men had taken a walk, spoke up, "You see, gentlemen, there has always been somebody attacking the island. We have enough contacts on the mainland that it's doubtful we will be in any danger."

Gabe got the feeling Sandra might actually be the British agent. But it was not just her, the husband and wife were a team.

Alan had said earlier that it would be better if they had not brought more British troops, but since they did, the least amount of resistance would be the best. Doctor Cook had related that the troops were to establish ownership and validate Great Britain's claim to the island, not just here and now but after the war as well.

Gabe could not help but feel that Doctor Cook and Leo had come to believe, possibly after talking with Sandra, that with England facing the combined armies and navies of Spain, France, the Dutch, and the Americans, the probability of winning the war was remote. He had hinted at this from the start. The Army Captain had been very optimistic that he and his company could stand off any assault from attacking forces. He was either brainwashed or as stupid as England's politicians. Hopefully, Lewis would see to it that Dunlap would not let his company be wiped out in a futile attempt to protect the island.

***

OVER THE NEXT TWO days the ship was replenished. Fresh water was brought aboard after the barrels were brought on deck, emptied and scrubbed clean to the combined satisfaction of Doctor Cornish and Doctor Cook.

Gabe was not eavesdropping but listened as Doctor Cornish explained that the problems he'd encountered that he felt were associated with the lack of fresh water, fruits and vegetables, and the problems with rancid meats. He also explained that on his previous ship the captain was far less concerned with the men's health and welfare. Therefore, the number of intestinal diseases which soon affected the whole body made it a constant battle to keep them healthy. Cornish then made Gabe feel good when he told Cook that both *Ares'* captain and first lieutenant were much more concerned about the men, believing that if the men were not healthy the ship could not function properly and certainly could not function as would be expected of a warship.

The discussion then turned to every sailor's night-mare...sexually transmitted diseases, or the pox. One of Cornish's surgery assistants was a better than average hand at sewing up condoms made from the gut of the sheep they slaughtered.

Cornish told Cook, "He actually makes three different sizes. They are not cheap but if saved and washed they can be used several times. I have noticed after talking to the men about the mercury treatments, more of the men have bought and used the condoms. Therefore, the number of men getting the pox is much less."

Gabe swallowed hard, thinking of the mercury treatment. His first sexual union had been with a girl his own age, but she, at thirteen, had been experienced. His other activity came with older, more experienced women, but not whores. His last unwedded experience had been on his eighteenth birthday. He topped a planter's daughter, who was a fetching lass who had watched her father's slaves. She knew more ways than he could count and he was not sorry when it was time to return to the ship. He'd met Faith then. What would he have done had he been poxed before they were married? Sighing, he thought, *that's one bridge I didn't have to cross*.

Con Vallin came over and asked about giving the men a make-and-mend afternoon before they sailed in the morning. Today was Friday, and sailors were a superstitious lot, so they wouldn't set sail on what was considered an unlucky day.

One of the midshipmen, young Vaughn Corwin, was almost thrown overboard when he wanted to bring a bunch of bananas aboard.

"Eat all you want ashore, but not a one aboard ship," Scott, the master had said. "They are considered an omen for disaster when at sea."

Doctor Cook smiled at Scott but didn't say a thing. Was it the poison gas created by decaying fruit that could kill, or the deadly spiders that was sometimes found in the stalks? Regardless, his medical explanation would not change a seaman's beliefs so he'd make sure he enjoyed his bananas ashore.

CHAPTER THIRTY TWO

L IEUTENANT LAQUA LISTENED TO his lookout. The man had slid down a backstay, rather than hailing the lieutenant, and run to the quarterdeck to report his sightings. Fifteen year old Zachary Massey was sent to wake the captain. The marine sentry had heard part of Lieutenant Laqua's instructions to the midshipman and didn't envy the boy's job of waking the captain.

"Shake 'is cot but don't touch 'is body," the marine sentry whispered his own advice. The middy nodded with a grin.

"Captain...Captain, sir. Wake up, Captain, it's urgent."

Gabe opened his eyes, blinked, and then blinked again, trying to focus on who was calling him. He sat up and swung his legs off of his cot, his feet touching the deck. His eyes focused enough to see Massey.

"Lieutenant Laqua's compliments, sir. He feels that you are urgently needed on deck as we have the enemy in sight."

Gabe became immediately alert. "The enemy," he said.

"Aye, Captain. The lookout said it looked like a whole bloody fleet. He has sent for the first lieutenant, sir."

Gabe nodded as he stomped his foot into his boot. Scott, the master, last evening had predicted that they'd sight Saint Lucia by mid afternoon on the morrow. "What time is it?" Gabe asked, putting on his second boot and standing.

"It's four bells in the middle watch, sir."

Why didn't he just say two a.m., Gabe thought. Tucking his night shirt into his britches, he ordered the midshipman to wake his cox'n. *Dagan would be on deck*, he thought. He was always there. Gabe reached the quarterdeck before his first lieutenant, but just by steps. The men at the wheel noticed that Gabe had not put on his uniform shirt and coat. They also knew that anyone not recognizing the captain was beyond help. Gabe had noted when he came on deck that a fresh breeze was blowing with large waves and white caps.

Lieutenant Laqua handed the night glass to Gabe. "Right off the bow, Captain, stern lights, and lots of them."

Gabe took the glass but asked, "How do you know they're French?"

Laqua smiled, he'd been waiting for that question. "A flare was sent up...a signal I would guess. The tricolor, however, was noted when the flare was sent up. Morris, the lookout, saw it as well, sir. I have taken the liberty to call hands to reduce sail, sir."

Gabe nodded and looked around. Most of his lieutenants were now gathered around as well as Scott, the master; Dagan, whom he'd already spotted, and Doctor Cook was approaching. Speaking to his officers, in general, he asked, "Any guesses where the fleet is headed?"

Turner, the third lieutenant, spoke quickly, "Martinique, sir, but they also could be headed to Saint Lucia."

"For what purpose?" Gabe asked.

"We have been out of touch for a month or so, Captain. The French may have attacked and captured the island, or they may have plans to do so. If not Saint Lucia, then Martinique for certain."

The young lieutenant was spot on, Gabe thought. "Have you any estimate of how many ships are in the formation?" he asked.

"Morris from his vantage point believes twenty-three to twenty-six. They are spread out."

"Do they all seem to be in formation?"

"We've searched the horizon but find no other sightings. Do we reduce sail, Captain?"

Gabe was about to reply yes but stopped. "How long would it take for us to close within range of our long guns?"

Scott thought a second. "Extreme range, three quarters of an hour."

Gabe nodded. "Increase sail," he ordered Laqua, "but go about it quietly. Then have the men go to quarters."

Laqua was aghast...attack a fleet with one ship. He didn't question his captain, though. He wasn't the only one shocked, Doctor Cook was as well.

Seeing Hex, Gabe ordered him to roust out Nesbit. Turning to Vallin, Gabe spoke again, "Have the officers not on duty, including the gunnery master, in my cabin." He then turned to Lieutenant Laqua, "Keep the ship darkened...and Mr. Laqua, a double tot for Morris at next issue."

"Aye, Captain," the lieutenant said as he turned to go about his tasks.

***

BRANDY WAS PROVIDED TO the men gathered in the captain's cabin. Neither Nesbit nor Simon Davis appeared grumpy after being awakened early. The news was enough to stir the two.

Gabe explained his plan of action, as the men

sipped at their brandy. "I intend to close with the last ship in line, gentlemen. I plan to skewer her arse and then come about. As we come about, we'll let go with a broadside. If there's another ship in range, we'll save half the broadside for it. Have both larboard and starboard guns loaded as we need to be prepared for either direction. After we let go, we will hastily make our retreat. I know that this is but an irritant to the Frogs but I want them to know that we know they are here."

"Do you think that we could increase sail and reach Saint Lucia first to warn them of the approaching fleet?"

"I doubt it," Gabe said, "but as Mr. Turner alluded to earlier. They may already have the island."

***

Ares steadily gained on the French fleet. With the ship totally darkened, the gunners went about the work of loading the ship's guns. The main batteries were double-shotted and the bowchasers had a measure of grape on top of ball.

One of the gun crew ran to the quarterdeck. "Mr. Myers says that we are in extreme range now, sir." Gabe nodded.

Crossing over to the larboard ratlines, Gabe climbed up several feet and peered through his night glass. The last ship in line was a large ship, but appeared to be a stores ship, not a warship. *This is better*, Gabe thought. The French, without supplies, would be hard put to carry on a war. As he continued to look both larboard and starboard, the nearest warship was identified as a small frigate, with thirty-two or possibly thirty-six guns. The ship could get in her blows, either way. A lucky ball at the right time could mean the death of *Ares*.

Gabe looked about at his crew. The men had a grim

determined look. Each of them expected the captain to smite the Frogs and then run for it. Gabe looked through his glass again. It seemed as if they had gotten almost in pistol shot range.

"We will attack the store ship yonder," Gabe said speaking to his lieutenants and the master. "We will then try the frigate to larboard. Mr. Turner, fire as you bear."

"Aye, Captain."

"Captain LoGuidice, I see no need to send your sharpshooters aloft but feel free to deploy them as you wish."

"Thank you, Captain," LoGuidice responded.

"Let's make this quick, gentlemen," Gabe said as he sent his officers to their stations. "Mr. Scott, you may fire the starboard guns as they bear once the bow chasers fire."

"Aye, Captain."

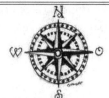

CHAPTER THIRTY THREE

THINKING OF HOW HE'D been awakened, Gabe wondered how the captains on the French ships would react when their ships were fired upon. The lookout would certainly be made to answer, but Gabe guessed that they only saw what they expected to see. The doubt swept over his body. What if they'd been seen and they were reeling him in. No! They'd never have let him get that close. Time for silence was over.

"Fire...fire, Mr. Meyers, fire!"

The four twelve-pounders in the forecastle thundered forth, breaking the nighttime silence. Gabe watched as orange flames belched forward and shattered the stern windows of the supply ship. Balls of flames lit up the darkness as the ship's aft cabin was on fire. Scott had the men at the wheel doing their best to swing the ship so that their broadside would bear.

Lieutenant Turner was excited. "Forward guns concentrate on the frigate. Aft guns pour it into the merchant ship."

Bugles and drums could be heard, but from which ship they couldn't be sure. *Ares'* gun ports were open and the aft guns fired on the supply ship, punishing her with twenty-four pound balls. The destruction was more than Gabe had hoped for. The fire in the stern cabin was growing so that flames leaped up from the skylight. Screams could be heard. The frigate was now being fired on by the main battery while the quarterdeck's carronades belched their forty-two pound balls. In the excitement, the frigate captain could be seen on deck shouting to his men, but it was no use. The twenty-four pound balls had holed the frigate in places that were big enough for a carriage to drive through. The carronades' balls had disintegrated the quarterdeck; the ship was completely destroyed. As quick as it started, the action was over. They had hit with speed and daring. Some would say doing little, but it was better than nothing at all.

Before the flames from the burning ship were completely lost from sight, the lookout still hadn't seen any pursuit. Dagan put his hand on his nephew's shoulder, with no words spoken but none were needed.

Not so with Doctor Cook and Leo. "I must say, Captain that was daring. I've never witnessed such a ferocious attack."

"We were lucky," Gabe replied. "I depended on their lookouts looking forward, not aft. Had we been several ships the plan would never have worked."

The other officers did not speak, but whispers could be heard as the men discussed the action and their part in it. Lieutenant Laqua still had the watch and started to silence the men but caught his captain smiling at some of the remarks.

The captain spoke rather loudly then, "Lieutenant Laqua!"

"Aye, Captain."

"See to it that the men get an extra tot at the next rum issue."

"Aye, Captain."

"Mr. Laqua, also inform the purser that I'll brook no complaints." This caused the men to smile even more.

The dawn's horizon was completely empty, but by

ten o'clock sails were sighted. After an anxious quarter of an hour, the lookout called down that it was a British squadron. Gabe found himself sitting in the admiral's cabin by noon, reporting to Sir Samuel Hood. After the pleasantries were over, Gabe reported the previous night's attack.

Hood was smiling at the report. "We need more daring if we are to survive the war." The word survive was used again, Gabe noted. Hood then informed Gabe that Rodney had finally sailed for the Colonies.

Hood continued, "It was said that De Grasse was sailing for the Americas as well, so it is doubtful that the French fleet spotted last night was his. It was more likely De Guichens. The French have increased their naval presence in the Caribbean while we lessen ours as the hurricane season approaches."

The climate and wind direction presented problems for the British held islands in the Lesser Antilles, while the French tended to ignore the possibilities and focused on taking many of the islands once held by the British.

Admiral Hood then asked Gabe how he happened to be sailing under private orders. Gabe had dreaded the question but knew it would come up. He diplomatically stated he'd been the unlucky officer that was available when the secret branch of the Foreign Office called.

"I...ah...brought the gentlemen on board in case you have need to question them," Gabe admitted.

"Damn nuisance, tying up such a fine officer and crack ship, I'd say. They, meaning the Admiralty, could have done as well with an officer-aged lieutenant commanding a brig," Hood growled. He then softened, "But I may as well see the gentlemen, otherwise, I'll hear from Whitehall how discourteous I was." With that, Hood bellowed for his flag lieutenant and had the 'Foreign Office' gentlemen escorted back.

The meeting went better than expected. Saint Lucia had been taken as expected. Hood's concern was now with Rodney sailing for the Americas, what would happen to the Dutch islands and Saint Kitts. When asked if he would reinforce Saint Kitts, Hood alluded to the possibility but did not get specific. He was more worried about Jamaica and Bermuda. Barbados was also a concern but the main concern was Jamaica and Bermuda. The interview ended with Hood praising Gabe's actions against French Admiral De Guichens. He's made up his mind it wasn't De Grasse, Gabe realized.

CHAPTER THIRTY FOUR

IT WAS AUGUST, 1781, the beginning of the hurricane season in the Caribbean. The British navy would, as was customary, reduce the number of ships in the area until after the season. It was hard to believe that nearly a year had gone by since the 'great hurricane of 1780' had laid waste to so many islands and ships...ships of every nation, including the French. *Ares* had been one of the few survivors. Gabe had captured her after a one-sided battle, but she served her new master well. Dagan had said that your last ship was always your best ship. Gabe wasn't sure. *SeaWolf*, his first ship, would always hold a special place in his heart, but *Ares*...well she was like no other. She was not as big, nor did she carry as many guns as *Leopard* or *Trident*, but she was a thoroughbred in a field of dray horses.

***

IT WOULD BE DIFFERENT returning to Antigua once Gabe's current assignment was completed. Gabe's friend, Admiral Dutch Moffitt, would be gone. The two men had said their farewells at dinner the night before Gabe had to sail. Faith had left the two men to their brandy and cigars, knowing that they may never serve together again. Dutch had discussed how the war had been mishandled from the onset. They'd talked about all the advantages the British navy had enjoyed at the start of the year that had for the most part been lost. The most recent news was dismal.

Saint Vincent and Tobago had been lost. Saint Lucia had been attacked twice. Barbados was in constant danger. It was now understood that Rodney was headed back to England to defend himself for plundering Saint Eustatius and spending weeks putting together a treasure fleet to sail to England. Rodney had sent Admiral Hood to support Admiral Graves in the Colonies after confirmed reports that De Grasse, with a fleet, was sailing to aid General Washington. With Admiral Hood sailing to America, Gabe had no idea who his superior would be in Antigua when he returned.

***

ARES' ANCHOR HAD BARELY come to grip when Gabe was summoned to weigh anchor and set sail again. He had once again transported his Foreign Office gentlemen to Saint Kitts, much to his dislike. This time he'd left them there. He'd pleaded his case that the island could be attacked and that their lives would be in great danger. The two insisted their cover was foolproof and if there was an attack, the fort on Brimstone Hill could surely repulse anything the enemy might send. Gabe had argued still, "No fort can withstand a prolonged siege. Supplies will run out and you can't resist the enemy without food, powder, and shot, even if you have water. I have learned, Sir Lawrence, and this holds especially true in war, there is no such thing as always or never."

"Sail ho! She be a Frog, Captain."

Gabe was standing at the fife rail when the call had come down. What would a lone French ship be doing off Saint Kitts and Nevis? The ship was headed south, sou-east. Had it been scouting the British islands? Was Saint Kitts and Nevis still controlled by the British?

Con Vallin, the first lieutenant, impatiently called up to the lookout. "What manner of ship is it?"

"A brig, I'd say, sur."

"Not one of our better lookouts," Vallin muttered to himself.

"Alter course to intercept the er...brig, Mr. Vallin."

"Aye, Captain."

The chase would be short, Gabe knew, so he didn't go down to break his fast as planned.

"I'll get your sword," Hex volunteered.

"Mr. Massey," Gabe heard his first lieutenant calling the midshipman. "You've been skylarking all morning. Take a glass and aloft with you, so it will do some good." Gabe tried to stifle a smile.

"It never ends, does it?" Dagan said, announcing his presence.

"Deck thar, yonder ship has come about."

"She's a merchant ship," Scott, the master said, breaking his silence. "No Navy ship would be so shabby."

"Mr. Meyers," Gabe called his gunner. "Put one across that ship's bow when convenient. I'm not in the mood for a drawn out chase."

"Aye, Cap'n. We'll sink 'er if you like."

Gabe smiled, that was confidence speaking. *The ship had certainly come together*, he thought, thankful for Con Vallin. Yet he'd never stop to think his leadership had anything to do with the crew's progress. It was no more than ten minutes when one of the bow chasers fired.

"Damme, sir," Lieutenant Turner swore. "I don't recall the captain telling you to give the bugger a shave."

The gun crews laughed. Had Meyers been any closer, he'd have knocked off the jib boom.

Captain LoGiudice was now alongside the rail.

"Marines are ready for a break in the monotony, Captain."

Gabe smiled. LoGiudice didn't allow much time for the marines to grow slack. He had the best detachment Gabe had served with. Hex was back with Simon Davis. Hex buckled on Gabe's sword while Davis held a glass of lime juice.

"Mr. Nesbit sends a bit to quench yer thirst until you can come down, Captain."

"Thank you, Mr. Davis." Gabe gulped down the tangy sweet beverage. He'd been more thirsty than he realized.

"Shall I go over, Captain?" the first lieutenant asked.

"Aye, and Con, take Mr. Turner with you and a few solid hands. We'll give him a few hours of commanding a ship."

Vallin, the Scotsman, gave a hearty smile. "Aye, Captain, it will do him good."

***

THE SHIP WAS A brig that had sprung a leak in a squall and was headed to Martinique, a French held island. The captain, like most merchant ship captains, was full of self-importance.

"Were it not for his cargo, Captain, I'd say let his bloody arse go. Maybe she'll sink before they get to Martinique."

The ship's manifest indicated uniform supplies and kegs of French wine, the good stuff, Vallin volunteered. There were also two racks of muskets and two six-pound field pieces with powder and shot for the lot. The rest appeared to be harnesses, saddles, and bridles.

"The Frog didn't destroy his papers either, Captain. They're probably the most important. He was part of

Comte de Barras' squadron headed to join Comte de Grasse in the aid to the Colonials."

Damnation, Gabe thought. Should he sail after Hood to let him know what they were up against? No, Hood would be joining Graves. He thought about sailing back to Saint Kitts but doubted he'd make a difference. No, he'd sail to Antigua. Who knew what may be headed there? "Damnation," he cursed out loud.

"There's nothing to do but go to English Harbour," Dagan said, speaking softly.

Gabe turned to his uncle, "Thank you, Uncle. It seems that is the only option we have."

"Aye," Dagan answered, thinking for once they were spared the task of being in the midst of the fight. No one's luck holds out forever, and they had more than most. Dagan was glad. They'd be spared from having to do battle, for now.

PART III

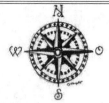

The Merchant Seaman

The war is going badly
Every man aboard knows
The captain has warned them
Of all of these foes.

It's not just the warships
It's privateers too
The Navy sends escorts
But it's little they can do.

Insurance is costly
From the losses they've taken
But they aren't the ones
The cannons be facing.

So we sign on a ship
When a billet be available
It's better than the press gang
Or some livery stable.

...Michael Aye

CHAPTER THIRTY FIVE

I recall...that devil woman
Silver combs...in coal black hair
I was taken...by her beauty
As she lured...me to her lair.

Soft breezes whispered
In the palm trees
The moon...shone on the sea
This dark eyed... gypsy lady
Lay her body...next to me.

Tender kisses...lit flames of passion
And they raged...out of control
How I've longed for...that gypsy lady
She was gone,..when I rose.

Oh devil woman I often wonder
If you ever ...really cared
How could you leave ...this lonely sailor
Who you woo'd into your lair...oh devil woman.

GABE AND DAGAN LISTENED to Hex as he sang. The tune sounded a bit mournful.

"He's not over that woman," Dagan said, meaning the lady who owned the Forbidden Siren Tavern on Grand Cayman. Maria Galante had been passing information to her brother, who was raiding the ships coming into and going out of the island. The woman had stolen Hex's heart and disappeared. She would have been arrested and probably executed had she stayed.

Doctor Robert Cornish was playing whist with his captain, Con Vallin, and Dagan. He was aware of the circumstances, like Vallin, but he had met the woman and knew the pull she had on a man.

"Medicine has come a long way since the Greek physician Hippocrates," Cornish said. "But even as far as we have advanced, we've yet to find a cure for a broken heart."

Dagan leaned back in his chair and took another sip of his brandy and said, "Nor a lonely heart." The group of men knew that Dagan loved the daughter of an American General.

The merchant vessel capture and subsequent transport of an extra pump from *Ares* to the brig had taken longer than expected. Once the brig had been pumped reasonably dry, Haycock, *Ares'* carpenter, went over with several of his mates to repair the leak. The repair would not be completely done until the ship was placed in dry dock. Until then the ship, had to be pumped one hour in four.

Since there was a delay in sailing for Antigua, Dagan went over to the ship. Devious soul that he was, he found a case of various French perfumes that would bring a nice return on the captain's investment when sold in the Caribbean. He also found a space in the planks near the captain's head that concealed several bags of gold coin...Spanish coins. The man had some connection to the Dons. His search was otherwise unremarkable. Gabe, as usual, wondered how much Dagan had kept compared to what he reported.

***

IT WAS FIVE BELLS in the middle watch when Gabe rose from his cot. He slid into his breeches and stomped into his boots, and then went on deck. Small waves slapped against the hull and to larboard he could see numerous white caps. A moderate breeze blew.

Lieutenant Laqua had the watch and everything appeared to be in order. A helmsman coughed and then coughed again alerting his lieutenant that the captain was on deck. *A good sign*, Gabe thought to himself. The helmsman might have kept his silence if Laqua had been an overbearing arse.

Lieutenant Laqua came over to Gabe and made the usual report. He followed that up with why he was at the rail. "We seem to have lost contact with the prize, Captain. One minute she was there and the next she was not. I sent Mr. Heath aloft with our best night glass." Gabe nodded his head. "Do you think the French retook the ship, Captain?"

Gabe thought a moment and then replied, "Not with her captain on board *Ares*. With her leak, I'd think it was something more along those lines." Gabe thought a moment and then quickly made a decision. Enemy ships might be in the area and sending up a flare might bring trouble. On the other hand, he did not want to lose his men that were on the prize. "Send up a flare, and then call all hands, Mr. Laqua."

"Aye, Captain." A flare was sent up, but the prize was not seen nor was there a response.

"Prepare to come about, Mr. Laqua," Gabe ordered, and then added, "Take us back to where you think you last saw the prize."

"Aye, Captain. I made a note with the time." Laqua looked at the log and then the ship's clock. "It has been thirty minutes, sir. You came up just after we lost contact."

The first lieutenant and the master had both come on deck and caught the last of the conversation.

"Once we come about, send up another flare and continue to do so every ten minutes unless ordered to stop."

"Aye, Captain."

Seeing his cox'n, Gabe ordered Hex to bring up the brig's captain.

"The ship may be in worse condition than we thought," Dagan volunteered. Gabe nodded, acknowledging his uncle's words.

A lookout called down a sighting to starboard, after the third flare. "It was more like the flash of cannon, sir, but I didn't hear a sound."

Gabe ordered the ship two points to starboard and had another flare sent up. It was several minutes before the flash was seen again, but everyone saw it.

"Two more points to starboard, Mr. Scott. Mr. Laqua, send up another flare."

The lookout called down this time, "There she be, Captain, dead ahead just off the starboard bow." Another flash was seen just where the lookout had said.

"Prepare to heave to, Mr. Laqua. Bring her as close alongside as you can, Mr. Scott."

"Why doesn't he light some lanterns," Marine Captain LoGiudice asked.

"I'm wondering the same thing," Gabe replied. "Have your marines ready, Captain, in case there's mischief."

"Aye, Captain."

Vallin came up to Gabe, "The Frog captain admitted that the hull has been leaking since the voyage started."

Gabe shook his head. "We pumped her dry and the carpenter only saw the latest damage. Go over, Con, and get a feel for the damage, and send Lieutenant Turner back to me."

The relief on young Lieutenant Turner's face was

obvious. The master's mate had the watch, but Turner felt a difference in the way the ship sailed compared to that afternoon. He bumped into a seaman coming on deck.

"The watch needs you," the seaman said.

Gordon, the master's mate, had noticed the lanterns were running low on oil. He ordered that they be refilled. When a crewman went in search of more oil, he noticed the water level had risen drastically. Gordon ordered the pumps manned just as he called for Turner. They'd been at the pumps for an hour but had made little headway. Pumps from *Ares* were again sent over and using three pumps, the well was soon nearly dry. Haycock, the carpenter, recommended that the main pump be manned ever other hour until they reached port and the ship was put in dry dock.

The dawn was breaking when the two ships got underway again. Land was sighted during the next watch. The crew felt that relief was now in sight.

English Harbour was the focal point of British Naval power in the Leeward Islands. Gabe thought, *were it to be taken we might as well surrender and return to England*. While he'd never considered that being a reality, he now knew that if Dé Grasse's combined fleet were to attack they'd never be able to stand a prolonged siege.

Who was anchored there now, Gabe wondered again. *Humph*! He thought to himself, *I'll know in an hour*.

CHAPTER THIRTY SIX

Antigua crept over the horizon until it was in plain view of the deck. It was a relief to every sailor to return to home port, no matter how long they'd been at sea. The wind was to the southwest and provided just enough of a cooling breeze to make the morning pleasant.

"Shirley Heights," Vallin commented. His comment was to stir his captain who appeared to be deep in thought.

"Call all hands to reduce sail, Mr. Vallin."

"Aye, Captain."

The sun was high in a cloudless sky. Once they were in the sheltered anchorage where there would be much less breeze, the decks would grow hot and become miserable.

"Make sure to put up awnings and open the gun ports once we are at anchor, Mr. Vallin," Gabe said.

"Aye, Captain."

A few feet will likely get blistered from oozing tar between the deck planks in this heat, Gabe thought. Doctor Cornish will likely be kept busy. Try as he may, Doctor Cornish had failed to get the men to wear shoes when on deck.

"Berkeley Fort," one of the helmsmen commented to Scott.

Gabe remembered when he'd been a youth and *Drakkar* had sailed past the fort the first time. He'd been in the tops, sent there by Mr. Buck for some slight mischief. God, it seemed an eternity ago.

"Flagship 'as gone," the lookout called down some time later.

Dutch was gone, Gabe thought to himself, feeling a bit lonely.

"How many ships do you see at anchor?" Vallin called to the lookout.

"Two navy ships," came the reply. *Two*, Gabe thought, *where is everyone*?

"Damned odd isn't it, Captain?" Vallin asked.

"That it is, Mr. Vallin. Most of them are probably headed to the Colonies with Hood and the others went when Admiral Moffitt sailed back to England."

"That means that you are likely the senior naval officer, other than the dockyard admiral," Vallin said, responding to Gabe's comments.

"More will be coming I'm sure, Con, the question is when."

Dagan had been standing aft. He'd taken a glass from Vaughn Corwin, the youngest of the mids. Sliding the glass closed with a snap, he walked to where Gabe stood talking to Vallin. When there was a pause in the conversation, Dagan spoke, "I see a ship at anchor with a Stanhope Crest on the flag. I'd say we have company."

"Are you sure?" Gabe asked.

Dagan had pulled out his pipe and was filling the bowl. He paused and looked at Gabe with a look that said, 'Am I sure, would I have spoken were I not sure.'

Taking the hint from Dagan's silence, Gabe muttered, "Of course, you are."

"I'm thinking that you'll be inheriting another middy," Dagan volunteered. Gabe looked thoughtfully at his uncle. Dagan merely nodded at Gabe this time.

Lieutenant Laqua approached his captain, "I believe that's your coach standing on the shore, Captain."

They had just dropped anchor. The usual 'captain repair on board' was not forthcoming as there was no flagship and, as his first lieutenant had theorized, he was likely the senior naval officer present.

Gabe ordered, turning to his cox'n, "Have my gig made ready."

Hex smiled and had anticipated this. "It's standing by, Captain," the cox'n responded with a grin.

"Are you ready, Uncle?"

Dagan walked over to the entry port and knocked the ash from his pipe and made his way down to the gig.

Gabe turned to Vallin, "Have the prize taken over to the dockyard. Make sure that enough men remain on board to keep her pumped until the dockyard accepts her. Also, tell the dockyard superintendant that I will be by this afternoon." It would give Gabe a reason to get away from the house with Lord Stanhope for a private conversation. He was certain that Dagan was right in his comments about a new midshipman.

By the time the gig ground into the soft sand, Faith, Gabe's mother, Maria, and Lord Stanhope were walking down to the water. Faith saw Gabe looking about and volunteered, "James is having his nap."

Gabe smiled; little James was a fussy little man when he missed his nap. Faith welcomed her husband home with a hug and a kiss. Gabe then embraced his mother. It was a most pleasant surprise to see her. He then shook hands with Lord Stanhope. "Noble is not with you?"

"He went over to Saint John with Lum. He'll be sorry that he missed you."

Hex walked up and was quickly greeted by Faith and Maria. Lord Stanhope gave a polite nod. "Will you need the gig this afternoon, Captain?"

Gabe fished a coin from his pocket and flipped it

in the air. Hex deftly caught it. "I think not," Gabe replied.

"Aye, Captain, and a wet for the crew before returning to the ship," Hex responded.

Gabe nodded with a wink. This was standard when dismissing his gig's crew. "Come on up to the house later," Gabe said in a whisper. Hex nodded but did not respond verbally.

The driver turned the coach around and drove to Lady Deborah's townhouse rather than the cottage. *It only makes sense*, Gabe thought. The cottage atop the hill lacked room for everyone.

Gabe asked, to make conversation, "Is this your first trip to Antigua, Lord Stanhope?"

"William, please, Sir Gabe."

"Then its Gabe," Gabe replied.

"No, but it's been twenty years."

"William's family owned a plantation here for a while," Maria volunteered.

Faith looking at her husband smiled. "William, is it?"

***

THE COACHMAN TRIED TO miss a few of the larger potholes but still Gabe and Lord Stanhope were bounced about as they made their way to the dockyard.

"I purposely arranged this trip in case you wished for a private conversation," Gabe said as soon as the coach had left the house.

"Thank you," Stanhope said. "First let me tell you that I'm in love with your mother and have proposed. She has not consented but she has not turned me down either. I believe that's why she so quickly agreed to come on this journey; so that she could talk with you and Dagan."

Gabe smiled, "You…you both have my blessings," he replied. "I do think that you have to understand there may be a reluctance to give up the Portsmouth house."

"I have considered that and have agreed to spend as much time there as she wishes."

Gabe was tempted to ask Stanhope his age, but refrained. The man had to be in his early to mid sixties.

"The second reason for this trip is Noble. I have grown to love the boy immensely. He is his father's son. He still has a bit of a rough demeanor. I think that while everything is coming around, he feels like he may not meet my expectations. That's nonsense of course, but I can see him catching himself when speaking. He's trying hard to speak correctly and not the foul language of…of. You know, Gabe, those he was forced to grow up around. In fact, the only time he seems to be completely at ease is when he is with your niece, Gretchen. He calls her Gretch." A smile broke out on Stanhope's face. "On one occasion, they stopped at the village tavern to water their horses. The owner's son, a fourteen-year-old bully, threw a bucket of water out the door, causing Gretchen's horse to rear. Gretchen, who was not expecting the animal to be spooked, was sitting easy and was unable to catch herself when the horse was frightened and was thrown to the muddy ground. Noble got off his horse and helped Gretchen to her feet, and made sure that she was not hurt. Wiping away tears, he handed her the reins to his horse. He then turned to the bully, 'Apologize to the lady.' 'Yer bleeding bonkers,' the boy snarled. Noble, without a word, knocked the boy to the ground and then started thrashing the boy with Gretchen's riding crop that she'd dropped. A crowd had gathered, and some of them had seen the entire incident. When the tavern owner walked out all full of bravado, he was quickly told by a bystander what happened. He cuffed his son a good one and then apologized to Gretchen."

Gabe was smiling. The tale did not surprise him, recalling how Noble had broken up the ambush.

"By the way, Gabe," Stanhope continued. "Did you know young Noble is betrothed? It seems after the incident, Gretchen asked Noble to marry her and he consented."

Gabe laughed now, but a thought entered his mind...*don't be surprised*. "Now as to Noble desiring to become a midshipman, how did this transpire?"

"Your friend, the captain at Deal," Stanhope replied.

"Captain Markham," Gabe responded.

"Yes, he was visiting your brother when Noble was visiting with Gretchen. Out of the blue, Noble told Captain Markham that he wanted to be in the navy like you and the captain. Gil and Markham explained how he'd have to be a midshipman first. They told him about the hardships, the dangers, and the benefits of the life they lived. Little Gretchen was not too happy about the possibility but sighed and said she supposed he'd be a hero like Uncle Gil and Uncle Gabe."

"I hope he never faces the hell I did," Gabe replied.

"I understand," Stanhope said and then changed the conversation. "The rumor is Gil will be given a new command after the first of the year. It is said that it will likely be Gibraltar."

"I didn't think that he'd be on the beach long," Gabe replied.

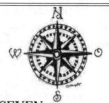

CHAPTER THIRTY SEVEN

THE NEXT MORNING GABE, Dagan, and Hex brought Noble back to the ship. Gabe had the first lieutenant assemble the midshipmen in the captain's dining area. Gabe introduced the mids by age and seniority. "Mr. Brian Heath is eighteen and the signal's midshipman, and the oldest. Joshua Delsenno is also eighteen and helps Mr. Heath with the signals when needed." Both of them were ready to take the lieutenant's exam when it was next given.

"Zachary Massey is fifteen and has proven himself brave and dependable in battle. The two younger gentlemen are Henry Easley and Vaughn Corwin. They are both ten years old." Gabe then introduced Noble as a possible candidate to become a middy.

Noble was to spend time doing everything required of *Ares'* midshipmen for the remainder of the day and each day for the next week. He was to eat and sleep in the cockpit and perform the same duties and take the same classes given by the master. One hour a day, at a time determined by Mr. Vallin, Noble would be allowed to talk with the captain. The rest of the times, he would be under the same constraints as the other mids.

"Are there any questions?" Gabe asked.

Heath stepped forward, "His clothes, Captain. They are not suitable for the ship."

Gabe nodded. It was a good question and showed forethought. He called Simon Davis over and requested his paper and a quill. He wrote a brief note to the purser to provide Noble with two sets of seaman slops to be billed to the captain. "Anything else?"

This time it was Delsenno. "I think between us we can provide anything else he will need."

Gabe nodded and dismissed the group except for Noble. He had Nesbit come forward. "Mr. Paul Dover will be coming on board. It may be temporary or it may be for the foreseeable future. He is young Noble's tutor. See that he has space enough for his needs. Also, I want you...and," Gabe said with an after-thought, "Simon Davis, if you see the need, to spend one hour each evening teaching our young friend how to be a gentleman and an officer. I will see that the first lieutenant sets aside time for instruction. Do you understand this, Noble?"

"Yes...aye, Captain."

Gabe smiled, "You are dismissed then, Mr. Stan-hope."

Noble turned to leave but at the use of Mr. Stan-hope, he paused. He swallowed and then spoke, "Thank you, Captain. I just wish me mom were alive to see it."

Gabe replied, "So do I, Noble, so do I."

After the boy left, Gabe briefly explained the boy's background to Nesbit. "No worries, Captain. A gen-tleman he will be."

***

A MONTH CAME AND went and Noble was still aboard *Ares*. He had on one occasion met the gun-ner's daughter due to lack of attention to the master's lectures. After twelve lashes of the bosun's rattan while leaning over a cannon, his attention improved considerably. Gabe had put to sea twice during the month, having established a routine of patrols with the other two frigates. Having Lord Stanhope as a guest had proven to be enjoyable, as had having his mother with them.

Lord Stanhope and his mother had visited *Ares* and were later invited to dinner by the wardroom. Doctor Cornish had made dietary recommendations for Lord Stanhope's gout, which was showing a big improvement. He'd also recommended a tea made from the bark of a willow tree to help with the pain.

It was now time to leave and also time for a decision from Noble in regards to becoming a midshipman. Gabe had called for the boy and told him to dress in his clothes he'd been wearing when he came aboard as they were going to dine at home that night. Gabe never once thought that the boy would think he was being taken from the ship.

Hex, seeing the concern on the boy's face, walked on deck with him. "Your grandfather and Maria are going to leave for home soon. This is nothing but a farewell dinner, so that you can say your good-byes. I think that you will be asked if you still desire to be a midshipman, if so, you will have to be outfitted."

A sense of relief flooded over Noble. "Thanks Jake," the boy shouted as he ran below to change. *I must write Gretchen before grandfather leaves*, he thought. The toughest part about being away from England was missing Gretchen.

***

HANDS AND COMPANY WAS the main tailor that specialized in military uniforms. The material, unlike that used in England, was lightweight and suited for the tropics. After getting Noble outfitted in uniforms, Lord Stanhope, Gabe, and Noble went to a shop specializing in blades.

"Most of our blades are long swords used by the

gentry and army officers. I only have a few naval officer swords and one midshipman's dirk that I took in on trade. I believe it is more for dress than a functional blade."

The dirk was bright and shiny, as the man said, with a few small jewels on the handle, but hardly something that would be used routinely.

"I believe that we'll pass on this one," Gabe said before either Lord Stanhope or Noble could answer.

Gabe then took his guests to a shop that he and his brother had visited when in the market for fowling pieces. Upon entry into the shop, they were surprised to see marine Captain LoGiudice. Gabe greeted his friend and introduced him to Lord Stanhope, who he recalled from visiting the ship and dining in the wardroom.

LoGiudice said, "I believe that I've seen this young sir aboard ship as well."

Noble shook hands with LoGiudice, who made Noble smile when he said, "I understand that you are the brave man who came to our captain's aid and thereby saved his life." Noble wasn't sure how to respond, so he said nothing.

LoGiudice placed his arm around Noble's shoulder, bent low and said, "I am an expert when it comes to rifles and pistols. Let me help you make your selection..." LoGiudice looked up at Gabe, "Pistols is it?" Gabe nodded. He then continued, "Then let me help you choose a pistol that's right for you and when time permits, I will teach you to shoot." Noble was all smiles now.

Gabe and Lord Stanhope stood back watching as pistol after pistol was examined, checking how it fit Noble's hand, and the weight and balance. When a choice was made, LoGiudice further surprised everyone when he purchased the pistol. "Not a word beyond us," LoGiudice made Noble swear.

"Now all we need are a dirk and the few books that I mentioned," Gabe said.

"Mr. Heath has promised his reference books to me," Noble volunteered. "They are not new but have things marked that are important." Gabe knew that it was not uncommon to share or pass down some of the basic books.

"All we have need of now is a dirk," Gabe said.

The owner of the shop spoke up, "Did you say you needed a dirk? Is that a small sword?"

"It could be considered as such, that or a large dagger, I guess," Gabe said, though that had never come up.

The owner left the front of the shop and a few minutes later returned with a magnificent blade. The dirk had been made by Thomas Gill. The overall length was twenty-one or twenty-two inches, with the blade at least eighteen inches. The blade was gray etched with an anchor and the royal seal. The hilt had a lot of gilt over the white sharkskin grip. A gold lion's head with a ring to attach a lanyard was in almost perfect condition. The sheath was in good shape also.

The dirk was a bit stiff when drawn from the scabbard, but that was probably due to shrinkage related to non-use. A little oil would make it better in no time. The dirk must have been commissioned by a wealthy person, Gabe mused. His own certainly was not so fine.

"How much?" Gabe asked.

The owner looked from Gabe to Stanhope and back. He recognized Stanhope as a man of means but he also recognized Gabe as a man of knowledge in regards to blades. The look of the young man wearing a captain's uniform meant that he'd proven himself, probably in battle. His name carried a lot of weight in most of Antigua's society. The owner of the shop had heard that Gabe owned a one hundred guinea presentation sword.

The dirk was at most a twenty-five guinea blade, with the shop owner having at most ten guineas in it. He was calculating an asking price when Gabe asked, "How much?"

"I've got..."

Gabe cut the man short. "I'm sure that you made up any allowance when taking the dirk in trade. We'll give you eight guineas."

"Fifteen," the shop owner responded.

"Ten and that's too much for what it will be used for," Gabe countered. "Ten and not a pence more."

"You bargain hard, Captain." Gabe smiled but didn't reply, and Lord Stanhope purchased the dirk.

Gabe paused, as they were leaving the shop, and turned. "I will send my cox'n by with my personal pistols. I need more shot, if you please."

The owner smiled, "I will make sure that it's perfect, Captain." He realized that by being fair, he'd just obtained a regular customer.

When Gabe and Stanhope were alone after dinner that night, Stanhope confessed how much he would miss Noble. "The young man has stolen my heart. It grieves me to leave him so soon. Maria has told me how she had to deal with the sea taking you from her. I have, at least, gotten to know the boy enough to know that he's his father's son. Smart, yet strong-willed and independent. Of course, he's had to survive. When he first came to the manor, his maid found him hoarding food away in case he had to leave suddenly. He's been quick to rely on his upbringing when he's dealing with some of our people's children, especially the stable boy. He still needs polish, but Mr. Dover and Gretchen have brought him around considerably, far more than I could have. Gretchen has informed him of the expectations that would be made of anyone who would be her suitor, so he had to learn to be a real gentleman. I expect that I will seek out your mother to help guide me through this."

Gabe smiled and said, "As long as you are a gentleman."

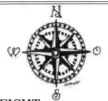

CHAPTER THIRTY EIGHT

IT WAS A PARTICULARLY hot day with perverse winds that had plagued *HMS Ares* since dawn, and if that wasn't enough, they sighted *HMS Pickle*. When Captain Nicholson had closed and come aboard, the news was not good. It was, in fact, a tremendous blow to the British war efforts in the Colonies. Admiral Hood had joined Admiral Graves in New York. However, the French fleet under Dé Grasse had sailed to the Chesapeake Bay, landing troops to supplement General George Washington's army as they fought General Cornwallis. The British fleet had fought the French fleet but was unable to fully engage the French. With the British Navy unable to oust the French, at what was being called the Battle of the Virginia Capes, Cornwallis was doomed. He'd surrendered at Yorktown on October 19th.

"Damn," Gabe cursed. "It was the hurricane last October and the French this year."

"Aye," Nicholson agreed. "It seems that there's a lot of criticism being passed around. Some are saying that had Graves struck hard and fast, the French would never have succeeded."

Gabe had met Admiral Graves. It was accepted that he held his position by being Lord North's brother-in-law. It was certainly not due to his fighting abilities. He was no Nelson, that was for sure.

Nicholson downed his glass of hock, wiped his mouth and spoke again, "Some are saying that if

Rodney had spent more time attending to his orders rather than plundering a helpless Dutch island, the French would never have gotten into such a favorable position to begin with."

"Aye," Gabe agreed. His thoughts now were to make sure that Doctor Cook, Leo and the Governor of Saint Kitts were aware of the latest news.

Seeing Captain Nicholson to *Ares'* entry port, Gabe shook his friend's hand. "Keep a vigilant lookout. With the war in the Colonies lost, the French and their new Spanish allies are sure to turn their combined focus on the Caribbean."

Gabe called to his first lieutenant, as Nicholson climbed down into his boat, "Have all the officers except the watch officer report to my cabin in a quarter of an hour."

"Bad news?" Vallin asked.

"It couldn't get much worse," Gabe replied.

It could, Dagan thought, *but there's no need to bring that up at this time. Yes, it could and would.*

***

LIEUTENANT BRYAN TURNER HAD the watch. The other two lieutenants, Marine Captain LoGiudice, the master, surgeon, bosun, and the gunner all stood around the captain's table while all the midshipmen except Mr. Corwin, who had the watch, stood behind their betters. When everyone had a glass of lime juice or tea, Gabe got down to business. He held nothing back in his news of the surrender of Cornwallis or the failure of the British to oust the French fleet.

"Does this mean what I think it does?" Vallin asked.

Gabe looked directly at his first lieutenant. "Tell us what your thoughts are?" Gabe said, not trying to put his lieutenant on the spot, but desiring to see how he grasped the overall situation.

"I believe, sir, that with the French in control of the Capes and Chesapeake Bay, and with our defeat at Yorktown, the war with the Colonies is essentially over."

Gabe agreed but asked, "And the Caribbean?"

"I'd say there are battles still to come," Vallin said.

"Aye," Gabe replied. He then added, "Unless we get reinforcements soon, I'm afraid we are ill-prepared to defend Antigua, and have no ability to defend our other islands."

"What about Saint Kitts?" Lieutenant Laqua asked. "Should they be warned?"

Gabe nodded. "Yes, as soon as this meeting is over we will come about and inform those there of the situation." The meeting ended with that. All hands were called and *Ares* came about on a heading for Saint Kitts.

Noble had learned that midshipmen were expected to listen and learn. Seeing Captain LoGiudice alone, he took a chance. "Does this mean that we stop fighting and return home, sir?"

LoGiudice frowned and then smiled, "No, Mr. Stanhope, I'm afraid, in the short term, we'll see enough action to satisfy even your young thirst." He was suddenly very serious, "Let's talk to your lieutenant and schedule some practice with your pistol and blade."

"I'm not afraid," Noble swore, trying to stand taller.

"That is ignorance speaking, my young friend. I've been in numerous battles and to be truthful I'm very scared." Seeing the boy's crestfallen look, LoGiudice placed his hand on the boy's shoulder, "I've no doubt that you're brave, Noble. Our captain has assured me of that. You've never witnessed the horror of war at sea though, with cannon balls flying and your ship being blasted apart, your friend being crushed by falling debris or overturned guns. There are others being mutilated and torn apart. No, being afraid is nothing to be ashamed of. It's how you handle your fear and how you do your duty in the midst of such chaos and destruction that counts. Your captain is a brave man, but if you ask him, he'll tell you there's never been a time that he didn't feel fear. Fear for his ship, his men, and for his family were he to fall. He'd be the first to tell you a certain amount of fear is a good thing. Just remember to do your duty, but unless it's life or death for you or the ship, you don't take any unnecessary chances."

"I understand, sir," Noble replied. As LoGiudice turned away, he spoke again, "Thank you, Captain."

LoGiudice smiled at the boy and again touched his shoulder. "Were I to have a son, Noble, I'd want him to be just like you." Stunned, Noble turned and walked away.

LoGiudice rose up to find Dagan watching him. "That was well said, Captain."

"True, every word of it was true," LoGiudice said, a little embarrassed at being overheard.

"Aye," Dagan smiled. "I've no doubt of it. I've found that I'm fond of the little bugger myself." Hearing Gabe speaking to the master, Dagan spoke again, "Reminds me a lot of someone else at that age."

LoGiudice looked over to Gabe and sensed who Dagan was referring to. "I can imagine. I can only imagine."

CHAPTER THIRTY NINE

"DAMNATION, THAT'S HELLISH NEWS you bring, Sir Gabe." Gabe listened to Governor Shirley as he paced about, digesting the news from America. "Is either Hood or Graves returning to the Caribbean?"

"I've not been told of any plans, Governor. Some thought has to be given to both Bermuda and Jamaica. They are much closer and are prime targets as well."

"Damn the French, damn the Dons and damn Rodney. He should have sailed after Saint Eustatius was taken. I hope that he chokes on his plunder. Graves has never been a fighting man. Rodney and Hood... that's who needed to be in the America's."

Gabe didn't agree or disagree outwardly. He just let Shirley rant until he finally calmed down.

"We have the fort. We can all hold up there if the French do come. Hopefully, we can get word out before it's too late."

If you have to send for help, it will already be too late, Gabe thought, but kept his opinion to himself.

A knock on the door was heard and one of the governor's servants eased his head through the door. "The good doctor from the Foreign Office and his assistant are here, sir."

While the governor told the man to send them in, Gabe wondered if anyone was left to believe in Cook's claimed reason for being in the Caribbean. Everyone seemed to have connected him with the Foreign Office.

***

HOMECOMING WAS BITTERSWEET. PULLING into Antigua and not seeing any French or Spanish ships was certainly a good feeling. Having Faith, little James, and Lum waiting when he came ashore was certainly pleasing; but seeing Lord Stanhope's ship was gone created a little melancholy. Noble had been in the tops as they entered the anchorage. When Vallin called him down, Gabe was on the quarterdeck.

Noble, without thinking, looked at Gabe and said, "Grandfather's ship is gone."

Vallin made to speak to the boy about his breach in protocol but he caught Gabe shaking his head slightly. It would set in now, Gabe was sure; the loneliness, the questioning of his decision to make the sea his life. Before, Grandfather Stanhope had been there. A lifeline in case he chose to go back on his decision about the sea. But now...now it was permanent, for better or worse. He'd not see his grandfather; he'd not see Gretchen or England, unless they got orders to return.

A thought came to Gabe's mind. "Mr. Stanhope."

Noble turned, "Yes sir."

"Did you get that letter off to Mistress Gretchen?"

Noble had looked like he was close to tears before Gabe had called him back. "Oh yes, Captain. Might there be a letter waiting?"

"There might," Gabe replied. "Your letter hasn't gotten there yet but when the mail comes aboard there may well be something for you."

The boy was all smiles now. "I certainly hope so, Captain."

So do I, Gabe thought, remembering his first cruise and the letters that he'd gotten.

***

FAITH RARELY FUSSED ABOUT navy protocol or discipline, but she wasn't having it now. "What do you mean, he must stay aboard ship. You're in port...at home. You're going to stay ashore."

"Yes, but I'm the captain."

"What about Hex and Dagan?"

"Hex is expected to be near me and Dagan's family."

"So is No."

"He's a midshipman aboard a warship. He has to live within certain constraints put in place for midshipmen."

"You got to go home."

"I was not on my father or relative's ship, and only when allowed and requested in advance."

Faith turned her head with her little nose up in the air. She then spoke softly, "I thought you loved No."

"I do," Gabe replied.

"Give him a chance then."

"What do you think they'd be saying on board ship?" Gabe asked. Faith didn't answer. Gabe continued, "He's privileged. He's the captain's pet. He gets special treatment. He thinks that he's better or above everyone else. Rules don't apply to him."

"That's not so," Faith retorted.

"I know that, but those that he trains with don't. The men he will have to lead or order into danger, they won't. No has to gain their confidence and respect. He's doing that and his lieutenant and the master have given him high marks. The men smile when he passes, not sulk like I've seen with a few. Do you want him to lose all that he's gained?"

Faith held her head down. "No, of course not."

"I didn't think so. We'll do some things so that he and the other mids can be included."

"We'll do something so that he knows you love him," Gabe said, softening his tone. "You could even write him a short note or letter."

Faith's face lit up. "He has a letter..."

Before she could finish, Gabe said, "From Gretchen."

Faith slapped her leg. "How did you guess?"

"By listening to mother and Lord Stanhope."

"We'll have Hex take it to him, and I'll hear no argument," Faith said.

Gabe smiled. It paid to pick your battles with the one who shared your bed at night. "I'll send a note to the ship inviting Con Vallin to dinner with another lieutenant, the surgeon, and two or three midshipman. I'll not name anyone but I'll bet my first lieutenant has perception enough to read between the lines."

"What about Phil and Holly?" Faith asked.

"Let's give them a few nights alone while ashore."

Faith smiled, "We'll make the invitation two...no three days from now."

Gabe replied, "Three is better."

***

CAPTAIN LOUIS HAVEN FROM *HMS Lark,* of twenty guns, sat in Captain Sir Gabriel Anthony's dining area aboard *HMS Ares.* Both men had a glass of hock. Gabe normally would have had Nesbit serve lime juice or Nesbit's new favorite, sweetened lemon juice. But one look at the haggard face of Haven when he came aboard caused Gabe to order something stronger.

"A privateer you say?"

"Aye, Sir Gabe. This ship had no flag...not French, Spanish, or Dutch. Although the first ship that we spotted, the sixty-four, was obviously Dutch, as I said."

The privateer had appeared astern of *Lark*, who was shadowing the Dutch sixty-four and two Dutch frigates. The Dutch frigates had been just visible and well forward of the sixty-four, so Haven had felt secure trailing the Dutch ships to get an idea as to their destination.

A sharp lookout had spotted the privateer overhauling *Lark* and called down not a minute too soon. The privateer actually looked like a converted slaver, maybe even an American built ship. She was pierced for twenty-eight guns, but as with most ships, she had at least four to six more if you counted bow chasers, quarterdeck guns, and stern guns.

Thinking of guns, the bang...bang...bang on the main deck was starting to play on Gabe's nerves and seemed to be distracting Haven also. Gabe had seen him look up a couple of times when a pistol was fired. Marine Captain LoGiudice was teaching the midshipmen how to accurately aim, fire, and reload a pistol. His goal had been three shots in a minute. Gabe was not sure anyone had made the goal. He was about to send Hex topside with a request to delay the shooting lessons for the time being, however, there'd been no further shots in the last couple of minutes. Hopefully, the lesson was over for the day.

Gabe, seeing that Haven's glass was empty, asked if he desired another. Seeing Gabe's glass had hardly been touched, Haven declined and then resumed his story.

Haven had come about to do battle with the privateer when the lookouts called down that the Dutch ships had all come about. *HMS Lark* then traded one broadside when the privateer then run for it. "The privateer had heavier metal," Haven said. "Twelve pounders at least."

Lark had been chased into the night but when dawn came the horizon was clear. The *Lark* still had three more days that they were to patrol but Haven felt his information was such that he needed to return. Gabe agreed with the captain and told him so.

The ships had been headed in a northerly direction when spotted, but that told Gabe little. They could have been headed toward Saint Kitts, but with only four ships Gabe doubted it; Puerto Rico, maybe. That made sense, with Spain being the Dutch's new ally. *Still?*

CHAPTER FORTY

H*MS ARES'* NEXT PATROL was uneventful. Boring would have been an apt description had Vallin not used his days and nights for drill upon drills. Fire drills at 2:00 A.M., gun and sail drills day and night, boat drills at midnight when changing the watch had to be interrupted. The men knew their jobs but now they could do them in their sleep. Not only were the jack tars drilled, but also the marines, mids, and the ship's lieutenants. Vallin even had Noble report to Lieutenant Turner that a broadside had just killed the captain, first and second lieutenants. The master was severely wounded. It was up to the third lieutenant to fight the ship and keep it from a lee shore. Such was the training that it kept the men from getting bored.

Gabe declared a make and mend day their last day on patrol. The men were exhausted and glad to have a free day. Hex took out his guitar after the meal that night, while a couple of other men had various instruments. Different men would sing and some would dance. Dagan and Gabe were enjoying the light breeze and a bowl of pipe tobacco when Midshipman Easley asked Noble to sing the 'smuggler song.'

Noble came forward and after a word or two with the musicians, he began:

If you wake at midnight and hear horses' feet
Don't go drawing back the blind or looking in the street
Them that ask no questions isn't told a lie
Watch the wall, my darling, while the gentlemen go by.

Chorus
Five and twenty ponies
Trotting through the dark
Brandy for the parson
Baccy for the clerk
Laces for a lady
Letter for a spy.
And watch the wall, my darling, while the gentlemen go by.

The song went on for several verses, but soon the men started pitching in on the chorus.

"The men appear in good spirits," the first lieutenant volunteered as he approached his captain.

"Aye," Gabe replied and then added, "I didn't know Mr. Stanhope had such a fine voice."

This time it was the first lieutenant who replied, "Aye," all the while he was starting to react to the tune being played.

"Voice like mine," Dagan japed, only to be glared at by Gabe.

With no one close enough to overhear their conversation, Gabe asked, "How is our young gentleman progressing, Con?"

The first lieutenant looked at Gabe a long moment. "He's doing well in all areas of seamanship, sir. He's surpassed Easley and Corwin and is approaching Massey in general expertise. He's made friends with all in the cockpit. He does better with the crew than the two older midshipmen. His weakness is navigation, but even that's improving. He's the best shot with both pistol and musket and is getting better with the sword and cutlass."

With all that Vallin was saying that was positive, Gabe could sense there was something he was not saying. To make it easy for Vallin, Gabe said, "And the bad."

Vallin smiled, realizing that his captain could read his thoughts. "He's a gambler, sir. He'll bet on anything from who'll make it to the tops first to who'll be last. While ashore last time, he bet the purser that out of five ears of corn, at least three of them would have the same number of rows."

This interested Gabe. "Did they?"

"Yes, the first three ears of corn had sixteen rows each. He then made a double or nothing bet that seven out of ten ears of corn would have an even number of rows."

Gabe asked, "And the purser took the bet?"

"Aye, Captain. In fact, all ten ears of corn had either sixteen or twenty rows of kernels."

"Damnation!" Gabe exclaimed. "He's not bet with the men, has he?"

"No, not that I know of, Captain. He did bet Captain LoGiudice that he'd hit bulls eye three out of five shots at twenty feet."

"And did he?" Gabe asked.

"Yes, four out of five but the target floated further away by the fifth shot."

"And LoGiudice paid him?"

"Oh, no sir. This was not a money bet. It was just a bet that he could do it."

"Have you talked to Mr. Stanhope about his gambling?"

"Er...no sir. I thought it might come better from Dagan or Hex."

Gabe nodded. *Possibly, or even myself on an occasion when we're ashore*, Gabe thought. Gambling...was that something held over from his previous life, or was that new? Either way it would have to be addressed.

***

THE SUN WAS CLIMBING high when *Ares* dropped her anchor at English Harbour. A lot of ships had arrived since their departure on patrol. Several merchant ships with a frigate and brig anchored near them.

Escort ships, Gabe surmised. This was likely the last convoy they'd see until after the new year. The merchant ships sat low in the water, which let Gabe know that they were heavily laden. Gabe heard Dagan and the master talking, as he walked over toward the wheel.

Scott, the master was saying, "I feel that they are headed to India and not coming back, since they only have two ships for escorts. Were they coming back they'd want at least two more escort ships."

"Who are they?" Gabe asked.

Randall Scott turned to face the captain, "Several theys, sir. The Honest Johns would lobby for it, as would the insurers. Lloyds has already told Parliament that unless they get adequate escorts, they would not insure the hulls or the cargo." He smiled and continued, "I've been told the majority of Parliament are investors in the East India Company, so I'm sure the Navy has been swayed."

Dagan grinned, "I'd bet more than a few of our admirals have invested in the Honest Johns, themselves," using the slang for the East India Company.

Gabe smiled but didn't comment. Walking to the stern, he could see a captain's gig pulling away from *HMS Ludlow,* but it was not Captain Hurley. The captain was in full dress uniform. *Damnable hot*, Gabe thought.

Hex walked up and, catching Gabe's eye, stated the obvious. "We have a visitor headed this way, Captain."

226

"I see him," Gabe replied. "Have Nesbit prepare a bit of refreshment if you will, Jake."

"Yonder captain looks up in age," Dagan replied.

Gabe nodded, "I see that." *I wonder if he's senior*, he thought. "Can you see the ship's name?"

"No, but she is a thirty-eight," Dagan replied. Gabe nodded his reply.

"Boat ahoy!" The sentry challenged.

"*Hebe* " came a crisp reply. Vallin called the side-boys together and the bosun was there with his pipe.

The captain was not only a great deal older, but he was out of shape. His face was flushed as he huffed and puffed his way through the entry port. His breathing was audible above the bosun's pipe.

Gabe stepped forward and formally introduced himself, "Captain Gabe Anthony. Welcome aboard *HMS Ares* of forty-four guns."

"Captain Sir Reginald Quattlebaum."

"Would you care for some refreshment, sir?"

"Of course," Quattlebaum answered in an abrupt manner.

Vallin spoke, not liking the man's emphasis on 'Sir Quattlebaum', "I will see to those tasks, Sir Gabe." It was his way of letting the visiting captain know that he wasn't the only knight aboard the ship.

Seeing Dagan, Hex, the master, and Turner all standing with smiles, Vallin asked, "Was it that obvious?"

"Aye," Dagan answered and then added, "and jolly well done, good sir."

Quattlebaum dismissed the offered lemon juice and asked for something a bit bolder. After Nesbit poured the captain a liberal portion of hock, Quattlebaum gulped half the glass in one swallow. Smacking his lips, he sat the glass down and spoke to Gabe, "I have need of your frigate and one of the others."

Gabe was shocked at the man's words. "I'm sorry, sir, but I can't comply with your request."

"Request be damned. That was not a request, it was an order. I'm sure that I'm senior to you."

Gabe looked at the man, who lifted the glass and finished the hock in one more swallow. "I am under private Admiralty orders, sir. The other two frigates have been assigned to Antigua and the governor to provide protection from invasion. I'm not sure if you have been made aware, Captain, but the French have defeated the combined fleets of Admirals Graves and Hood. The French, Spaniards, and the Dutch are now raiding shipping lines and islands with little or nothing to oppose them. We need, at least, a ship of the line and several more frigates just to protect Antigua. I may be called upon to weigh anchor at any moment, which would really hurt the island's defensive capabilities. There are Dutch ships and a privateer patrolling these waters now."

"Damnation, man," Quattlebaum roared. "Don't I know about the bloody Dutch and privateer? I lost a frigate, a brig, and six ships in the convoy to the damnable whoresons."

So that's why the man is pressured, Gabe thought. *He's liable to be put on the beach, with such losses.*

"I understand your need, but still Sir Reginald, I can't help you," Gabe said, trying to put concern in his voice.

"Humph...I could order you, sir."

"I would have to refuse the order and send a report to the Admiralty and the Foreign Office. Were I to do that, sir, I'm sure the consequences would be most unpleasant."

"Damn you," Quattlebaum roared.

Gabe had had enough. He rose up from his chair slowly and deliberately. "I am sympathetic to your need, Captain, but I will allow no one to raise their voice and curse me in my cabin on my ship. In fact, sir, one more outburst and I will seek satisfaction. You may not have noticed, but the skylight is open so I'm sure you were heard by many of my officers and crew."

Quattlebaum looked longingly at his empty glass.

"Nesbit," Gabe called, and then nodded at the glass when he entered.

"Please accept my apology, sir," Quattlebaum muttered after a hasty swallow of the hock. "The pressures are getting to me."

Gabe had already recognized that. Clearing his throat and trying to purge his distaste for this man, Gabe spoke. "Captain, tomorrow Captain Hurley will go out on patrol. I see no reason why he can't assist you in escorting your convoy as far as Barbados. The island is recovering from a devastating hurricane, but there is likely to be a naval presence there with enough ships to assist you."

Quattlebaum downed the hock and made ready to go.

"Captain," Gabe called, refusing to use the man's title. "Had you come aboard and politely asked for assistance rather than throwing your seniority and title around, you would have been given assistance readily and probably an invitation to dine with the governor. That would have allowed your officers and crew a brief respite."

Quattlebaum hung his head but did not reply. He made his way up the companion ladder instead, and over to the entry port. Gabe waited a moment before he left his cabin. As he stepped out of his door, Phil LoGiudice was standing there with Noble. He had sensed that all was not well and asked the marine captain to come.

"A dullard," LoGiudice volunteered.

Gabe shook his head, the anger he'd felt was subsiding and he felt drained. "Noble sent for you?" he asked.

"It was more like I was the first one he spied but he was ready to intervene himself. He said that he couldn't abide a lout disrespecting our captain."

Gabe smiled now, "Let's go ashore, Phil."

"Aye, Captain. I'm sure that our reception will be much better."

"Undoubtably," Gabe responded. "Undoubtably."

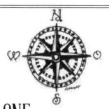

CHAPTER FORTY ONE

"IT'S NEARLY CHRISTMAS AGAIN," Faith said, snuggling close to Gabe. He'd been home two weeks and would leave the next day for another weeklong patrol. Faith had gotten used to him being home more. Little James really liked having his father around. James not only played with his father, but also with his Uncle Dagan and Uncle Jake, who were usually around for whatever game James wanted to play. At least, they spared Lum. Young Noble Pride found little James crawling up into his lap when he came by to pick up his mail.

The windows to the bedroom were open and a gentle breeze stirred the mosquito net. Gabe and Faith had made love and now, spent from their passion, lay in each other's arms. Faith liked to talk in moments like this while Gabe muttered his replies. His thoughts were more on sleep than small talk.

"Would you like to have another child, Gabe?"

"Huh...what was that?"

"Would you like to have another baby?"

"I guess I really haven't thought about it."

"Men," Faith retorted. "Ships and the sea, and a wench in port."

Gabe had been on his back, and now rolled over. "I meant that I just figured it'd happen when it happened. We don't use one of those condoms that Doctor Cornish stresses to the men as a means to protect one from becoming a father and from the pox and such. Neither of those is of concern to me being a married man."

Faith suddenly rose up, "Did you know that the planter Martin's wife became pregnant while he was in England. The talk is that she brought a slave, a rather large...if you know what I mean into her chamber and was so enamored with him, that he suddenly became a house servant. The talk is that he'd better be gone by the time Mr. Martin returns."

Gabe thought a minute and then asked, "What about the pregnancy, surely Martin will know that it's not his."

Faith rose up on her elbow, exposing her breast. Gabe's gaze suddenly dropped from Faith's face to her chest.

"Men!" she snapped, and sat up in the bed, momentarily exposing the second breast. She quickly pulled the sheet up covering both breasts. "Now, may I have your attention?"

"You had it, probably more than you realize," Gabe responded.

"Hush now and listen. Marilyn is going to go down to the area where the free blacks stay and she will see this voodoo woman. She blows something in your face that makes you sleepy. Once you're asleep, she goes down "there"...with special hooks that she made and when you wake up your not pregnant anymore." Gabe was not sure that he had heard Faith right. "Nanny says that this has been going on for years in the slave quarters."

"I don't care how long it's been happening," Gabe said. "It sounds dangerous to me."

"She doesn't have much choice the way I hear it," Faith said. "She's sure that Martin will kill her if he finds out."

"If...if," Gabe repeated. "Don't you think he will

find out, Faith? How did you find out?"

Faith looked sheepish, "Livi told me, but Nanny knew about it too."

"That means that probably the entire countryside knows about it. What did Martin's overseer think? He had to know something was amiss, for the mistress of the house to have a large field hand brought to the house. What do you think it will cost the Mistress Martin to keep the overseer quiet?"

Faith looked perplexed, "You think he'll talk?"

Gabe smiled, "I bet he already has. I hope Marilyn doesn't die at the hands of this witch woman."

"Voodoo woman," Faith corrected him.

"All the same to me," Gabe responded.

"She couldn't go to the doctor, he's friends with Martin," Faith said.

"I'd think he would be the one man that she could trust to not talk," Gabe said, remembering conversations he'd had with *Ares'* surgeon Robert Cornish. As a youth, he'd heard of women drinking a bitter tea or pushing herbal concoctions into the uterus to create a miscarriage. He'd also heard of women prostituting themselves to come up with the fee required by some physician or midwife to pay for the procedure. Sadly, he'd also heard of women bleeding to death from certain procedures. All that he could think of was the mental and physical pain the Martin woman would go through trying not to get caught for her dalliance. He'd known one navy captain who found himself poxed. He wrote a letter asking for forgiveness and then shot himself.

"When is Martin due back?" Gabe asked.

Faith looked at Gabe seriously, "He was supposed to have returned with the convoy that was just here."

Gabe said, "Several ships, including a naval frigate and a brig, were taken. He may not return. The Dutch are usually good about letting prisoners go for ransom, so he could still show up...but who knows. In the meantime, if you feel comfortable doing so, try to persuade Marilyn to see a real doctor before seeing that witch."

"Voodoo woman," Faith said, speaking each word one at a time.

"Now come to me, you wench. You've gotten careless with the covers so that your breasts are no longer covered and the sight of those delicious melons has stirred up my humors."

"Who said I was being careless, kind sir. What would you say if I told you that it was deliberate?"

"I'd have the same humors only more happily so," Gabe said reaching over to kiss his wife, first on the lips, then on her neck, and then with delight, the taste of those beautiful ripe melons.

"Gabe."

"Yes."

"What if I get pregnant?"

Gabe pulled his mouth away from Faith's delicious fruit and muttered, "James needs a playmate."

Faith groaned and crushed his head to her chest. "No more talking," she whispered. Gabe didn't argue.

CHAPTER FORTY TWO

H*MS LUDLOW* RETURNED CHRISTMAS Day along with another ship, the dispatch vessel, *Rose*. Captain Robert Hurley was directed to Gabe's residence by Lieutenant Laqua, the duty officer on board *Ares*. At the same time, the captain of the *Rose* went on board *Ares* with dispatches, mail, and an important official who sought the captain.

Captain Hurley and the official shared a ride in a rented coach. Hex answered the knock at the door. They had just finished Christmas dinner, and a stuffed Hex decided to stretch his legs for a moment.

Faith had acquired the services of a new slave, as Nanny was getting older. Faith promised her that she would be freed at the end of five years. Nanny was teaching the girl how to do things the 'Nanny way.' When it came to cooking, the girl, Bella, was an apt pupil and had done an outstanding job preparing the Christmas dinner.

Gabe, Faith, and Dagan were getting up from the table when they heard the knock. Hex, already up, volunteered to get it. Hearing the voices, Gabe automatically recognized Captain Hurley's, but the other voice also sounded strangely familiar.

"Lord Skalla," Gabe exclaimed as the trio entered the parlor.

Faith smiled as the men entered the room, but her smile was strained. It wasn't that she didn't like Lord Skalla well enough, but past experience had proven that when he showed up, Gabe left on a dangerous mission.

She remembered all too well their mission to the Indian Ocean and Madagascar. Dagan had been severely wounded, as had Admiral Buck, and trouble had been made for Gabe. It had all worked out, but it had been nothing less than a miracle that they had survived at all. Gabe had returned looking haggard. The patch of gray hair along his scalp where he'd been creased by a pistol ball had turned white. His eyes, it was hard to explain, but they had looked dull and empty. She and little James, with time, had changed all that. And now...now Lord Skalla was back. Would it never end? Hadn't Gabe said that the war was all but over, so why did they need him now?

Faith, being the proper wife, rose up and politely greeted their visitors and inquired about refreshments. She was sorry that dinner was over, but there was dessert to be had. Both of the men turned down dessert but did agree to a glass of wine. After Bella served the glasses and left, Faith made her excuses and left also, but didn't go far, just out of sight but not out of hearing.

Nanny placed a hand on Faith's shoulder; the girl she had raised, the girl that she thought of as her own daughter. Bella came out of the kitchen and saw the two, sensing that this was how it was...a special bond. She backed into the kitchen.

***

GABE, UNDERSTANDING THAT WHATEVER Lord Skalla had to say would be confidential, asked Hurley how his patrol and escort duties went. Hurley was smart enough to give his report and leave. He knew that whatever Lord Skalla had to say would have nothing to do with him or the *Ludlow*. Or would it?

"We reached Barbados without incident," Captain Hurley began. "Once there, Captain Quattlebaum was most appreciative of our services. It turns out this was his first command in years. It seems he's been on the beach for a while."

And likely to wind up there again if he doesn't change his ways, Gabe thought, but didn't say.

Hurley continued his report, "Barbados is still recovering from the hurricane, as you would expect, but it seems to be coming along well, the island's defenses especially. Lord Ragland sends his regards and says he's gotten word that he's being replaced. Not unexpectedly, as he's been there nearly ten years... since before the war."

Gabe wondered what was next for Ragland. He had proven to be a good friend and ally. He's miss him but felt sure their paths would cross again.

"The evening before we were set to sail, a coastal trader came in. It seems she and another trader almost fell prey to a big privateer."

This caught Gabe's ear. Small coastal vessels were usually left alone. They were often stopped, searched, and interrogated in an attempt to gain information. But these little vessels were generally left alone, that is unless there was a need for subterfuge. He'd done it himself. So this might prove to be useful information.

"My cox'n tells me the gossip along the waterfront is a French privateer is sailing with a small Dutch squadron and taking prizes left and right."

Gabe looked at Hurley, "This we know."

"The captain is thought to be a man named dé Corsia. It seems that he's been raiding shipping in these waters for years, even before the war."

Gabe looked at Hex, who just shrugged. There had been a woman using her tavern in Grand Cayman to gather information on ships with valuable cargo. Hex had fallen for her, fallen hard. It was then discovered that she was in league with her pirate brother. They had both escaped apprehension. Was it the same man? The name didn't mean anything to Hex, so maybe not. Such raiders often had other ships that sailed with them. So they may or may not be connected.

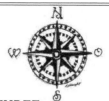

CHAPTER FORTY THREE

L ORD SKALLA HAD WAITED patiently for Hurley to report and make his departure. Once he'd left, Skalla stood and apologized for interrupting Gabe and Faith's Christmas. "Were it not important, I would not have done so."

Gabe nodded his understanding but did not speak. Skalla glanced at Dagan and Hex as he gathered his thoughts. Some would ask if Gabe minded dismissing the two men...some would, but not him. He'd long since learned the two men were strict confidants. Anything said to him would be repeated to them anyway, so why waste time.

He took another sip of the wine. *Excellent wine*, he thought, probably liberated from some French ship. He then thought *Ares had been a French ship. How many such ships had Gabe and his brother taken as prizes? More than enough to overlook the source of his wine and just enjoy it for what it was, an excellent wine.*

"The war with the Colonies is lost," Skalla said abruptly. "Lord North had a fit when he got the news of Lord Cornwallis' surrender. He blames Admiral Rodney for not immediately sailing to the Colonies and supporting Graves."

"He's not the only one, I hear," Gabe said.

Skalla nodded, "There will be much said, but enough plunder was brought back to England to quiet the talk, so it will soon be forgotten. A delegation is being put together to officially end the fighting."

"That's good news," Gabe said.

"It should be," Skalla said. "The Americans are as tired of this war as we are, but not the French or Spaniards and, after Rodney's activities, neither are the Dutch."

Gabe felt his momentary elation sink. "So what now?" he asked.

"I'm sure the French will do everything in their power to capture as many of our islands in the Caribbean as they can, if for no other reason than to use them as bargaining chips. We just heard your Captain Hurley talk about the French privateer sailing with the Dutch. You, of course, know about all the attacks on our possessions. The only question now is what's next. Admiral Hood is now trying to locate the French fleet. Word is that dé Grasse had it in mind to attack both Bermuda and Jamaica. I've not heard anything yet as to what's happening in those areas. When I left England the rumor was that the Navy wanted to get Rodney back at sea, so he may be on his way to us now. Regardless of what else you can say about the man, he is a good commander in battle."

Aye, Gabe thought. *I'll give him that.* "What about Antigua?" Gabe asked. "We've little enough to protect the island."

"I understand," Skalla said. "Admiral Moffitt has stressed the need for reinforcements here, even going so far as to say that even as capable as you are, one ship cannot hold off a fleet."

"One ship?" Gabe asked.

Skalla nodded, "I think he forgot about the *Ludlow* and *Lark*. After all, they were only ordered here for repairs. I would imagine that he assumed they set sail long ago. It's to our advantage that everyone seems to have lost track of those ships. Rodney sent them away and then sent Hood to the Colonies. With

. Hood having no knowledge of them and Rodney in England, I think they've forgotten them."

Gabe smiled, "Until some clerk realizes they're gone."

"Aye, there are always the clerks hovering over their columns."

"Just so," Gabe replied, "just so."

***

AFTER BRINGING GABE UP to date on the war, Lord Skalla asked about his agents. "Where might I find Sir Lawrence and Mr. Gallagher?"

Gabe, shocked that Lord Skalla didn't know, managed to reply, "They're on Saint Kitts."

"What! Why are they there?"

"I assure you I don't know, but when I was last there, I was told they planned on staying. We've not heard from them since, and frankly I wondered if they'd returned to England."

Lord Skalla was upset. He seemed to be having difficulty with coming to a decision but finally he slapped his palm with his fist and cursed, "Damnation." He took the last swallow of his wine and sat back down obviously perplexed.

"Another?" Gabe asked.

"Please," Skalla replied.

Hex stood at once and went to the table for a bottle of wine. He refilled Skalla's glass and when Gabe placed his hand over his own glass, Hex placed the bottle on the table.

"How did his cover as a physician looking into how the tropical diseases affect our sailors work?"

"It went well for about a week," Gabe replied.

Skalla sighed, "He is a noted physician."

"I understand," Gabe replied. "His subterfuge was quickly dismissed with our sailing him all over the

Caribbean at the drop of the hat. Leo was not the best sort to act as his assistant. He is a good agent, I'm sure. I would have lost a good man, were it not for his quick action."

"I was opposed to the assignment. I felt that there was little our Leo the Lion couldn't find out on his own, but Sir Lawrence needed to start somewhere. And I've no doubt our troubles as a nation are soon coming to an end."

"I believe they are just beginning." Dagan said as he stood up and left the room.

Something was up, Gabe knew. Otherwise, his uncle would not have just up and left.

***

THE TALK BECAME GENERAL, with Lord Skalla surmising France's objectives in the Caribbean. "The control of the entire West Indies would be my thoughts," Skalla was saying as Dagan returned.

"My apologies for interrupting, my Lord," Dagan said. "There is an urgent need for Sir Gabe."

Gabe thought it must be urgent for his uncle to speak so formally. He excused himself and fell in behind Dagan, leaving Hex to entertain Lord Skalla. Dagan led Gabe through the kitchen and onto the back porch.

Lum was there with a rather large male slave. "This is Sampson," Lum said. "Mistress Martin named him that when he first came to their plantation, suh."

"I heard that he'd run away," Gabe said, not liking the idea of the man seeking refuge at his home.

"I know it ain't good, Cap'n," Lum said. "The folks tell him that Mistress Martin is gonna die and he's gonna be whipped and skinned alive. The slaves have told Sampson that the overseer done had his fish knives sharpened so they'll shave a man."

Damn, Gabe thought. *I want nothing to do with harboring a runaway slave.*

Lum saw Gabe was deep in thought and spoke again, "He's from a fishing village, Cap'n, so he knows his way on a boat."

"A boat is one thing," Gabe snapped. "A ship is another." Lum hung his head when Gabe snapped. Seeing that, Gabe immediately felt guilty. "I'm sorry, Lum, but the ships we have here would be a poor place to hide him. He'd eventually be spotted and then we'd have to answer to Martin and maybe even the governor."

"What about a ship that's just stopping here," Dagan suggested.

"It might work," Gabe admitted as he went back inside to speak with Lord Skalla.

***

HMS ROSE, OF TEN guns, was sleek and fast, as were most dispatch vessels. Her guns would do little against a warship of any size, but her captain, Lieutenant John McCay, was very proud of her...his first command. When he received a note from Captain Sir Gabriel Anthony requesting a meeting with him, he was at first elated, and then doubts took over and he found himself worried. What had he done? Nothing that he could think of. Had he offended the Foreign Office agent? He didn't think so. Sir Gabe had requested to meet on board the tiny *Rose* and that was puzzling. Most captains would have him to 'repair on board' their ship. He was still pacing the deck in his cabin when he heard the sentry challenge...'boat ahoy.' The reply came back, '*Ares.*'

McCay looked around one last time, making sure everything was as it should be, and rushed on deck.

Gabe came to the point, after being greeted, "I have a favor to ask."

"Certainly," McCay responded, ready to do anything possible for the man who'd charmed all of England with his exploits.

When they got to the cabin, small as it was, they sat at the small table to keep from bumping their heads on the overhead beams.

Gabe started speaking once a glass of passable wine was served. "What I'm about to tell you, sir, must be held in strict confidence."

This caused McCay to straighten up and scoot forward in his chair. "Of course, sir."

When Gabe finished his story he took a sip of his wine, and then took a larger swallow, finding the wine more tasty after telling the young captain his distasteful story.

McCay seemed to be in a quandary. He'd never heard of a white woman bringing a black man into her bedroom. He found himself thinking ill of the slave. Gabe pointed out that Sampson had little to say about the matter.

"I'll do it, Sir Gabe. We weigh anchor and get underway tomorrow morning. When can you bring Sampson on board?"

"He's already on board," Gabe responded. McCay nodded.

"I thank you, Captain McCay. You have, in all probability, saved a life. I'm in your debt, so please don't ever hesitate to call on me should you require my assistance in anyway."

The men shook hands and Gabe took his leave. The next morning *Rose* got underway with one more volunteer. He was entered into the books as Sampson Martin, a free black.

CHAPTER FORTY FOUR

NEW YEARS DAY, 1782, was warm but not hot. A nice breeze caused the palm trees to groan as their trunks leaned and the palm fronds were bristling. Gabe and Faith were visiting Commodore Gardner and his wife in Saint John's. Seeing Gardner brought back several fond memories. Gabe recalled when the war broke out, Gardner had retired rather than fight the Colonials. Several of them were his good friends. As Gardner was a senior captain, he'd been promoted to admiral but he was a yellow admiral assigned to a non-existent squadron. Several captains had done this, opening the path for Gil to be promoted early. The conversation turned to the soon-to-end hostilities with the Colonies.

"Who can say if the Frogs and the Dons would cease hostilities when the Americans stopped? One thing positive, Gabe, and this is confidential to a degree. The importance of Antigua has been driven home to Parliament. The dockyard has certainly made its worth noted...so much so, it will be an admiral's assignment, not just temporary like now. I have talked to the First Lord and I'm strongly being considered to fill the position. It's felt my knowledge of the works and my relationship with many of the Americans will help normalize relations between England and our cousins."

"That would be great," Gabe responded, happy for his friend. "When will you know?"

Gardner smiled, "When official orders arrive. I expect them to be here within the month. You know Admiral Gordon has claimed to be in failing health from tropical humors and has requested to be relieved." Gabe smiled and Gardner asked, "What?"

"It's rumored that Admiral Gordon's wife considers the local society beneath her. She has not gained many friends. It's also been said several of their young female servants have been dismissed. It would seem our admiral likes young women and is not particular about color. When Mrs. Gordon finds out she sends that girl away. They do leave with a fat purse," Gabe said.

Thinking about Admiral Gordon's habits made Gabe think of Marilyn Martin. She'd taken care of the pregnancy with few side effects other than bleeding, but even that hadn't been too significant. So while she'd recuperated physically from her indiscretion, her social well-being had suffered more than even Gabe would have imagined. Slave talk was expected but it had been the overseer that had caused the biggest problem. The overseer, a known drinker, had not been discreet about his mistress when he got drunk. To make matters worse, he felt like she looked down upon him. The woman would take a black slave to her bed but had the nerve to tell him that he was repulsive. The more he thought about it and the more he drank, he decided he'd show the slut. He entered the house, with a belly full of cheap rum, broke down the bedroom door and attacked her. He ripped her nightgown off and flung it on the floor. He started pawing at her breasts, at her nakedness and when she fought back at him, he slapped her face, leaving his hand print. He then slung her across the bed, fumbling to undo his britches, and that was his last mistake. Reaching under her pillow, Marilyn pulled her husband's pistol out. The man looked up when he heard the metallic click of the hammer being drawn back. Marilyn pulled the trigger as he looked up. The ball hit him between the nose and upper lip. The commotion alerted the house servant, who sent one of the boys to get the watchman. Her maid helped her into another gown and housecoat. Water was brought to wash her face but everything else was left as it was for the watchman to see.

Mr. Martin still hadn't been heard from and the plantation was suffering due to inactivity and lack of leadership. While no one mourned the death of the overseer or condoned his actions, a good many felt she had brought it on herself. Others, the more open-minded, said what was good for the goose was good for the gander. Mr. Martin, apparently like a good many others, had taken pleasure with the young slave girls.

There were rumors that if Mr. Martin didn't return soon, she planned to leave the island. The only good that came from it was that the overseer had told everyone he was going to skin Sampson. Everyone now thought the slave was also dead and no one put any effort into looking for him.

***

THE VISIT WITH THE Gardners went well. Gabe and Faith invited them to stay as their guests if they needed to look for quarters when they returned to English Harbour. A house for the admiral was planned but hadn't been built yet.

"The money has been set aside to build quarters for the admiral in charge in close proximity to the dockyard."

Gabe wondered, with all the problems inherent to a dockyard, if that might not prove to be a double-edged sword. Time would tell.

***

FIVE DAYS LATER, ON the 6th of January, Captain Louis Haven of *HMS Lark* returned to Antigua. His gig was lowered right away and made its way to *Ares,* even before being summoned.

"Looks like Captain Haven's gig is approaching," Lieutenant Vallin told Gabe as he entered the captain's cabin. "It must be something urgent for Haven to rush about." Gabe smiled at that. Haven was a good captain but believed if you had to rush...rush slowly.

"It's the damn French, Captain," Haven exclaimed. "I had an easy trip to the south but came upon a French frigate as I sailed toward Saint Kitts. My lookout declared her to be a large frigate. We came about and almost immediately came in sight of a small frigate or corvette. I intended to approach this ship and do battle if needed, when the lookout called down that more sails had been spotted. I came about again and headed westerly toward Jamaica, with the big Frenchie giving chase. We spotted a squall and headed into it. We followed the squall line for an hour and lost the frigate. I came about to an east-south-east course, turning north when the Peaks of Saint Lucia was spotted. When we made our way into English Harbour, the lookout spotted more sails to the north."

Damnation, Gabe thought, *it sounds like Lord Skalla's fears are coming to bear*. Gabe called for his gig and headed to talk with the governor. This was a scenario where any choice could potentially turn out bad. If the island was left with only the forts to defend it, it would likely fall. If Gabe sailed, even with *Ludlow* and *Lark,* would that make a difference for Saint Kitts? He felt sure an attack was imminent, with all the sightings in that area. What if it was only a feint? A feint to draw in ships to defend the island, only to find out the real threat was somewhere else.

The governor did not like the idea of venturing out from Antigua. However, Lord Skalla stated the matter was more critical and urgent than perhaps the governor or even Gabe realized.

"We have two agents who have specific knowledge that cannot be allowed to fall into enemy hands." The knowledge was more important than a ship or even Antigua. "As soon as we find out what the enemy is doing, we must deal with our agents," Lord Skalla said emphatically. His words left little room for argument.

***

HMS LUDLOW DEPARTED THE next morning with strict orders. "If you sight a fleet you return at once. Do not be provoked into action. We need information more than anything else."

Lord Skalla was standing there. "Do you need that in writing, Captain?"

Hurley looked at Lord Skalla and, unable to hide his anger, he retorted, "If you feel the need, my Lord, but I've been following Sir Gabe's orders long enough that I'm sure he knows that I will follow orders, whether they're written or not."

Gabe was proud of Hurley but he also understood the reason for Lord Skalla's words.

"Forgive me, Captain," Skalla said. "I was out of place. I'm sure Sir Gabe has every confidence in your abilities."

"Thank you," Hurley responded. He held out his hand to Gabe and then almost as an afterthought he held his hand out to Lord Skalla, who shook it.

CHAPTER FORTY FIVE

HEX WAS PLAYING DRAUGHTS, or checkers, as it was referred to in the Colonies, with the surgeon. The game was going on in Doctor Cornish's office. On the main deck above, the thud of boots on the planking echoed down into the sick bay.

Captain LoGiudice was having small arms drill and sword drills, not only with the marines, but also with the older midshipmen as well. The thudding seemed to be distracting Doctor Cornish as he made a move that was a big mistake, allowing Hex to jump three of Cornish's pieces and was now waiting to be crowned. Hex could go forward or backwards with a king. This was his third king. Cornish threw up his hands and resigned, "Your game."

They heard footsteps on a ladder and then a knock on the surgeon's door. It was Vaughn Corwin, the youngest of the mids. "Please sir," Corwin fairly shouted, "you are needed on deck. Mr. Massey has been injured."

"How bad," Cornish asked, gathering himself to go on deck.

"Maybe dead," Corwin cried out almost in tears.

"Young sir, get a hold of yourself," Hex said, letting his hand slide over the boy's shoulder as they made their way out of the office and up on deck. Massey was lying on deck, unconscious.

Cornish went to examine Massey and Hex asked a marine, who looked pale, "What happened?"

"They were going through drills with Massey being the man attacking with a sword, and the marine trying to fend off the attacker with his musket. It appeared when Massey lunged with his sword, he was off balance and fell just as the marine used the butt of his musket to block the lunge. Trouble was, when Massey fell forward, he fell right into the marine's thrust and the butt of the musket caught him just above the ear. He fell out cold."

"He is alive," Cornish was able to ascertain this right away.

A large bruise was already showing over the ear and there was substantial swelling. Doctor Cornish asked Hex to see if the captain had any ice. Hex nodded and hurried off. Cornish had found out before the war that injuries obtained in cold climate did not swell as bad as those in warmer climates.

His examination showed no further injuries other than a scrape on the side of the mid's face from hitting the deck and sliding a bit. By the time Hex was back with the ice, which was faster than the surgeon had anticipated, Massey was coming around. He let go with a slight groan and raised his hand to the side of his head.

"Easy now," Cornish said, speaking softly. "You've taken quite a blow." He allowed Massey to sit forward, but it caused him to be dizzy and vomit, so he was laid back down.

Gabe was now on the scene. Seeing the men step back, Cornish, who was wiping the vomit off the mid's face, looked up at the captain.

Cornish spoke, without being asked, "A bad concussion, Captain, if not more. I dare say he may even have an intracranial bleed. Hopefully, the ice will help but if it doesn't his head will have to be opened and the clot evacuated. We will need to have him taken to the hospital."

Gabe nodded and looked at Con Vallin, the first lieutenant. "I will see to it, Captain," Vallin said before Gabe could speak.

As Cornish left the ship with Massey, Con Vallin called to Noble. "Mr. Stanhope!"

"Aye!"

"You will assume Mr. Massey's duties until his return."

"Yes, sir," Noble answered in a subdued voice. Massey was his closest friend on board ship.

"Mr. Stanhope," Vallin called again.

"Sir."

"Are you with us?"

"Yes sir. I was just saying a small prayer for Mr. Massey. Our captain's mother says 'above all else say a prayer.'"

Vallin was now speechless. Vallin knew the captain's mother and could picture her telling the boy just that. "She's right, I'm sure," Vallin managed.

Noble looked at Mr. Dover, his tutor. The two had rushed on deck when they heard the commotion. Dover now looked at Noble and smiled. The boy was learning nicely. He'd learn even more now.

***

THE MARINE OUTSIDE THE captain's cabin came to attention, stamped his musket's butt on the deck and announced, "Captain LoGiudice, sir."

"Enter," Gabe called and rose from his desk to greet the captain. He heard the bell clanging on the main deck. Seven bells in the forenoon watch. The morning drills would now cease.

Kegs of rum were being brought on deck as men lined up to get their ration. The men would be fed at eight bells.

"I'm sorry about the injury to Midshipman

Massey," LoGiudice said. "Private Sutcliff is most upset that he struck the blow."

"There's no question that it was anything other than an unfortunate accident is there, Phil?"

"No sir. Sergeant Daniels and Corporal Merle both witnessed the accident. Corporal Merle did say the blow sounded like a watermelon being squished."

"Damn," Gabe said. "Hopefully, the boy will live."

***

YOUNG NOBLE STANHOPE HAD been trained well by Mr. Massey in regards to his duties. What he liked the best about filling in for the injured Massey was that in battle he would be the captain's messenger, and if boat work was called for he'd be in the captain's boat. He'd had time since being on board to reflect back on the day the captain and Captain Markham had come to his aid and the subsequent attack on the two captains in retaliation.

There was ample time for reflection when he was on watch at night. Was it his destiny to be a naval captain like Gabe? Would he spend as few years at sea, and then go back to live with his grandfather? He felt guilty, at times, for leaving his grandfather so soon after being accepted as his father's son. All of these things played on his mind. He mentioned them to Mr. Dover, who replied, "Your grandfather expects you to become somebody. The sea is an honorable occupation."

It was during these quiet nights that the loneliness crept in. He thought of his mum. God, how he missed her. Some had condemned her for being little more than a whore; a discreet whore for sure, but still a whore. It had troubled him until Dagan sat him down.

"Was there ever a time your mum didn't care for you?"

"No."

"Was there ever a time she didn't make you feel filled with love?"

"No."

"That's what you remember, then. She loved your father and you are a product of their love. Society, being what it is, lets or causes bad things to happen, most are very unfair. Therefore, your mum did what she had to in order to take care of you. Meeting Gabe and Francis Markham was in a way making up for all the injustice you've experienced in your young life. It's up to you now, what you do with this new opportunity. You can be an upstanding young man and remember the circumstances from which you came and vow to improve your life and the way you treat others. Or you can lie in self pity and disappoint all those who offered you a helping hand."

Noble had vowed that he'd not fall into self pity. He was now in a position to be recognized. That could be good or bad, depending on how he responded when the chips were down. He'd not disappoint anyone, he vowed to himself. He not only wanted to please the captain, Dagan, his grandfather, and even Hex, but there was that girl back in England whom he wanted to please. Gretchen was still in his thoughts on such nights. Mr. Dover helped Noble read her letters at first but now he was able to do it himself. Yes! He'd been given a new opportunity to succeed in life and he planned to take full advantage of it. There were too many people counting on him. With this new set of duties, he'd make the most of the opportunity, regardless of how long it lasted.

PART IV

A Sailor's Lot

Ships are in the harbour
There are big guns ashore
The enemy has dug in
We know what's in store.

The captain, he's honest
Says there's hell to pay
But we have a chance
Just do what they say.

They say the island is crucial
But not to a sailor's lot
We can't help but think
Of all the islands they got.

...Michael Aye

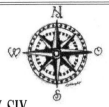

CHAPTER FORTY SIX

THE *LUDLOW* WAS LATE in returning from patrol. Lord Skalla was antsy and even Gabe felt ill at ease. Hurley finally returned on the 20th of January, and immediately boarded his gig and made his way to *Ares*. Gabe met him at the entry port and, seeing the look on Captain Hurley's face, took him directly to his cabin, motioning his first lieutenant to follow. Nesbit was now able to recognize when light refreshments were called for and when something a bit stronger was necessary. Today, without asking, he brought in four glasses. He'd seen the three officers but knew Dagan was usually lurking about. Setting the decanter on the table with the glasses, Nesbit looked at the captain.

"Shall I pour, sir?" Gabe nodded and Nesbit filled the glasses halfway and departed.

Hurley took a swallow and started, "The French are out. On January 11th, dé Grasse anchored his fleet in the Basse Terre Roads on Saint Kitts. It's reported that the French have landed over six thousand troops under the command of Francois Claude Amour, the Marquis de Bouillé. Reports are that Admiral dé Grasse has twenty-four ships of the line and two fifty-gun ships."

"Damn," Gabe swore. He called Nesbit and told the servant to get Hex and tell him to find Lord Skalla and meet at the governor's office. "What about our people?" he asked Hurley. "Any news there?"

Hurley understood that Gabe was not only talking about the British garrison but also Doctor Cook and Leo Gallagher. "I understand the governor had the garrison withdraw to the fortress atop Brimstone Hill, while the general population surrendered to the French. They have generally been allowed to go about their daily business. The French have not only established themselves on Saint Kitts, but Nevis as well."

Gabe nodded and said, "I will ask you now, Captain Hurley, off the record of course, as you will surely be asked on the record by the governor and Lord Skalla, why you took so long in returning?"

Hurley set his glass down and removing his handkerchief from his pocket, he wiped the sweat from his face. It was hot in the cabin and Gabe had felt sweat running down his spine.

"There was no damn wind. I sighted the French ships," Hurley began, "and so I came about. Rounding Nevis, I was going to heave to and send a party ashore to gather more information about the French invasion, with the understanding that they might be left ashore. We then spied a fishing yawl and closed with her and obtained most of the information in my report. We were still talking to the fisherman when the lookout called down a French frigate had rounded the island and was closing. We immediately got underway only to find another frigate closing off our bow, and that began a chase that I'll not soon forget. Every time I thought I'd eluded the Frogs, I found out it was only wishful thinking. They had to have cleaner bottoms, as they got between me and Jamaica so that I couldn't seek refuge there. It was doubtful Grand Cayman would offer much protection. We ran into a squall and as dangerous as it was, we came about. There was no sign of the frigates that night, but at dawn the lookout spotted them at first light. We sailed into the Gulf and, as dusk overtook us, sailed into the bay at Galveston. Our master had knowledge of it. We anchored and were prepared to give battle if the French were sighted on the dawn. I had the men sleep at the guns and extra sentries put out in case the French sighted us and planned a boat attack. No attack ensued, but when we were ready to set sail, another ship was sighted. The lookout felt it was a Don, so we lay at anchor until dusk and got underway. The weather then turned perverse. We had only light air for a full day, barely making headway. We were then blessed with a moderate breeze, but nature was fickle and the wind died again. Luck was with us on the dawn with a fresh breeze. We then made our way directly back to port."

It was a good report. Hurley was a good captain. He was lucky to have evaded the two French frigates, especially, when every other officer and crewman wanted him to fight.

They now had to report to the governor and Lord Skalla.

***

GABE WAS MENTALLY EXHAUSTED by the time he got home. The news Captain Hurley brought back had created a lot of fear and anxiety. Lord Skalla wanted to sail with the evening tide and mount a rescue for his agents. The governor would not hear of turning loose even one ship when the island was in danger.

Gabe understood the fears of each man. He liked Doctor Cook and Leo very much, but what made the men prefer staying at Saint Kitts rather than at English Harbour? It had to be related to contacts with other agents. Their attention to duty might be their undoing, Gabe knew.

Hex had been waiting for Gabe outside the

governor's residence. Knowing Lord Skalla would not give up in his persistence to rescue the agents, Gabe handed his cox'n a handful of coins.

"Check around and see if you can find someone familiar...I mean really knowledgeable of the coast around Saint Kitts." Gabe thought for a moment and then added, "Especially the northwestern aspect."

Hex took the money. "I'll have them on board ship in the morning if such a person is found." Gabe smiled at Hex, knowing if such a person existed, they'd be aboard *Ares* in the morning, one way or another.

***

FAITH, REALIZING THAT HER husband was completely exhausted, refrained from discussing the day's events. When he went straight to the brandy decanter and poured the snifter half full, she knew something was up. He smelled strongly of cigar smoke and his eyes were red. The biggest thing though, was that he was rubbing his old scalp wound where a streak of hair had turned white.

He must have caught a scent of himself as he asked Faith, "Is a bath to be had?"

"Aye," Faith answered with a smile, and then added, "And not too soon I'm thinking."

Once a tub was filled and Gabe relaxed as much as he could in the tub, he filled Faith in on all the latest news.

"Do you think they will come here next?" Faith asked.

"I wish I knew," Gabe answered honestly.

Faith took the sponge from Gabe's hand and started washing her husband. She looked at him when she finished. His head was laid back on a towel and his eyes were closed. She leaned over and kissed him, hating to wake him, but she had to so that they could get to bed. He stirred and smiled up at Faith and pulled her closer to him.

"Stop," she hissed. "You'll get my gown wet and I'll have to take it off."

"What's wrong with that?" Gabe responded.

"Nothing," Faith answered as she slipped the gown from her shoulders.

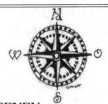

CHAPTER FORTY SEVEN

THE NEW DAY BROUGHT big changes to the island of Antigua. A fleet was spotted in the distance, causing a panic, as the news of the French taking Saint Kitts had spread quickly. Then the British flag was sighted; it was not the dreaded French but a British fleet. Rear Admiral Sir Samuel Hood, acting Commander in Chief to the Leeward Islands had arrived with twenty-one ships of the line and nine frigates.

Hurley, who was aboard *Ares*, spoke to Gabe, "I wonder if he even knows we are a part of his command?"

"I'm sure that I'll be called aboard the flagship and I'll make it known you were sent on separate orders by Admiral Rodney."

Hurley smiled and had little doubt that Captain Anthony would cover their activities. Gabe was summoned at once, as expected. Lord Skalla, without being asked, accompanied Gabe to the flagship, undoubtedly to plead his case for rescue of his agents.

Hood's flagship was the *HMS Barfleur,* a second rate of ninety-eight guns. Her captain was Alexander Hood, who Gabe had met some years ago at the Admiralty. He was the older brother to Sir Samuel Hood and Gabe wondered how it felt to be the older brother of such a decorated officer.

Captain Hood was a good officer and probably would hoist his own flag soon. It was not only deserved, but nepotism was alive and well in the Royal

Navy. *Hypocrite,* Gabe thought suddenly. Were it not for his father's reputation as well as Gil's, he might still be a lieutenant.

Captain Hood greeted Gabe cordially, but frowned when Lord Skalla was introduced. "Sir Samuel is waiting on you, Captain Anthony. I will slip a note to his flag lieutenant to see if he has time to see our friend from the Foreign Services branch. He gave Gabe a knowing look as he shook hands.

As the flag lieutenant whisked Gabe away, Captain Hood said, "If time permits, I'd certainly like to have you dine with me."

"I'd enjoy that," Gabe called his reply.

Admiral Hood welcomed Gabe and asked about Gil, who was now in Gibraltar. When Gabe finished his report, Hood paused and then spoke, "You were quite right taking *Ludlow* and *Lark* under your wing. Had they gone to Jamaica, they'd have been lost from us. Governor Shirley is a good man as far as the army goes, but he knows naught in regards to employing a naval ship." Hood then said something surprising to Gabe. "Rodney should have been clear in his orders to Hurley and Haven. Written orders, damn him. I'm glad you took responsibility and kept the ships diligently employed. It would not do to have two frigates standing idle when they are needed so."

Gabe knew senior officers often found fault in one another, but it was rarely spoken in front of a junior captain. It let Gabe know that he was in good standing with Sir Samuel.

"Now, about the damnable spy," Hood said. "It seems they've an anchor on your arse, my boy. Do what you can to distance yourself, Gabe."

Gabe took a breath and said, "I thought I had, sir," feeling guilty when he said it. He knew some officers, especially army officers who would not even dine with members of the secret branch of the Foreign Services. Apparently some naval officers felt similar.

"I guess I'll have to see the man," Hood said.

Gabe was deep in thought and only caught the last of his words. He could only think of one response, "Yes, sir."

***

GABE WAS IN HIS cabin on board *HMS Ares*. He'd just interviewed the man that Hex had drummed up. He claimed to have extensive knowledge of the entire coast of Saint Kitts, having worked for years for his uncle, who was a coastal trader and then carried sugar cane from the northern fields to Basseterre. Gabe felt much better about his assigned task after the interview. He'd been made to wait while Lord Skalla made his plea for help in rescuing his agents. Lord Skalla was very courteous and diplomatic, unlike his conversation with the governor yesterday, understanding that he'd get nowhere making demands of Sir Samuel.

"I have a French fleet to bring to battle," the admiral started.

"I doubt one frigate would change the outcome," Lord Skalla pleaded.

Sir Samuel asked, knowing the answer already, "Do you have a particular ship in mind to carry out this attempt?"

"I was hoping Captain Anthony's ship would still be available to us, sir."

Hood was looking down at a paper on his desk. He lifted his eyes and a hint of a smile escaped his lips. "I thought so, Lord Skalla, but do be careful. Sir Gabe has a promising career ahead of him with the Navy. I'd hate to see it sullied." Hood then made a signal by raising his finger. The flag lieutenant entered and the interview was over.

Gabe was surprised at the admiral's last comments to Lord Skalla, but understood that the admiral had made them in an attempt to protect his future. If Lord Skalla took exception, he didn't mention it.

Captain Hood saw Gabe off as they left the flagship, "No time to have you dine with us, Sir Gabe. It's the admiral's desire to weigh anchor upon the morrow."

As his gig made its way back to *HMS Ares,* Gabe watched hoys carrying supplies out to the ships and barges and rowing troops to other ships,. He'd heard a lieutenant on board the flagship mention that they were taking a thousand troops. Would that help? He put it from his mind.

The plan was to put to sea tomorrow evening and make the fifty-mile voyage so as to arrive at Saint Kitts with the dawn on the twenty-fourth. *Ares* would be one of the last ships to get underway, anchored as she was. *HMS Lark* and *HMS Ludlow* would sail with the fleet. He'd miss Hurley and Haven, but if they survived it was very likely they'd meet up again...if they survived. With that thought, he sent for Hex to get his boat crew together. He was going home to see his wife and play with his son. Dagan had been scarce the last few days, Gabe realized. Was he thinking about tomorrow, or of Betsy Manning back in the Colonies...Colonies, not anymore? They were now being called the United States, Lord Skalla had said.

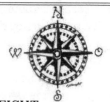

CHAPTER FORTY EIGHT

GABE STOOD BESIDE DAGAN on the quarterdeck by the fife rail. As the stern lights of Hood's fleet raised and dipped with the sea, he had time to reflect on his uncle...at his side. It had always been thus. When Gabe grew in rank and seniority, Dagan had transferred many of the tasks and duties he used to fulfill to Hex, but he was always there. Were it not for the vow he'd made all those years ago, would he still be here...or would he be in America with Betsy. No one ever questioned what Dagan's exact rank was. He came and went as he pleased. Some of the younger lieutenants and midshipmen were seen to salute him on occasion. He moved freely about the ship and was known to be invited into the wardroom to play cards, cribbage, draughts, and on occasion was invited to dine. His rank...he was the captain's uncle and advisor. He could be found most anywhere on the ship until the ship sailed into harm's way. At those times he was there...by the captain.

"I see our master is picking our new pilot's brain," Dagan volunteered.

Lewis Lester.

Gabe had almost laughed when he heard the man's name. He had certainly impressed Gabe and Scott with his knowledge of the coast of Saint Kitts. He recommended that they sail into Pump Bay. They could anchor and it was a short pull to a black sand beach. A path existed that would take you up through the coconut and palm trees. The path was steep, but the climb was not overly long. When you reached the top of the path a fig tree stood. You turned to the left to go to Sandy Point Town, and right to reach the fort. A regular wagon road would lead you up to the fort entrance. On the beach, there would be several rock formations and a few along the path going up the hill. They were not difficult to get past but would offer good cover should skirmishes be encountered. The distance from the beach was around two miles. It was ten miles to Basseterre. The French may have posted soldiers out this far, but hopefully they were still establishing themselves ashore.

"The sea is getting up," Dagan said. "I fear that we are in for squalls."

Gabe nodded and looked aloft. No need to take in a reef at this point. "Mr. Vallin," he called.

"Aye, Captain."

"I will leave the deck to you."

"Aye, aye, Captain."

Gabe turned and felt ocean spray hit his face and lips. The spray stung but Gabe hardly thought of it. "Let's see if Nesbit might have something warm, Uncle."

Dagan smiled. He didn't wear a coat, like Gabe, and only had a thin shirt on. With the sun down, a good breeze, and the ocean spray, he'd gotten cool as well...damp and cool.

***

DAWN FOUND HOOD'S FLEET off the southeast coast of Nevis at dawn. Squalls had followed them for the entire voyage, short as it was. The squally morning would help with launching a surprise attack but would make ship handling difficult at best. As the fleet made for the French anchorage at Basse Terre

Roads, *Ares* went northwest.

Lord Skalla was on deck, looking like he'd slept very little. He was not the only one. Over by the starboard rails, Captain LoGiudice watched his sergeants inspecting his marines. They would take two squads. One would go with Gabe to the fort, and the other would be under Sergeant Jackson, who would secure the landing and hold it for the party's hasty departure should they meet up with the French.

Captain LoGiudice was taking Corporal Dunn with them to scout the path. "He's part mountain goat," the marine captain had japed.

Lewis Lester would lead the way. They were at Sandy Bay and ready to heave to before Gabe realized it. He'd been expecting to hear cannon fire by now. He hoped that they'd launched the attack, as that would help distract any nearby French soldiers.

***

HEX HAD LINED UP his boat crew. Standing next to Hex was Noble. *What is he doing there*, Gabe thought for a second and then remembered that he'd taken over Mr. Massey's duties. Noble looked up and saw Gabe looking his way. A broad smile broke out on the mid's face. Seeing the boy smiling, Hex nudged him and leaned over and whispered to the boy.

"Reminding the lad of his duties," Dagan said.

"Morning Uncle," Gabe said, not even realizing that he had walked up. "Did you get a nap in?"

"Aye, short as it was," Dagan admitted. "It probably would have been better had Nesbit learned how to make coffee like Silas."

Silas was Vice Admiral Lord Anthony's servant. His coffee was famous. Lord Sandwich, First Lord of the Admiralty had even bragged about the man's coffee. Nesbit had tasted the coffee and tried to duplicate the recipe, but had not perfected it. Silas had smiled when asked what his secret was. Smiled, yes...but he did not tell.

Lieutenant Vallin broke Gabe's reverie, "The boats are ready, Captain. This mist will make things tougher, but hopefully it will help keep the Frogs' heads down or under cover."

"Thank you, Con." Pausing once again, Gabe asked, "Have you heard any cannon fire?"

"No, I haven't, now that you mentioned it."

***

THE SURF WAS UP a bit and lifted the boat again, after the bow had ground into the gray black sand, pushing it further forward on the beach. Captain LoGiudice's marines were well trained. They'd landed first and set up a perimeter around the landing. When Gabe made to get out of his boat, Noble was there offering a hand, which Gabe took, thanking the boy.

Once they were situated on the shore, Lewis and Corporal Dunn set off up the path with Sergeant Daniels right behind them. Hex followed Daniels, with Gabe, Lord Skalla, LoGiudice, Dagan, Noble, and the rest of the marines all in a single file.

Gabe was gasping for breath by the time they'd reached the top of the path. He made a vow that he'd exercise more even if it meant walking laps around the deck. He took guilty pleasure seeing the marine captain was faring no better than he. Lord Skalla, on the other hand, showed no ill effects whatsoever.

Lewis allowed the men to catch their breath and then they set off down the road at a fair pace. It seemed they'd been walking forever, but in reality it had only been fifteen minutes when Lewis raised his hand to halt. Corporal Dunn was there. The road up to the fort was just across the road, easily visible in the early morning light. The boom of ship's guns could be heard in the distance.

"Damn late," Gabe muttered to no one in particular but several ayes responded.

They'd only gone a couple of hundred yards up the trail when they were challenged by a sentry. "Halt!" the voice sounded excited, with a bit of a tremor.

"He thinks that we are the French," Dagan whispered.

Gabe took a step forward, glad that he'd worn his complete uniform. "I'm Captain Sir Gabriel Anthony of his Majesty's ship, *Ares*. I'm part of Admiral Sir Samuel Hood's fleet. The distant cannon fire you hear is the British fleet attacking the French. We are here to see the governor."

The sentry called a corporal, who sent word for an officer. A captain soon showed up on horseback. He recognized Gabe from his previous visit with the governor. "Captain, it's good to see you. I will send for a carriage and have someone bring transportation for your soldiers." Gabe saw LoGiudice wince when his marines were called soldiers.

"We have no time for niceties," Lord Skalla spoke out. "Let's get our men some water and then we must get on with it."

The battle in the distance was now in full force with the continuous thunder of the ship's guns. The carriage arrived rather quickly and Gabe and Lord Skalla were whisked away. Marine Captain LoGiudice preferred to stay with his men.

They were greeted by the governor once they were inside the fort. Gabe stood back and let Lord Skalla speak; this was now his show. Doctor Cook and Leo Gallagher arrived and seemed shocked to see Lord Skalla. Another man accompanied them and was not introduced, but Gabe felt he must be the local agent.

Even with the governor's assurance that the fort was impregnable, Lord Skalla insisted on Cook and Leo making ready for immediate departure. Gabe had known the man for some time and had never seen him be so forceful. He obviously had his reasons. He had proven his bravery in battle in the past so Gabe knew the French did not overly concern him. He had his reasons...secret reasons that were not intended for Gabe or any of the others. Gabe said his goodbyes and they departed.

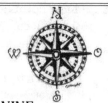

CHAPTER FORTY NINE

THE GROUP HAD ALMOST made it to the path that led down to the beach when Corporal Dunn came running up. "Frogs headed this way from Sandy Point Town."

"Did they see you?" Captain LoGiudice asked.

"No sir."

"They're likely headed down to the anchorage," Gabe said.

"The path is just up that rise," Dunn volunteered. The sound of the French soldiers now reached them.

"We'll never make it to the path. Let's divide our men and position them in the brush on each side of the road. We won't fire unless we have to, but if we do we will have them in crossfire."

The men had just gotten in position when a French officer mounted on a horse rode by. It looked like there were three squads of French soldiers behind him. Damn near a company. Two of the squads had passed by when something attracted a man in the last squad. He shouted something that Gabe didn't recognize, but he recognized the intent as the soldier raised his musket to fire.

"Damnation what luck," Gabe swore. He raised his pistol and fired, dropping the unlucky soul. When he fired, several of the men on his side also fired and the road was suddenly cluttered with bodies. Some were dead, but some of the men were only wounded.

"To the path," Gabe shouted.

He saw LoGiudice, who managed, "You go and we will stay back covering your escape."

"I'll form up at the path to cover you," Gabe replied.

The French officer had now gotten his frightened horse under control and had turned his men, urging them on to meet the enemy. LoGiudice had his men divided into sections. Two men fired, and turned back as two more picked out targets and fired. They repeated this until they made the path where Gabe had positioned his men. They let go with a volley as the marines ran by to take up positions behind trees and rocks on the path.

LoGiudice called out that they were now in position, so Gabe's men fired and retreated down the path. The French were now on the path and firing downward and had the advantage. A thud was heard next to Noble. Turning, he saw a marine grasp his chest while crimson ran between his fingers. He looked at Noble and said, "I'll never see me mum." He then fell forward dead.

More grunts were heard as the French poured a haze of lead balls down at the British. They were almost at the bottom of the path and the marines there were now firing up at the French.

"Hurry," Gabe said to Skalla, "get your men into the boats."

There were more marines falling now. "Damme, but they know their business," LoGiudice swore.

"It's that officer," Gabe said. "He's pushing them."

Several of the French were now down but there were still enough to make getting to the boats and escaping nearly impossible. Corporal Dunn gave a grunt and fell into Noble, with blood already pouring from a shoulder wound. Noble took the marine's musket. He checked to make sure it was loaded and then stood and climbed up on the bolder he'd crouched behind.

Everyone looked in awe and fear as the midshipman stood. With balls ricocheting off the rock, one of them burned the side of Noble's face. He took careful aim and fired the musket. The French officer dropped his sword, grasped his face and fell dead.

The British sailors and marines gave out a cheer and fired up at the French, who turned and ran back up the path.

Gabe walked over as Hex spoke to Noble, "That was dangerous."

Noble handed Corporal Dunn back his musket, looked at Hex and said, "I'd had enough."

Gabe and LoGiudice stared at each other. Finally, the marine captain muttered, "Did you see that shot?"

"Aye," Gabe replied, but his feelings were torn. Noble should be awarded a medal for his bravery. He'd saved the lives of several men, maybe all of them. Gabe was also angry, in a fatherly way. The boy had risked his life. Proud yes, Gabe was proud of Noble. But how do you balance pride and anger?

***

THEY MADE IT BACK aboard *Ares* without further difficulties. The sailors and marines in the shore party quickly spread the word of Noble's actions, not only his bravery but that shot...that magnificent shot.

Vallin approached his captain. Gabe said, "Let's get underway as soon as the wounded are all aboard."

"To the Roads?" Vallin asked.

"Home," Gabe replied, his job was done.

Dagan followed Gabe into his cabin, where without calling for Nesbit, Gabe took the bottle of American whiskey and poured stiff drinks into two glasses, downing his own in one gulp. The fiery liquid burned his throat and made him cough. His eyes watered and Gabe swore, but poured another drink, only two fingers this time. He wiped his eyes and saw Dagan smiling.

"You care for the boy," Dagan said.

"We all do."

"You can't hide him under a bushel. He'll live and learn. We have survived, in the meantime."

The sentry called out, at that moment, "Midshipman of the watch, sir."

"Enter," Gabe responded. When the midshipman entered, Gabe asked, "What can we do for you, Mr. Delsenno?"

"Mr. Vallin's respects, sir, but could you come on deck? It appears the enemy is attacking one of our ships." Gabe hurried on deck.

"It seems the enemy is trying to take one of our ships, Captain. The lookout thinks the main ship is a Dutch sixty-four and the other is a frigate. He didn't see a flag but thinks that it's a French frigate. Another set of sails appear to be approaching to leeward. Two, possibly three enemy ships have attacked one of our ships."

"Have you identified our ship, Mr. Vallin?"

"The lookout says that he believes it's the *Lark*, Captain."

"Clamp on all sail, Mr. Vallin. When we get in full view, have Mr. Heath hoist the signal enemy in sight. Hopefully, that will worry the buggers a bit."

"Are you going to attack the sixty-four?" Vallin asked.

Gabe looked at his first lieutenant. "Are you afraid of an old Dutch scow, Mr. Vallin?"

"No sir, not if you're not." Several of the men in earshot laughed.

Gabe spoke again, "Hopefully, we won't have to, Mr. Vallin. Let's be prepared, though. Clear for action."

"Aye, Captain."

The Foreign Office gentlemen found a spot out of the way as *Ares* made ready for battle. Decks were being sanded; and tubs were being placed between the guns for wetting sponges. Nets were spread under the mast to catch wrecked debris from aloft. Loose articles about the deck were picked up or secured. Cabin bulkheads were being struck down and carried below. The gunner and his mates were checking balls in the garlands and a couple of men, those that would be in the magazine, were putting on leather slippers.

Doctor Cook spoke out, "I'm sure Doctor Cornish and his men are getting the cockpit ready for the wounded. I shall go down and attempt to make myself useful."

Noble Stanhope was standing at his station when Lieutenant Vallin walked up. "Ship prepared for battle, Captain."

Gabe looked at his first lieutenant, "What...no time set, Mr. Vallin."

Vallin smiled and reported, "Seven minutes, sir."

"Damnation, the men are getting better," Gabe explained.

Noble stood there thinking but didn't say a word. He knew damn well the first lieutenant's watch was broken and so did the captain.

Dagan, seeing the lad's look, leaned over and whispered, "A game, Noble. It's a game to encourage the men." The youth shook his head in understanding. Dagan then placed his hand on the boy's shoulder and spoke again, "Have a care today, Noble. Do your duty but no heroics."

"Aye, Mr. Dagan."

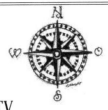

CHAPTER FIFTY

THE LOOKOUT OVERHEAD CALLED down, "Sails to leeward be a brig, Cap'n, one of ours."

That's a relief, Gabe thought. *No help but it's not the enemy either.* The ship battle, if you could call it that was now visible from the deck.

The French frigate was alongside *Lark* and the Dutch sixty-four appeared to be coming about to do battle with *Ares*. A frigate normally would be no match for a sixty-four, but *Ares* was a razee who had been laid down as a sixty-four so her timbers were much stouter. Still, it was not on Gabe's mind to trade broadside for broadside with the Dutch ship. She was an old ship, which was obvious from the way she was built.

The Dutch were known to build stout ships but they were not racehorses. *Ares,* on the other hand, was. He was sure that he could outmaneuver the sixty-four and hopefully disable her, and then close with *Lark,* and give aid fighting the frigate.

Scott, the master, also had his eye on the Dutch. "She is slow, Captain, much too slow. She's probably got tentacles of weed growing off her hull. I'd bet that until Rodney attacked Saint Eustatius, she probably hadn't seen deep water in years."

Gabe had been watching the ship and agreed with Scott. "Mr. Vallin."

"Aye."

"I intend to bear down on yonder ship, but instead

of passing down her side, we are crossing her bow and letting go. Have Mr. Laqua tell his gun captains to fire each gun separately as we cross her bow." Vallin nodded.

It was a daring move if it worked. If not...if anything went wrong, they'd have the fat Dutchman on their quarterdeck. Hex walked up and handed Gabe his pistols. He'd taken them below, cleaned them quickly and reloaded them after their foray ashore.

***

THE TWO SHIPS SAILED closer and closer toward each other. Scott had put two men on the wheel. He spoke to them, "Steer small." Nowhere else did a person speak. Men were at their stations, all ready to give battle when the captain called for it. LoGiudice had his marines deployed, all standing as if ready for inspection.

"Mr. Stanhope."

Noble jumped, "Aye, Captain."

"My compliments to Mr. Laqua. We are about to cross."

"Yes sir."

Gabe stood on the quarterdeck and watched. Too soon and the Dutch would turn and they'd have to face his broadsides. Too late and *Ares* would likely be rammed.

"Be ready, Mr. Scott," Gabe spoke, stringing out the 'be ready'. "Now," he shouted, "Now."

The helmsmen expecting the order spun the wheel before the master could speak. The helm answered as it dug in and the deck canted at an acute angle. Scott bellowed again and the wheel spun back. The angle corrected and Laqua had the guns firing.

BOOM...BOOM...BOOM.

Noble, who'd damn near fell, watched as *Ares'*

twenty-four pounders belched orange flames and destruction. The first shot went down the length of the ship, gouging the hull, but the next three or four hit the Dutch ship's bow hard...hard and often. By the time *Ares* had crossed the enemy's bow, a whole section of it was missing. The jib and boom were down and hanging in the water. The forward mast was leaning at a dangerous angle. The Dutch had not fired a shot, the surprise had been complete. She was still a dangerous adversary though. With the jib and boom hanging in the water, the ship was slewed around, which brought her broadside to bear.

"Put your helm down, Mr. Scott. Let's not give the buggers any more of a target than we have to."

The gun ports on the Dutch ship opened and the black snouts of their guns rumbled forward. Several guns thundered but the shots were wide.

"They'd planned on the obvious," Scott said with a smile.

"Let's cross her stern, Mr. Scott."

"Aye, Captain."

"Mr. Stanhope."

"Yes sir."

"My compliments to Mr. Laqua. We intend to cross the enemy's stern. I want every shot to concentrate on the rudder."

"Aye," Noble responded and took off.

Ares came about and crossed the stern of the Dutch ship with surprising ease and very little return fire. The rudder was shot away, leaving the Dutch warship disabled. It had been so easy that Gabe almost felt sorry for the ship's captain. He'd probably never fired those big guns in anger. In fact, had they not befriended the Americans, they'd probably still be in port somewhere.

"The enemy frigate is getting underway," the

lookout called down.

Gabe turned his gaze toward *Lark*. The small frigate had been battered...battered hard.

"To *Lark* or the enemy, Captain?"

Gabe closed his glass with a loud snap. Haven would have to deal with his ship for now. *Ares'* duty was to destroy the enemy frigate. The frigate did not come about to do battle as Gabe expected, but he was determined to force the issue. "Give chase to yonder frigate," Gabe snapped.

Everyone realized that they were closing the distance between the two ships, after a quarter of an hour. The enemy fired its stern guns after a half an hour, but nobody saw where the ball landed. The next ball was short and wide, and the third was high, holing the fore main sail.

"Bring her up two points," Gabe ordered. "Mr. Vallin, it appears our foe is ready to dance. See if Mr. Meyers can provide some music more to my liking."

Noble smiled as the first lieutenant called for the gunner. Would he be as calm under fire as the captain? He hoped so. It was only a few minutes before the twelve pounder bow chasers fired. The first two shots were short, and the third ball hit the water and slammed into the enemy ship but the fourth shot was a good hit. A huge hole opened up in the stern. The next ball did similar damage. The ball after that missed as the enemy captain maneuvered. A gaping hole was seen after two more hits, and they were close enough to see the last hit to the stern chaser. The big gun leaped in the air and tumbled out the hole and down the ship. The ropes and tackles held the gun for a moment and then it slipped further and fell.

"Hell's fire look at that," Vallin shouted.

The frigate slewed to larboard. Dagan volunteered, "Fouled her rudder. The gun's ropes and tackles has slid down and fouled the rudder."

"Reduce sail," Gabe shouted. "Reduce sail, Mr. Vallin, fighting sail only."

The sail handlers jumped to it and the evolution was quickly carried out. The frigate was disabled, like the sixty-four, but for how long? Could it be cleared without sending someone over the side? Would the debris clear itself? Gabe stood watching.

The enemy apparently could not maneuver to larboard or starboard. They were already defeated but would they surrender? A man appeared in the hole of the stern and looked down.

"Mr. Vallin, go forward with a speaking trumpet and ask if they surrender. I will close a bit more."

Vallin did as asked but the man only shook his fist in reply. *Do I continue to pound her into submission,* Gabe wondered. As the outcome was basically decided, she would prove a good prize if the enemy gave up now.

"Damnation," Gabe swore. "To larboard, Mr. Scott, to larboard."

The damn French captain was a sly devil. He must have had men ready with axes. The sails were off the French ship in an instant. *Ares* swung to larboard to keep from ramming the ship and as they sailed past the French opened up with their guns, blasting away much of the rail and bulwarks. The fiery hell knocked over guns, cut men in half and started a small fire. The only saving grace is they were quickly past the frigate.

Gabe had been knocked down. One of the helmsmen was a headless rag. Scott had a splinter in his side. Men were down writhing in pain and crying out. Others lay still in deathly silence. Noble was getting up. He appeared to only have a slight scalp wound. Dagan and Hex were unhurt.

Vallin was walking toward the quarterdeck. He appeared to have a few lacerations, but was otherwise fine. "Damn that man," he shouted.

He'd used grape on top of ball. He'd done his best to destroy the British ship with one broadside. Out-foxed, Gabe seethed. He'd been outfoxed, and his men had paid for it. The Frog would pay now.

"Mr. Vallin, get everything cleared away. Mr. Scott, are you able to continue?"

The master gritted his teeth, "Aye, Captain, I'll be with you."

"Prepare to come about then. We'll show this whoreson what happens when he draws British blood."

Ares came about; all the guns were loaded, including the carronades. The swivels were loaded with grape.

"Mr. Stanhope, tell Mr. Laqua that I intend to pass down her side and then cross her stern. We will pass to starboard."

"Aye, Captain."

Scott heard the captain and automatically he look aloft. The commissioning pennant stood out. The wind was still brisk, the sky was clearing, and the clouds were moving out. Dagan looked at the crew. Determined angry faces all looked toward the quarterdeck. Many of them had just lost some of their mates. They expected the captain to make the Frogs pay.

Ares closed with the French frigate, which lay dead in the water. The captain had gambled on destroying the enemy with the one pass. He'd put everything into it, and it had almost worked, almost but not quite. The French flag still flew, proud, brave, but ridiculous. The man should have surrendered...he didn't. He was about to receive his reward now.

"Now, Mr. Scott," Gabe called firmly.

The helmsman moved the wheel and where *Ares* had shown she'd pass to larboard, she passed to starboard instead. Every gun fired and poured out its version of hell. The twenty-four pounders thundered forth, raining death and destruction down on the French. The thunder and smoke filled Gabe's ears and eyes, blurring his vision as his eyes watered from the acrid smoke.

Gabe ordered, "Once past, prepare to come about."

"They've surrendered," Noble shouted.

The French flag was down and a white flag was raised.

CHAPTER FIFTY ONE

TWO BOATS MADE THEIR way to the French frigate. Gabe, Dagan, Lieutenant Turner, Noble, and several sailors were in one of them; the lead boat was filled with Captain LoGiudice and several of his marines. Hex ordered a sailor to hook on and they went up the battens and through the entry port.

LoGiudice had his marines lined up, with bayonets on their muskets and all pointed at what was left of the French men. Gabe realized immediately that they were not regular French sailors, but privateers, as not a one of them wore a uniform.

A woman was being held up across the way. Her side was crimson. A man lay at her feet, and had been cut nearly in half. The deck was turning black where he lay. The woman held a sword in her hand. Gabe took a step toward her only to be passed by Hex.

"Marie...Marie," he called.

The woman looked at Hex, taking a step toward him and then collapsed. Hex knelt down beside her and tried to cradle her in his arms. Gabe and Dagan sidled up to him.

Marie looked at Hex with tears in her eyes. "Mon Cherie," she gasped. "The only man that I have ever loved." She looked at Gabe and tried to lift the sword to him but was unable. "My brother," she said. She touched Hex's face with a bloody hand and kissed him. "Do you believe in the hereafter," she asked, gasping for breath. Then she was gone. Dagan leaned over and placed his hand on Hex's shoulder.

"Let's be about it," Gabe said to Lieutenant Turner.

The ship was thoroughly searched. The planter, Martin, was discovered in the hole and was brought on deck. His eyes were blinking and watering, as he tried to shade them from the sun with his hands. Gabe was not sure finding the man was a good thing, but that was not his concern. The man and his wife could work that out.

Several barrels of French wine were found, along with crates of trade goods and a few weapons. A cabin next to the captain's was searched. Dagan found a jewelry box and took a ruby ring from it. He looked at Gabe but didn't say a thing. On deck later, he discreetly gave it to Hex. A memory of the woman he loved.

Dé Corsia had, in fact, been the frigate captain's name. He was Maria's brother. He'd been raiding the British since before the beginning of the war. His ship's log, more detailed than a lot of his kind, spelled out his prizes and captures. A chest was found that held both gold and silver coin but not any more than most captains would have to use providing for his ship and crew. He's placed his ill-gotten gains ashore somewhere, Gabe decided. Well, he'd be taking no more.

Back on the main deck, Gabe called to his lieutenant, "Mr. Turner, I will send men over and see if we can clear up the rudder. Make sure that you keep a watch on the prisoners. Captain LoGiudice will remain on board with his marines to help."

***

GABE WENT BACK TO *Ares*. He spoke to Hex once they were on deck, "Go below and get yourself a drink. Young Noble will take over your duties until I need you further." He then made his way down to the cockpit.

Doctor Cornish was just taking off his apron. "We've just finished. Doctor Cook was a big help. He was able to remove the splinter from Mr. Scott's side, so he should do well."

Gabe made his way to his cabin with that news. Nesbit had just poured him a drink when the sentry announced the first lieutenant.

"The rudder has been cleared on our prize," he announced as Nesbit, without asking, poured him a glass.

"Good," Gabe replied. "When you're ready, get us underway. Hail to see if *Lark* is in any need of assistance." With that, the lieutenant left to attend to his duties.

Hex came forward and said, "I was shocked to see her."

"Aye," Gabe said. "I'm sorry for how this all turned out, but Jake..." he paused, trying to get his emotions in check. "At least you know that she loved you. You can better understand her disappearance now."

Hex nodded, wiping a tear away, "There's that."

Closure, Gabe thought, but did not say it.

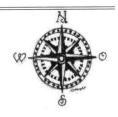

EPILOGUE

GRAY CLOUDS FOLLOWED *HMS Ares* across the fifty miles that separated Saint Kitts from Antigua. *HMS Lark* had gotten underway by the time *Ares* had buried their dead. Con Vallin had put Lieutenant Laqua aboard the prize to sail her back to Antigua. A full squad of Captain LoGiudice's marines was sent over to guard the prisoners.

Lord Skalla felt the mission was a total success. Gabe thought differently. Total success to him meant that you had accomplished your mission without loss of life, and that hadn't happened. The raid on Saint Kitts was, in Lieutenant Vallin's words, 'a shitten mess'.

Admiral Hood, seeing the French fleet anchored haphazardly, had ordered his fleet to form a line of battle. *HMS Alfred,* of seventy-four guns, almost immediately collided with *HMS Nymphe,* a thirty-six gun frigate. This accident prevented the surprise attack that Hood had desired. The attack continued through the next day and following morning. As determined as Hood was, he was unable to dislodge the French from Saint Kitts. The Fort at Brimstone Hill still had not surrendered but Gabe knew that it was only a matter of time.

HMS Pickle pulled into port the following week. Captain Nicholson stated that Parliament was already discussing a war with France.

"Have they not seen what the war with the

Colonies has cost us?" Gabe asked.

The Foreign Office men took passage back to England aboard the *Pickle*. *Mal is severely stretched for space,* Gabe thought as the little ship got underway.

Faith had invited Doctor Cook, Lord Skalla, and Leo to dinner their last night on Antigua. She and Gabe had really enjoyed the men's company. After the meal, Hex and Leo made their way down to the waterfront. Doctor Cook and Lord Skalla discussed the possibilities of a war with France and Spain.

"They'll not want to give up at this point," Lord Skalla was sure of that.

"It's coming," Doctor Cook agreed, "but I believe it will be a few years yet."

"I hope it never comes," Faith interjected, having heard the conversation. The men agreed, but all knew that it would.

Gabe told Faith about Jake's woman, later that night in bed. "That's so sad," she said, and then added, "How many lives has this war destroyed?" That comment caused Gabe to think.

He had a letter for Noble from Gretchen. Would their young love withstand the war, time and distance? Only time would tell, but right now he was content. He had Faith beside him. He reached over and pulled her closer and sleep came at once.

HISTORICAL NOTES

For the sentence of hanging a seaman as detailed in the opening of this book, I referred to the Royal Navy Articles of War 1757, Article 27. The Articles of War, a purely naval code of discipline, stems from "Laws of the Sea and Punishments."

The attack on Saint Eustatius: Britain, tired of the way the Dutch handled their neutrality during the American Revolutionary War, especially with recognizing the American flag and giving aid to American ships, declared war on the Republic of the Seven United Netherlands on December 20, 1780. The British outfitted a massive battle fleet to take and destroy the weapons depot and vital commercial centers on Saint Eustatius. The command of the fleet was given to Admiral George Brydges Rodney on February 3, 1781. Rodney, after taking the island, was to sail to America to assist in Britain's war effort there. The fleet was made up of fifteen ships of the line and numerous smaller ships. Some were transports carrying over three thousand soldiers. Once the fleet arrived at Saint Eustatius, Governor de Graaff, having no prior knowledge of the war, surrendered the island after firing two rounds as a show of honor. The wealth Admiral Rodney and General Vaughan found far exceeded expectations. When the British Fleet arrived, one hundred and thirty merchantmen lay at anchor in the bay, along with a Dutch frigate and five smaller American armed merchantmen.

Instead of sending his fleet on to engage the enemy in the Caribbean and provide reinforcement in America, Rodney delayed his departure until July or August, 1781. He had weakened his fleet greatly by sending a strong defending force of ships to guard his treasure ships. During the time between his arrival and departure, Rodney uprooted and relocated all the Jews on the island, which created an outcry and call for condemnation against Rodney. A personal letter that Rodney wrote to his family was noted to promise a new home in London, and for his daughter the best harpsichord money could purchase. A marriage settlement was to be for one of his sons, and a commission purchased in the foot guards for another son.

When Admiral Graves, in command of the ships Rodney had sent to support General Cornwallis, arrived outside Chesapeake Bay, he realized that they had arrived too late. A French fleet had already arrived. The battle between French Admiral De Grasse and Rear Admiral Thomas Graves became known as the Battle on Chesapeake Bay or as the Battle of the Capes. It was one of the most pivotal battles in history. The battle went on for several days. Some individuals were blaming Admiral Graves for his lack of aggression. When French Admiral Barras arrived with eight more French warships, Graves found himself seriously outnumbered, and sailed away. Cornwallis was trapped. While the Battle of the Capes was tactically indecisive, it was clearly a French victory. With the Royal Navy unable to break the Franco-American stronghold, Cornwallis was doomed. He surrendered at Yorktown, October 19, 1781. This basically ended the war on American soil. Many blamed the defeat on Rodney's greed. The defeat at Yorktown in October 1781 marked an escalation of war in the Caribbean.

Fitting out a midshipman: Most midshipmen

went to sea sponsored by a father or guardian with enough means to not only fit out the youth, but to also give further support by providing the captain of the midshipman's ship with enough funds to dole out an allowance at given times. When in England the fitting out was easy enough with tailors at Portsmouth, Plymouth, and London ready to provide all the uniforms that would be needed...tailors like M. Hand and Company, Hatter, James and Lock Company and Spitalfield's Silk Weavers. When it came to the small sword or midshipman's dirk as it was commonly called, the boy and his sponsor had only to go to one of the many makers of edged weapons to obtain a worthy blade. A name like Henry Wilkinson, by Royal appointment, was one such maker of the dirk. Other well known crasftsman included Thomas Gill - sword cutler and gun maker, and Samuel Harvey. All provided quality blades. Most of them had engravings or etchings of the crown to show their authenticity. Some had scrolls and nautical emblems, such as an anchor etched into the blade.

The blades were on an average of 17 ¾ inches long, with the etching in gray and a gilt hilt. The grips were done in fish/shark skin. The sheaths were usually made of a fine leather and metal (which looked brass to me.) A locking pin mechanism prevented the dirk from coming out of its sheath inadvertently. Generally, the grip of the dirk had a lion's head pommel. The problem with the fitting out of a midshipman at overseas bases was the finding of a good blade. Nowhere in my research did I find where it was common for a midshipman to be routinely outfitted with a pistol or brace of pistols.

The Battle of Saint Kitts and The Siege of Brimstone Hill: The battle of Saint Kitts, also known as the Battle of Frigate Bay, took place January 25th and 26th, 1782.

When Rear Admiral Samuel Hood left America after the Battle of Chesapeake Bay, he was in independent command, as Admiral Rodney had returned to England. During this time, French Admiral Comte de Grasse was attacking the British islands of Saint Kitts and Nevis. He had with him fifty warships and seven thousand troops. His flagship was the one-hundred ten gun, *Ville de Paris*. The attack on Saint Kitts began on January 11, 1782. The British on the island retreated to the fort on Brimstone Hill, starting on January 19, 1782.

Twenty-two British warships under Rear Admiral Hood were sighted on January 24th, and de Grasse sent his ships out to intercept the British fleet. However, contrary winds prevented the French from bringing the British fleet to battle. Hood circled north around Nevis and anchored off Basseterre. The French attacked the British fleet on both the morning and afternoon of January 26th, but were beaten off. The British suffered seventy-two dead and two hundred and forty-four were wounded. The British killed one hundred and seven and wounded two hundred and seven of the French. While damages on both sides were heavy, Hood was unable to stop the French land action.

Defending the fort at Brimstone Hill were the First Battalion of the First Foot, (approximately seven hundred soldiers), flank companies of the Fifteenth Foot (approximately one hundred and twenty), a Royal Artillery detachment, as well as many militia. The fort was also full of families and many British laborers. By the 12th of February, the fort had lost over one hundred and fifty men killed in addition to many sick and wounded. The French had breached the lower walls. The British commander, Fraser, had no option but to negotiate surrender, which included marching out with the honors of war. On February 14th, Hood managed to escape when the French fleet sailed to meet a convoy filled with supplies.

Author's Note: On one of our research trips, Pat and I visited Saint Kitts and walked the shores of Frigate Bay, toured Basseterre and spent most of a day at the Fortress on Brimstone Hill. This was a massive fort for its day. It had innumerable gun placements of virtually every caliber. Most of them were still in good condition, considering that they were so old and out in the weather. Brimstone Hill sits on top of a hill or a bluff with a commanding view of the ocean and surrounding areas. If the French had had artillery, the fort could have been taken from above easily, but in the end it was sickness and starvation that caused the surrender.

A Smuggler's Song

IF you wake at midnight, and hear a horse's feet,
Don't go drawing back the blind, or looking in the street,
Them that ask no questions isn't told a lie.
Watch the wall my darling while the Gentlemen go by.
Five and twenty ponies,
Trotting through the dark -
Brandy for the Parson, 'Baccy for the Clerk.
Laces for a lady; letters for a spy,
Watch the wall my darling while the Gentlemen go by!
Running round the wood lump if you chance to find
Little barrels, roped and tarred, all full of brandy-wine,
Don't you shout to come and look, nor use 'em for your
play.
Put the brishwood back again - and they'll be gone next
day!
If you see the stable-door setting open wide;
If you see a tired horse lying down inside;
If your mother mends a coat cut about and tore;
If the lining's wet and warm - don't you ask no more!
If you meet King George's men, dressed in blue and red,
You be careful what you say, and mindful what is said.
If they call you" pretty maid," and chuck you 'neath the
chin,
Don't you tell where no one is, nor yet where no one's
been!
Knocks and footsteps round the house - whistles after
dark -
You've no call for running out till the house-dogs bark.

Trusty's here, and Pincher's here, and *see* how dumb they
lie
They don't fret to follow when the Gentlemen go by!
'If You do as you've been told, 'likely there's a chance,
You'll be give a dainty doll, all the way from France,
With a cap of Valenciennes, and a velvet hood -
A present from the Gentlemen, along 'O being good!
Five and twenty ponies,
Trotting through the dark -
Brandy for the Parson, 'Baccy for the Clerk.
Them that asks no questions isn't told a lie -
Watch the wall my darling while the Gentlemen go by!

The Smuggler's song sung by Noble in this book
was written by Rudyard Kipling. I have not been able
to discover the exact date it was written.

About the Author

Michael Aye is a retired Naval Medical Officer. He has long been a student of early American and British Naval history. Since reading his first Kent novel, Mike has spent many hours reading the great authors of sea fiction, often while being "haze gray and underway" himself.